PRIDE

"I don't like bein' called 'boy' neither." Roosevelt fixed his stare upon the coach.

"You don't like a hell of a lot." Hammer wheeled on Mando. "Where I come from 'greaser' don't mean much. It's like the way we talk."

"I was born in Los Angeles," said Mando. "You can call me 'Chicano' if you can't use my name."

"G'wan, how do I know your doggone name?"

"Mando Cruz. I play third base. I run good and I hit good. I'm here on a thirty-five hundred dollar bonus. You want to know any more?"

CHICANO CRUZ

Chicano Cruz

by William Cox

BANTAM BOOKS · TORONTO · NEW YORK · LONDON

RLI: VLM 4 (VLR 3–5)
IL 6-up

CHICANO CRUZ
A Bantam Book / March 1972

| 2nd printing .... *July 1973* | 4th printing ... *October 1974* |
| 3rd printing ... *October 1974* | 5th printing ... *October 1976* |

ISBN 0-553-10480-2

Published simultaneously in the United States and Canada

Bantam Books are published by Bantam Books, Inc. Its trade-
mark, consisting of the words "Bantam Books" and the por-
trayal of a bantam, is registered in the United States Patent
Office and in other countries. Marca Registrada. Bantam
Books, Inc., 666 Fifth Avenue, New York, New York 10019.

Chicano Cruz

1

The ancient rattletrap Ford turned off the San Diego Freeway and rolled wearily down the ramp and onto a busy main thoroughfare. The California sun was wan; it was very early springtime; a clot of yellow smog hung over the ever-present low mountains of the San Fernando Valley. The two passengers in the car had driven from Arizona without sleep, but they were young enough and strong enough to be wide awake.

Mando Cruz said, "Next turn left."

"I remember," said Jack Kelly.

"Back to the *barrio*, but not for long," said Mando. He was nineteen years of age. He was five feet ten inches tall. He weighed one hundred and seventy pounds, mostly bone and muscle. He had olive skin, almost brown from the sun, and his black hair curled on his head. He had oversized hands and forearms, like an old-fashioned blacksmith.

"It's not the real *barrio*," objected Jack Kelly. "Your folks pulled out of there long ago."

"Sure, they did." Mando wiped sweat from his brow. It was not that hot; he was going to a conference which could end only one way. "And Uncle Luis made good. So what? So they built another *barrio*. The Hollenbeck area, or here in the valley, you get chicanos together, you've got a *barrio*."

1

Jack Kelly was red-haired and blue-eyed and tall and strong. Like Mando, he had the big hands. Like Mando, he wore a short-sleeved pullover jersey and tight jeans and the kind of composition-soled athletic shoes used by Olympic athletes with the distinguishing black slash marks. He spoke lightly, but his glance was serious.

"You've been talking that way for miles. Get with it, man, we've made up our minds. Haven't we?"

"We have." Mando stared straight ahead. They made the second turn and came to a street where children shrieked and ran and played loud games. "Smell it? You're the one pointed it out to me. It smells strong."

"I didn't mean anything by it," protested Jack. "It smells different every neighborhood. Chicanos eat the hot stuff, cook with the oils. So what?"

"We're different from you. Foreigners."

"Aw, you're chewin' it. You're Americans, whether you come from Mexico, Texas—or Hollenbeck." Jack was uncomfortable. "We've been through all that night after night. I dig you. You dig me. Don't start up with me now."

Mando said, "You know what *bato loco* is?"

"You told me. Like your brother Ricky. The Brown Berets. The wild ones. They want everything overnight."

"Yes. *Sí, señor.* They want it quick, like the Black Panthers. Like they should always have had it."

Jack said, "Look, man, I know all this. I'm with you, remember me? I never had it so great, either. Why don't you face the music, meet me later, and we'll take off? Why bug me?"

"Because you know all the answers. Because you've been my roomie for a year. Because we're college chums, man."

"You mean because you're uptight about leaving school," said Jack.

"Yeah."

The houses were all ticky-tacky alike, despite various paint jobs. The little square lawns were all geometric but not all well kept. It was midafternoon, and stout

2

women sat on the porches or in patios back of the kitchens. Several men lounged, indifferent; a few waved without enthusiasm. He had come home, Mando the ball-player, Mando the student, he had come home to tell them it was no use, he had quit school and was not going back this year—if ever.

Jack pulled into a narrow driveway alongside one of the houses which was newly painted—its neighbors were not so fortunate. There was a pickup truck and a Volkswagen ahead of the old Ford, so that the rear end was at the sidewalk as the two young men got out of the car. The boys saw them, and one yelled, "Mando the Man," and threw a baseball hard. Mando reached up and plucked it from the air and tossed it around his back and straight to the boy, who cooed his pleasure, black eyes shining.

Jack unlocked the rear deck, and they lifted out a box of books. The boys ran to help, chattering. There was a somewhat battered record player and a stack of recordings and one suitcase.

Mando said, "Leave the duffel bag in there. You be back soon, man?"

"I've got to tell my story. Then it's quicker than possible. My folks aren't going to like it, either."

Mando said, "You still think we're right?"

"I don't think we have another way to go," Jack told him. "I truly don't, *amigo*. Stay loose in there, now. Take two and hit to right."

"No way, man," said Mando. "It'll be rough. Thanks for letting me rave."

"You're my man." Jack got into the Ford and backed it out of the driveway. The tappets were clacking. The car needed work, but they couldn't afford it, Mando knew. It would do for their purpose as of now. It only needed to stand up for a week or so; then all would be decided.

The boys were clamoring. Mando tossed a high one for them, and they all ran after the ball. Then he threw them another, a used one from college but in better condition than the one they were playing with. They waved and cheered, and he went up the steps and into

3

the house, from which no one had come to welcome him.

It was his nineteenth birthday.

They were all gathered, not the cousins or the grandparents or the friends for his natal day, just the immediate family. There was Papa with his leg in a cast; Mamma sitting in the corner with her arms folded over her ample bosom; Enrique Jr., "Ricky," with his brown skullcap; Consuelo, prettier than ever; José, with his mop of mod hair; María, at fourteen too fat, and who would always be fat. And there was Uncle Luis Guzmán, who was Mamma's prosperous brother, in his neat gringo suit and close haircut, also too stout but trying hard to be with it, with the business establishment, Uncle Luis the Talker. They all loved him, he knew, but they also looked upon Mando as the enemy.

In his resentment he said, "Happy birthday to me."

"Happy?" As always, Uncle Luis took over. "You make us happy? You quit the college, and that makes us laugh and play?"

"A lawyer," said Papa. "We send him to be a lawyer so that we are not cheated by the gringo."

There was a general murmur of assent. Only Ricky snorted contempt.

Uncle Luis said, "Did I not tell you that I would take care of Papa? Did I not assure you all would be well here? What do you want from me? Why do you do this to your people?"

Ricky said, "Why should he be a lawyer for you, Uncle Talker? You are *gabacho* in your heart."

"Do not speak so of my brother," cried Mamma. "He has been good to us all. This very house ... everything we owe to my brother."

"Your brother the *gabacho*, the gringo," said Ricky. "He grows rich off us. He gives us jobs, nonunion. He makes the down payment on the houses—we carry the mortgages. Don't tell me about Uncle Talker."

"Silence!" roared Papa, thumping his heavy cane on the floor so that it shook beneath them. "It is not of Luis

4

that we speak. It is of this one who quits his college, who goes against the wishes of the family."

Mando carried his small possessions into the rear of the house. There were three bedrooms among them, and one and a half baths. In the ghetto it would seem ample, true enough; it was clean, and because Uncle Luis was a contractor in the painting business, it was bright. He put the books in Consuelo's room and the record player in José's room, which he shared with Ricky. He returned in the midst of high discussion.

Ricky said, "Yes, we had things, the Chicano Studies, Head Start, NAPP. We had them. Now there is a recession. We don't have them."

"It is because of your violence. *Bato loco,* crazy guy. Like the Black Panthers. Because of you, nobody will support the movements for the good," said Uncle Luis.

"We supported them. We WERE them," shouted Ricky. "You and the other taxpayers, you took them from us. It grows late for you gringos to make amends."

"Threats," said Uncle Luis. "The police will take care of you."

"And the National Guard," said Ricky. "They will shoot us down, *sí?* That is what you want, no?"

Mando said, "Okay, knock it off. What's the use of it? You two, the right and the left of it. Nowhere."

"What do you mean nowhere, you who quit the college?" demanded Uncle Luis.

Mando reached into his hip pocket and took out a piece of paper. He said, "Papa is behind on the mortgage. You are about to take a second trust deed. Give him time. And add onto the payments and the interest."

"It is a kindness," said Mamma.

"Please, Mamma. Remember Tito Gonzales? He was sick and couldn't pay. Uncle Luis took care of him. To the veterans' hospital he went, and someone else has the house. Don't tell me about Uncle Luis."

"The gringo," said Ricky.

"And you," said Mando. "You take his wages. You take his pay, and you yell at him and talk against him."

"Don't you start on me." Ricky was twenty-one, and he had been among the bully boys of the *barrio*.

Mando said, "Enough. You know me better than that." He extended the piece of paper to his father. "A birthday gift from me to the family."

His father squinted at the check. "This is genuine? What is this? What have you done?"

"I didn't steal it."

They all crowded around, Ricky jostling Uncle Luis away. They exclaimed in loud voices.

"Three thousand dollars? Mando has robbed a bank!"

Mando said, "It will pay back Uncle Luis on the mortgage, and it will keep you in tacos and beans for a while, until Papa can work again and maybe Ricky will help a little too, instead of drinking beer and running with his *bato loco* friends accomplishing nothing."

"I demand to know," said Papa. "Where did you get this amount of money?"

"From the Gold Sox, where else?"

"Baseball? You signed with the Sox?" Ricky was confused. "But you can't do that. You're not twenty-one."

Mando produced another piece of paper. "For you to sign," he said to his father.

"No!" said Mamma.

"No!" said Uncle Luis.

"Yes!" said Ricky, standing up and waving his arms. "It is for the benefit of all. Three thousand dollars!"

"I will take care of you," said Uncle Luis.

"Gringo! *Gabacho!*" snarled Ricky. "Mando is right. Remember Gonzales!"

"Never the baseball," said Mamma. "My boy, he is to be the lawyer."

Mando said, "Sign it, Papa. I have to report tomorrow for tryouts. It's for the best."

His father held the check in one hand and the contract in the other. He was forty years of age, and he looked fifteen years older. He had come to California from Mexico as a wetback and had gained citizenship only after great troubles. He had married Constancia Guzmán when they were young and strong, but the strength had

6

gone out of them, her with child-bearing, him with bone labor and bad health. All his hopes lay in his children.

"Mando, Mando. Why do you do this?" he murmured.

"Because it is the time. Because of the money."

"But the law?"

"I can make it up between seasons. Many have done so."

They were speaking in Spanish now, liquid accents softly exchanged. The older man was not listening to the protests of Uncle Luis, nor to the mournful, sad tones of Mamma. He looked up at his second son, and his eyes were humble.

"You do this. You have the excellent marks in college, you do not have to do this."

"For you, Papa. For the family. Maybe I will not be great at baseball. But for now, it is the best way."

"You were unhappy at the college, maybe?"

"No, Papa."

"No trouble?"

"No trouble, Papa."

"It is hard to understand."

"Look, Papa, how could I go to school, study, play ball, knowing you were here with the fractured leg? Knowing that you could not make the payments, knowing Uncle Luis? Do not try to tell me about him, I will not listen. The Italians have a name for him—*padrone*. He grows rich from the sweat of his family because he is clever. He has the heart of a turnip. Ricky may be wrong about a lot of things, but he is right about the Talker. Sign the contract, Papa, and let me go in peace."

"I do not like this, my son."

"I do not like it very much, either, my father. So— sign, and what will be will be."

Enrique Cruz sat with his chin on his chest for a moment. The voices of the others reverberated in the room, which was not quite big enough to accommodate so much sound. Uncle Luis and Ricky were shouting against each other. Enrique Cruz raised his head.

"Luis!"

The head of the family spoke in that one salutation.

7

Silence came upon them all. Luis stepped forward, bound by tradition to obey.

"A pen, please, Luis."

"You are not . . ." The Talker stopped. He handed over a golden ball-point pen.

Papa wrote his signature with great care. Mamma pressed a handkerchief to her mouth, but no one dared interfere. Mando kissed his father on the cheek, put the contract in his pocket, and hurried into the kitchen. There were tears on his cheeks. He did not hear the clash between Uncle Luis and Ricky and Papa; he knew what it had cost to sign the piece of paper; he knew that it meant defeat, acknowledgment that the Talker was dishonest; and he knew it hurt Papa to allow him to quit college.

Consuelo came silently and went to the ever-present pot on the stove and ladled out soup and put a small pan of refried beans on a burner and warmed a small, well-oiled steak. He sat in the corner at the table. His sister was a beautiful eighteen; she was slender and long-legged and slim of ankle. Like Mando, she resembled Papa's side of the family. They had always been close for brother and sister in the modern world.

She asked, "Is Jack going with you?"

"How did you know?" It was good to tease her, to use the light tone for a change.

"Is he?" she demanded.

"Yes, Jack's going. His mother's in the hospital. We're a couple of emergency cases."

"It's not right. You both should finish school."

"So that you should go to work as a waitress?" he asked.

She flushed deeply. "Jack told you. I begged him not to tell you."

"My sister begs my friend not to tell me about herself," he said, grinning at her. "Shame. What would our parents think of that?"

"All right," she said. "A girl doesn't matter. Right? Only the boys matter. What is a girl? A potential mamma. Beyond that, *nada*. Nothing."

8

"You don't believe that. I don't believe it."

She set a taco before him, succulent with chopped meat and greens shredded to hold the tomato sauce. "I study sociology in the junior college. It is not a very good course. We are crowded. The blacks are militant. There is more noise and confusion than concentration. I could leave for a while, until things are better for the family."

"And when will things be better?"

She sank onto a chair opposite him. Her brown eyes were very large. "I do not dare to ask."

"Then stay in school. If I make it with the Sox, there will be plenty for all."

"For all," she repeated. "But what about you? Mando, the athlete, the student? What of him?"

"He will be a ballplayer, God willing."

The talk in the living room went on in Mexican-Spanish, but the key had altered. Now it was liquid, lilting, overlapping amidst soft laughter. Uncle Luis was telling a story; he was very good at story-telling.

She said, "You see how they are? They already accept. They scream and holler. Then they accept."

"What else? For hundreds of years they have been taught to accept. Only Ricky, he will continue to protest. And bat his head against walls."

"You were hard on Uncle Luis," she said. "The Gonzales thing—he is a *borracho*, a drunk. Uncle Luis had to protect his property. Without his properties, the family would suffer."

"Yes," said Mando. "But Papa—I had to get Papa to sign. He will never be an Uncle Luis."

"Mando the actor," she said, but she smiled, understanding. Then she sobered. "And what of Jack?"

"You worry too much, sister," he told her. "Jack is a big boy. He can take care of himself."

"Yes, I worry. I am *mexicana*, a woman. I worry about my men."

"You're a good sister." He reached out to touch her hand. "Let Jack do what he's got to do."

"What else? As you say, he is *muy hombre*." Again she blushed, but there was pride in her, along with fear.

It was difficult for her, Mando thought. If Papa and Mamma knew she was in love with Jack Kelly, there would be another flurry, another time of protesting and weeping. No Cruz had ever married a gringo.

Jack Kelly sat beside the swimming pool in the Encino middle-class section of the valley. His father was a huge man with a moustache and sideburns and hair down the back of his neck. The senior Kelly had been a college athlete. He was now going to fat.

"You've got to be crazy. Or is it that chicano buddy of yours? What is it with you?"

"Thirty-five hundred bucks," said Jack. "My own money. Not yours to dole out to me. Mine."

"I could keep you from gettin' it. You're under age."

The contract lay on a glass-topped table held down by a very dark bourbon highball. Jack looked at it, at his father.

"Mother wants you to sign it."

"You went to her first." The tone was hard, accusing.

"I've always gone to her first." His voice was as tough as his father's. "You've always been too busy."

"Making a living for you two."

"And spending. A Cadillac. This pool. You can't even afford the house in this neighborhood."

"I want things nice for my family!" He was shouting. "I gave you a car when you were in high school."

"And I'm still driving it," said Jack. "And it took you three years to pay for it, a secondhand car. We don't own anything except that car."

"Don't talk to me like that, my boy. You're not too big to get a whippin'." He started to rise from the beach chair.

Jack said, "Yes, I am too big. You know why Mother's in the hospital?"

"Just nerves, that's all. She'll be all right." But he was uneasy, shifting his bulk.

"Worry," said Jack. "Money worry. You've got a thirty-year mortgage on the house. You want to turn in the Cadillac because the ashtrays are full or the white sidewalls dirty or something."

"Now, you look here . . ."

Jack interrupted ruthlessly. "Father, I've been away a year, I've had plenty of time to think. All our lives we've lived off the top of things. And we always owed money. Sure, you've been generous with me. You wanted me to go to S.C. You had credit there. But Mother worried. I knew it then, and now she's having a breakdown because of worriment. She comes from a solid family."

"Are you running down my family?"

"Could be. They died broke. Big houses, all that. You had to pay their debts. Maybe you still owe on that, too. I won't live that way."

"You're quitting college to be a baseball bum, and you talk about how you'll live. You and your pachuco friends."

"You had it right the first time. 'Chicano,' they call themselves. Mexican-Americans."

"I remember the zoot-suiters. They're all alike. They smoke marijuana and booze it up. They want to bust up everything worthwhile. They're animals. They're no better than the niggers."

Jack said, "You'd better sign the contract."

"I won't do it! You go back to school. Or transfer to S.C., where I can keep an eye on you."

Jack said, "Father, you'd better sign the contract."

"Don't you threaten me, you young whippersnapper."

"One more time: Mother is ill. She thinks baseball is best for me right now. She knows I'm disturbed, and she believes in me. Sign it."

"No!"

There was a silence. Then Jack stood up and said, "Okay. It hasn't been too nice knowing you, but you are my father. I'll be leaving."

"You'd better not."

"I'll have to get a job. One that will take care of Mother and me."

His father came to his feet in a leap. "Your mother? What are you saying?"

"She feels better already. She made her own decision. Like, either you sign or we take off, Mother and me. I know a man in Arizona, he'll give me work, and I can play semipro ball on weekends. We'll make out. And we won't owe everyone."

The big man was scarlet. "No!"

"This man, he's a chicano," Jack said. "He likes me. I'll be working with black people. Whether I take the job or play ball, I'll be working with all sorts of people. I like all sorts of people. I don't know why. I wasn't taught it at home, not by my father."

"You can't do this."

"Mother did what she could. I guess I listened more to her than to you." He reached for the contract on the table.

His father put out a hand. "I want to talk to your mother."

"She has a phone by her bed." He turned his back and walked to the other end of the pool. He had managed to get through the scene without blowing his cool, he thought. It hadn't been easy. He had rehearsed it every yard between the hospital on Ventura Boulevard and his home. He heard his father go into the house—without slamming the door.

For a moment he gulped, remembering when his father had been his idol, the first baseman. Also he had been the great defensive end, not good enough for the pro football mart, but All Pacific Coast. Jack had his first mitt when he was four, his first football earlier than that—a wee one to tumble with on the grass of their first valley home, a modest place in Studio City. Father had been his teacher, his coach, and a good one.

Father had not taken a science degree. He was not a man for books. He was fine in the clubs and the bars, and an alumnus had offered him good starting money in sales—fertilizer it had been—and on the strength of that he married the gentle Marion Temple.

Mrs. Kelly had never been strong. The ebullience and

gusto of her husband relegated her to her natural place, smiling quietly on the sidelines; and after the first child was born, they were informed that she might not bear any more. Jack remembered her as the refuge from Father's blasts of wrath induced by alcohol or by a failure someplace in his business life.

Because fertilizer had not been it, the Los Angeles megalopolis turned to building lots, the orchards and farms were asphalted over, and the buying and selling of property became the thing. At least, Jack's father had believed in it. At times it seemed he was correct, but somehow he had never quite made his fortune at it. Now he had an office, a bit too elaborate, several sales people, male and female, and an overhead that kept his nose to the grindstone in order to maintain the front he thought was necessary.

The old-time athletes, thought Jack. They were always around with their big automobiles and their flashy wives and their positions as doctors, lawyers, merchants, chiefs. It was either match their status or fall out. Wise men had chosen to fall out, but not Big Kell. No matter the cost, he had tried to stay with them.

Jack could remember when he first became disenchanted. It had been because of his mother, seeing it as she saw it, suffering with her and her nervous headaches. It would have been better if she had openly complained, argued her side. She was not formed that way. She suffered in silence. He could understand her. He could never understand the crassness and belligerence of his father.

It had all boiled to a head one day when he was attending Harvard Prep School in the valley. Playing baseball for fun in a pickup game on a Sunday, he had encountered Mando Cruz.

Jack was playing first base, and on the opposing team Mando was playing third. It had been a circumstance, a real circumstance he knew, looking back. The game had been supposedly one-sided, several of the championship Harvard School players against sandlotters and high-

13

school boys. There had been this one chicano, Mando Cruz, who did not believe in defeat.

Instead of a lopsided victory, Jack's team found itself leading two to one in the ninth. Their pitcher was tiring, and they brought in an outfielder to finish the last half of the ninth. Mando Cruz had hit a home run for the sole counter for the opposition and was on deck when the strong-armed outfielder lost control and walked the third hitter.

Mando came up swinging two bats, discarding the lighter one, wielding a dark brown heavy stick. He had let two strikes go by, and then it was down to the final whiff, and the game would be over. The pitcher brought everything to bear and came down through the middle with a big-league fast ball.

Mando, protecting the plate with two strikes on him, did not apply full power. He hit sharply into the hole between Jack and the second baseman. The runner went all the way to third, and Mando turned the corner and threatened to take second. Only a strong throw and a smart cutoff prevented him.

The pitcher was annoyed. The game had been all sewed up; now the tying run was on third, and the winning run on first. That was when things began to happen.

Mando had learned that the man batting behind him was not a sure hitter. Therefore, when the pitcher came out of his stretch and aimed for the plate, Mando took off for second base. It did not seem that he was running very fast. He was glancing toward the catcher. Jack had an inkling of what he was trying—a bad throw—and yelled, "No, no, play the hitter."

But the catcher was proud of his arm. Thinking to end the game, he committed a baseball tactical error. He threw to the shortstop covering the bag.

Mando seemed to fly through the air feet first. He rammed into the shortstop. He kicked the ball loose and into center field. The base runner scored easily from third. Mando went down the line and took possession of the same sack, meantime knocking down the third base-

14

man. Now the ball, thrown from center field, went over the head of the frantic pitcher backing up the base.

Mando trotted home with the winning run. As he crossed the plate, the shortstop whom he had decked came racing in with the third baseman close behind. They were teammates of Jack's at school, and they were raging. They grabbed Mando and began shoving him around, howling that he had interfered with them, fouled them, adding that he was a dirty greaser and if he had any guts he'd fight them, or words to that effect. Other members of the team, including Jack, had boiled around in a matter of seconds.

The first thing Jack noticed was that Mando was not answering his accusers. He stood crouched, his eyes going around. He was looking for teammates, Jack thought, but it was only a pickup game; nobody wanted any part of the fight, it was all his.

The second thing he noted was that Mando wasn't scared. His nostrils widened, then narrowed when he saw he was alone. He almost smiled, as though to accept his dilemma as one which had occurred before and would happen again.

Then he suddenly hit the shortstop, who was closest to him. The boy went backward, taking a couple more with him. Mando could have run through the hole then, and nobody would have chased him, not after witnessing that sort of wallop. He did not.

He hit the third baseman. Another opponent came close, and he batted him negligently, dropping him where he stood. It was then the others dived low and high at him, unbalancing him. One of them had a bat in his hand. They were hammering and kicking at Mando, and this fellow had the bat poised.

That was when something cracked. All those involved were from Harvard School. Jack felt this sound in his head. His eyes closed, then opened.

Then he had the bat. Using it as a poker, he was ramming it between Mando and his attackers. He was yelling and using swear words he scarcely knew the meaning of, and he was sending his own classmates right

15

and left. He got them all away from Mando and lifted the bat, and they knew he could hit a ball out of any park, and what the bat would do to them if he wished to use it.

And he told them, "Get away from him, you dirty jerks. Can't you see he's a better man? Can't you see he's not scared of you? You want to kill him, you damn fools?"

They stood back in awe, and then they were outraged. They were angrier at Jack than at Mando. Jack had deserted his own; he had resigned from the crowd.

And he had, indeed, he realized. He had driven Mando home and eaten his first *chile relleno* and tacos and tasted refried beans, and he had met Connie, Consuelo. Life had not been the same after that.

His father had ranted. It was one time that his mother had spoken up, had taken his side. His mother was fond of both Connie and Mando, but Jack had managed to have them over for a swim only when his father was busy with a prospect for a sale of real estate or otherwise occupied.

It was a foregone conclusion that they would go to college together. The Arizona institution was not fancy, but it had a great baseball team and a fine coach. Jack and Mando had roomed together through their first year and played on the varsity, because there was no freshman rule, and the Gold Sox scout had discovered them. It was no big deal, he reflected; they might have received a much bigger bonus if they had remained in school. It was simply the time for them to strike out on their own. They had talked about it for weeks, day and night, and had arrived at the same conclusion—they must make their move—win, lose, or draw.

His father came out of the house and toward the glass-topped table. He picked up the contract and signed it. There was pain on his face, and some bewilderment, as though he had been bitten by an aging pet dog or kicked by a friendly horse. He simply did not understand, Jack knew.

"Thanks, Father."

16

"Don't thank me. You're on your own. Your mother says you want it that way. Okay."

"Yes, I'm on my own."

"See what good a couple thousand does you. See what good your greaser friends are to you. I should've known when you turned against the Harvard boys. I should've known."

Jack said, "Okay, Father. Good-bye."

His father turned his back. His shoulders twitched, but he did not allow Jack to see his face.

It was time to fetch Mando and leave for the training camp. It was time to speak to Connie for a moment and let her know how he felt about her. Jack hesitated, but it was time to go.

2

The Gold Sox represented the burgeoning Bayside City of coastal California in the American League, thus giving a semblance of balance to the organization known as "the junior circuit," as opposed to the National League, which was the first major league to make money and remain in business. The club was owned by a corporation which included several Hollywood millionaires, including an actor, a comedian, and an independent producer. It was managed by a veteran of baseball named Joseph "Buster" Condor.

The corporation had chosen wisely. They had millions of dollars invested in a couple of dozen ballplayers who were either castoffs from other teams or new boys up from the high minors. Buster Condor knew them all; he had been around and about baseball all his fifty years. He was a tall, balding, immaculate man, deceptively mild, capable of violent tempers and also of sudden, sometimes clever decisions. It took a man like him to handle a catastrophe like a first-year expansion team.

The first thing Condor had done was to hire Samuel "Dutch" Muller, another veteran, a former great catcher, a sometime minor-league manager, a man whose ambition was limited only by cynicism acquired over long years of great hopes and larger disappointments. Thirty thousand dollars a year opened horizons for the bowlegged, gnarled Dutch, even though hopes of better than a last-place finish were, he well knew, less than his hope of heaven ... and Dutch had not led an exemplary life off the ball fields.

Condor and Dutch then got their heads together and picked a scouting team and a coaching staff. One of the scouts, Charlie Denver, had found Mando Cruz and Jack Kelly. One of the coaches would check them out in the camp where over a hundred tyros would show their wares.

This coach was called Harry the Clawhammer, baseball nicknames being less than highly imaginative. Hammer was a hulking two-hundred-pounder with ham hands and a voice like a file raked across the edge of raw metal. He had been a dropout of high school in his first week. This was back in Texas, and no one noticed, because Harry didn't stay around; he ran away and became a baseball bum. He had been a great hitter, and spent some time with the Giants in New York, but he wound up in the minors until his eyes failed him. He never was even a fair fielder, and "Clawhammer" had nothing to do with his glove. It related more to his predilection for settling arguments by hitting people on the head.

The candidates wore their school uniforms when they reported. There were fifty or so infielders in the group, all sorts, sizes, races. Hammer put his hands on his ample hips and spat tobacco juice and roared at them.

"How many youse guys got your military comin'?"

Feet shifted; no one understood. Hammer glared at them.

"You tongue-tied, all of youse? How many got lucky and skipped their numbers, like? Ain't gettin' called as of right now?"

Mando and Jack raised their hands; they had been fortunate. About half of the other aspirants had also not been drawn in the draft lottery.

Hammer said, "All right, yawl git over there. The rest of you, I dunno, the club's got plans, you move yonder. Now, I got a list here, all the names and stuff. I ain't

19

about to try and remember. Way I sees it, yawl show me what you got. Then I know you. Nothin' means nothin' to me 'ceptin' can you run, hit, and throw. Okay, you that ain't army bait, line up for sprints."

It was a huge complex, the training camp of the Gold Sox. It was an expanse of land otherwise valueless, located near the Mexican border in California. It had been equipped by the management with four baseball diamonds overlapping as in public parks, a barracks, an administration building, and a sprawling motel designed to house fans and possibly tourists attracted by the climate and the excitement of being around baseball players.

Mando lined up alongside Jack as Hammer walked fifty yards onto the outfield grass and sighted along an imaginary line. Every move made by the coach was ponderous, Mando thought; he was a pachyderm of a baseball man. On the other side was a short Negro, and Mando extended a hand and mentioned his name as introduction.

The black boy slapped in the skin salute and said, "Sandy Roosevelt," without friendliness. He had wide-spaced eyes and hardly any neck, and his shoulders were ax-handle wide.

Mando nudged Jack. "This is what could be called a motley crew."

"Including us," said the tall first baseman.

Roosevelt was wearing a sweat suit from which letters had been cut; others wore baseball shirts and jeans or baseball pants and T-shirts. But everyone had spikes, Mando noted; not even the most woeful specimen was without his official baseball shoes. This was an important test; the swiftest runners would complete the first hurdle atop the list. The slower men who could throw and hit would have their chance, but the fastest would be ahead of them.

They were all nervous, Mando thought. A few edged forward to gain inches on the remainder, and a rumble went up and down the ragged line.

Roosevelt growled, "Let 'em cheat, the sons."

He was down in the sprinter's start—a track man, thought Mando, a tough competitor. Jack was also on his mark. Mando, who had run little track, merely bent his knees. Coach Hammer lifted a loglike arm and bellowed something, then dropped, pointing his finger at them.

Mando was off in the ruck; Roosevelt ahead; the taller, heavier Jack close behind. They ran twenty yards, and Roosevelt began to fly. Mando flew right along in his wake. Behind them the others strung out, with Jack in third place.

Mando saw Roosevelt take a quick glance over his shoulder, thereby noting that he had company. The squat Negro swerved into Mando's path. In order to avoid him, Mando would have had to cut in front of Jack. Therefore he drove ahead with all his might and speed.

His shoulder struck Roosevelt as they came to the imaginary finish line. Both went sprawling. Jack crossed the line yards ahead of the others.

Roosevelt kicked out, and one spike nicked Mando's elbow. In the next moment the two were rolling over one another throwing punches that had little or no effect. Hammer reached down. He got one of them in each hand and easily lifted the pair to their feet.

"Whatinhell is this?" he roared. "A damn nigger and a greaser fightin' already?"

Roosevelt swung first. He hit the coach on the shoulder; Mando kicked out for freedom. He got Hammer on the knee. Both wriggled loose, and Hammer backed off, his arms up, yelling for help.

Jack grabbed Mando from behind and swung him around, saying, "Is that a way to make friends and influence people?"

Roosevelt was still trying to get at the big coach, but his arms were not quite long enough. One fist caught Hammer on the shoulder, and then both Mando and Jack went in and yanked Roosevelt away and held on to him. The black youth was cursing a full stream.

Hammer demanded. "What's goin' on here, anyway?" He was surprisingly calm.

"Nobody calls me that name," panted Roosevelt.

"He's right," Mando agreed. "Nobody should."

Roosevelt's odd eyes rolled toward Mando. "He called you 'greaser,' didn't he?"

"Only once." Mando did not look at the coach; he kept his gaze on Roosevelt. "People generally try you once."

Hammer blustered, "All right, yawl guys. Everybody over to the battin' cage. All 'ceptin' you three jaspers."

Mando watched the others run. Everybody wanted to hit; it was the nature of all ballplayers. The slower boys would be anxious to make character with muscle. Now it seemed they three would be at the end of the line when observers were weary with the whole procedure.

Hammer said, "What started this here ruckus?"

Again Roosevelt's eyes slanted to Mando. "I lost my stride. I ran in front of him."

Hammer said, "You lost nothin', boy. I seen you. You got speed to burn. You got balance. And you think you're smart and tough. Well, you may be tough, but you ain't too smart."

"I don't like bein' called 'boy,' neither." Roosevelt fixed his stare upon the coach.

"You don't like a hell of a lot." Hammer wheeled on Mando. "Where I come from, 'greaser' don't mean much. It's like the way we talk."

"I was born in Los Angeles," said Mando. "You can call me 'chicano' if you can't use my name."

"G'wan, how do I know your doggone name?"

"Mando Cruz. I play third base. I run good and I hit good. I'm here on a thirty-five-hundred-dollar bonus. You want to know any more?"

Hammer appealed to Jack. "You ever see two such feisty punk kids in your life?"

"Mando's my roomie," said Jack. "I'm on his side."

The big man scratched his head. A grin tugged at the corners of his wide mouth, and he looked suddenly human. "I be dogged. Three of 'em. Look, I didn't mean nothin'. Anything in this world I cotton to it's a fighter. That is, if he's got somethin' he believes in which he will battle for. What do you play, tall boy?"

22

"I'm Jack Kelly, and I play first."

"Bonus?"

"Like Mando."

"And you?"

"Sanderson Roosevelt. I play short. No bonus. No nothin', but I can run, and I can hit, and I'm a glove."

"From the sandlots?"

"New Jersey. Best semipro country there is."

"How old are you all?"

Mando and Jack said, "Nineteen."

Roosevelt said, "Free, black, and twenty-one."

Hammer said, "Go with them others. And I'm gonna pitch battin' practice to the three of you. And watch out for your ears, 'cause I might stick one in 'em. Yawl are too damn fresh."

He lumbered off. The trio surveyed one another.

Mando said, "I think I made a mistake about him."

"He's somethin' else," said Jack. "I figured we were all fired."

Roosevelt still stared at Mando. "I cut you off. I'll do anything to make it in baseball. I ain't sorry, but I appreciate your ways."

"Cool it, man," said Mando. "We all want to make it."

"Yeah. But I got to."

"Okay. All God's chillun got to," said Jack. "We all have good and sufficient reasons, right? First, short, and third. All we need is a second baseman, and we're an infield."

"I don't care who I play with," Roosevelt declared as he walked away. "I ain't nobody's buddy."

When he was out of hearing, Mando said, "Nice kid."

"If he had a neck, he'd be as tall as you," said Jack. "You should've cut my way; he's a rough customer."

"I'm a rough customer, man," said Mando.

"I seem to remember."

They laughed. They walked toward the batting cage, where the infield hopefuls were taking five cuts each at pitches thrown to them by an old pitcher who had nothing left but control and a thorough knowledge of his craft, Ace Holder. Some of the kids were scared, some were overconfident, some were simply inept. It seemed as if every youth who owned a glove and a pair of spikes had turned out for the Gold Sox trials. They waited patiently enough until all were finished. There didn't seem to be a good prospect in the lot.

Hammer beckoned to them. Roosevelt grabbed a bat and ran to the plate as the coach took ball and glove from Holder and toed the slab.

"He's got to be first," Jack said.

"Like he said, he's got reasons." Mando stationed himself where he could watch Hammer's style of delivery.

The big shapeless man seemed transformed on the mound. The ball was like a marble in his hand. He threw three-quarters without effort. The pitch came at Roosevelt's head, and the black youth flung himself backward. A dinky little twist, and the ball was over the plate for what would be called a strike in any league. Several bystanders guffawed. Hammer stared at them.

"You didn't see no curve balls," he rumbled. "You seen nothin' a baby couldn't hit."

He stretched again. He threw a fast one down the alley. Roosevelt came around on it. There was a satisfying whack, and the hit went into right field.

"All righty, lemme see you pull," said Hammer.

He threw one on the outside edge of the plate. Roosevelt got out a bit ahead and fouled it off to the left. Hammer grunted and picked up another ball. He slammed it with terrific speed low and inside. Roosevelt slapped it on a line into left field.

"Here's an easy one," said Hammer.

He pulled the string on an off-speed pitch. Most rookies would have leaped upon it and probably foozled it. Roosevelt waited and hit it into center field.

"Now, I'm warnin' you, boy. The curve."

Hammer threw it well, so that it was around the knees after it broke. Roosevelt pounced, and his neck swelled as he whacked through. The ball took a long flight into the ozone.

Hammer said, "Jest a loud out. Okay, next."

24

Jack went to the plate. He was left-handed all the way. He stood in daintily, his toes angled, his style as natural as paint, Mando thought with pride. Jack had class; it stuck out all over him. Hammer surveyed him for a moment, then tried the same trick he had essayed on Roosevelt, aiming the curve at his ear.

Jack did not give. He followed the flight of the ball. He came around with the level, perfect swing of the natural baseball hitter.

Hammer turned and watched the ball vanish against a cloudless sky. He did not say a word. He looked hard at Jack, threw four more pitches. Jack hit every one of them into the outfield.

Hammer said, "All right you, Cruz. Lemme see you."

Mando took the same stick used by Jack, a heavy one. He decided not to look for the curve. Hammer let fly, and it was only at the last moment that Mando snatched his head from the flight of the pitch. He staggered back and finally fell.

Hammer said, "Fooled ya, huh?"

"Do that again and see what happens," said Mando.

"No point." Hammer shrugged. "Try this one."

He came in sneaky fast but across the plate. Mando swung. He felt the satisfying thud all the way to his shoulders. Of all the balls hit that afternoon, this one went the farthest. It started low and rose and went out of sight altogether.

"Touch 'em all," said Hammer. "You a slugger, Mando?"

"I hit 'em out," Mando told him grimly.

He hit three more out, all fast balls. Then Hammer gave him the slow one, and Mando knocked it into the outfield.

"That'll do," said the coach. "Yawl go play catch and stuff. You—skinny fella there, you a second baseman?"

A thin boy said, "Er—I'm a shortstop. Jones, sir."

"You're a second sacker. Yawl others, get around. You— you fellas there, take the outfield." He picked the kids who had come closest to finishing fast in the sprint, Mando noted.

Hammer picked up the fungo bat and took his position near the plate. "Okay, youse punks. Let's see if there's a glove among yawl."

He started, traditionally, at third, knocking a nasty hopper down to Mando, who fielded it cleanly and made the long throw to Jack, who was graceful as a ballet dancer around first base. The next went to Roosevelt. He charged it, grabbed it, and slung it in one motion. He lacked fluidity, but his throw was on the money, and his speed was unquestionable. The second baseman was adequate, obviously not in the class with the other three rookies. He did manage to cover first when Hammer hit a grounder for Jack to field.

Now they went into the double-play routine, with Jack covering as Mando relayed to Roosevelt, who fired like a machine gun. On the next play the shortstop fed the ball, but the second sacker's pivot was not very good.

Roosevelt snapped, "You can't make it, don't try it, man."

"Try shuttin' up," said Hammer, and again knocked the ball down to short.

Roosevelt grabbed it and threw hard at second. The raw rookie fumbled it. Roosevelt stamped his foot and muttered.

Hammer said, "Too hard. You didn't lead him."

"Give it to me again!"

Hammer obliged. Roosevelt figured the bounce, took the ball in both hands, and lobbed to second. The toss was just right, and the second baseman made his relay in good form.

"You'll learn." Hammer said.

Roosevelt talked to himself but made no further comments to the others for the remainder of the drill.

Hammer finally called a halt after the bunting practice. He said, "You, Jones, you'll get a chance at short."

The thin boy looked at Roosevelt with respect. "I don't think I want it. Can I practice at second?"

"You're an infielder, aintcha? Go on, now, with the others." Hammer watched him, shaking his head. "Won't

26

make it, no hands. You guys, you got hands, I'll say that. You got a lot to learn. But you got guts and hands and good eyes. I mean all of you. Roosevelt, you fight everything too much, mainly your own self. Dig?"

"I got my ways."

"You got a knot for a head," said Hammer. "Tell yawl somethin'. You three got a chance to stick. Not with the big club, don't get no crazy notions. Even this club ain't got no room for raw rookies. You ain't seen nothin' yet. I know yawl don't believe it, but wait. There's some pros in camp, believe you me. On t'other hand, I'm gonna get you unies and put yawl with the possibles. You'll room in the main buildin'. There'll be more, but you three got it made from this bunch."

"You mean none of the others will get a chance?" Jack ventured to ask.

"No way," said Hammer.

"But—you scarcely saw them work out."

Hammer scowled. "What you think they hire me for? My good looks? Mister, I can SMELL a prospect. I can pick 'em blindfolded. I don't know too much about yawl—but you're prospects, and golly knows this club needs all the help it can get."

Roosevelt said in his dour way, "I got no contract."

"Come with me," said Hammer. "You all go to that building yonder. The bigger one. They'll take care of you when I give 'em the word."

He waddled away, Roosevelt in his wake. The Negro shortstop did not turn to say so-long; he rolled, slightly bowlegged, head high, determination oozing from every pore.

Mando said, "Did you hear the big, bad man? 'Golly knows,' he said. Golly knows?"

"Yeah." Jack shook his head. "People is critters, my grandpa always said."

"My grandpa can't speak English," Mando said. "Hammer would call him a dumb greaser."

"And then throw him a baseball."

"The old man couldn't catch it. Should we make the scene in the big building?"

27

It was all new. The parking lot was graveled, and they retrieved their bags from the dusty, somnolent Ford and trekked into a foyer somewhat like that of a hotel lobby without the luxuries.

Ace Holder was waiting for them. "You're the chosen people?" he asked, grinning. He was gray-haired, and his eyes had the far look of an old athlete, and one arm hung oddly away from throwing too many curve balls. "The guy at the desk will give you beds."

"Thank you," said Mando.

"Don't thank me, I didn't even throw to you." He eyed Mando without warmth. "So you're the long ball hitter?"

"Can I help it?" Pitchers always hated hitters, he knew. Custom demanded this of them.

"Wait'll they start to curve you," Ace said somberly.

"I'll be in there."

"You'll be outta there often enough." The amenities observed, he grinned at them. "Hope you make Class A. This club might need you in a few years."

He went about his own business. There was a minor club official at the desk. He assigned them to Room 16, and they took their bags and wandered down a long hall until they found the designated number and entered a big room. There were two bunk beds, oversized, two closets, and four small bureaus with four drawers each.

"Two more to come," said Jack. "Let's grab the lowers."

"Why not?" Mando began to unpack. There was a huge window looking over the parking lot, and in one corner was an air-conditioning unit. "First class all the way. Now, if we can only keep up the hitting."

"And the fielding," said Jack. "There were some pretty good ballplayers out there who won't be here tomorrow."

Mando said, "Look!"

They peered out the window. Cars were vanishing from the parking spaces. Would-be ballplayers were leaving for home, for other tryout camps. It was a sad sight, but Mando could not suppress his feeling of relief and excitement.

28

"Many are called but few are chosen," Jack murmured.

"Amen."

The door opened, and Roosevelt came into the room. He had a battered little overnight bag in his hand. He stared around, then scowled at them.

"Pigs grabbed the best bunks, huh?"

"First pig gets most slop," Mando told him. "What would you have done?"

Roosevelt didn't answer. He went to a dresser and opened his bag. It contained clean underwear and socks and one pair of white jeans and a pair of white sneakers. He arranged everything neatly and closed the drawer and went to the window. Cars were still leaving.

"Huh," he said. "Everybody got a car. Me, I travel on my thumb."

"You're here," said Mando. The black youth rubbed him the wrong way at every turn.

Roosevelt flung open a closet door, found towels on a shelf. He removed his soiled shirt, displaying a torso corded with rippling muscles. "I dunno about you white pigs, but us niggers like to be clean." He started for the door to locate the shower room.

Mando ripped off his shirt. "Take a look, man. Who's got darker skin, you or me?"

It was true. Roosevelt was café-au-lait; each was of a warm shade of brown. They glared at each other.

Jack Kelly drawled, "Us white folks loll on the beach to try and get your color. Why don't you two knock it off? There won't be any way to live with you if you don't."

"You don't want a nigger livin' with you, right?" demanded Roosevelt.

"Why, you jerk, I'm chicano," said Mando. "I'm proud of it. Jack's a Wasp. Who knows what the fourth guy in this dormitory's going to be? While you're in the shower you better wash your mouth out with soap."

Roosevelt dropped the towel and started a punch swinging at Mando's head. Jack grabbed his wrist and spun him. Roosevelt went all the way around, and Jack applied a hammerlock. Kicking, squirming, grimacing, Roosevelt tried to get loose.

Jack said, "I also rassle some." He put pressure on the hold. Roosevelt's head went down, and Jack rammed into Mando's bunk and held him there.

"Like I say, this has to stop," said Jack. "We're here to make the club. Fighting's another business. Both of you better knock it off."

He stepped back and let Roosevelt free. The black boy arose slowly. He picked up the towel. Without another word he left the room.

Jack went on, "You've got to lay off him. He's got a big monkey on his back one way or another. Why don't you let his monkey fight your monkey?"

For a moment Mando was outraged. His best friend ... Then he subsided; the steam went out of him.

"Okay. You're right. Nigger and greaser, what's the difference? I have to learn to control the thing." He managed a wry grin. "It's crazy to come out of the *barrio* and have to fight a guy from the black ghetto, now, ain't it?"

"Crazy is the word, man."

"Yeah. . . . Yeah." He sat down on his bunk. Worse was to come, he knew. He must force himself to adjust. He had chosen this world; if he was to make a place for himself, he had to find a key to open the door ... many doors.

Jack said something he scarcely heard. He grunted as his oldest friend went to join Roosevelt in the showers. Oldest friend? He had no other close friend. He had reduced himself to family and Jack Kelly. He had closed other doors that he might assail this one, he reminded himself. As to family, Uncle Luis the Talker would never give him the time of day again, his mother was weeping, his Brown Beret brother never was close to him in thought or deed.

There was a tap on the door, and he called, "Come in, it's not locked," without thinking that his tone was surly. When the boy named Jones entered, he stared blankly, then with recognition.

30

"Jones?"

"Gilbert Jones," said the youth. "They sent me here."

"Well, you make four. All infielders," said Mando. "You suppose they've got method in their madness?"

"Maybe." Jones looked around. He was carrying a lightweight piece of airplane luggage, a weekender which was not inexpensive. "May I put away some things?"

"Over there," said Mando. The young man had no color. His hair was fair, nondescript. His eyes were pale gray. His face was thin and without expression. Only his jaw was, on closer inspection, solid, fleshed.

"Which bunk?"

"Upper. Over the great first baseman, Kelly." Mando pointed. "Over me the great shortstop, Roosevelt. I think you got the best of it. I'll bet Roosevelt twists and turns in the night."

Jones said, "Yes, Roosevelt. That was the mistake, you see."

"Uh-huh. Mistake, huh?" Mando was curious.

"Well, I'm a shortstop too." Jones unlocked his suitcase. He was methodical in every move. He took out brightly colored shirts. He hung up sleek slacks. There were shiny boots and two wide-lapeled, colorful jackets. There were handkerchiefs and underwear, and all spoke of good taste and good money.

"I see." Mando did not see at all.

"Hammer wanted to get rid of me. But Mr. Condor said that they should take another look." Jones threw Mando a surprisingly sharp glance. "I don't come on strong."

"And you never played much second base."

"No. Short and third."

"Third?" Mando was amazed.

"I have an arm," said Jones, stating a plain fact.

"I see. And you hit?"

"I get on."

"Uh-huh. Lead-off?"

"In college."

"Whereabouts?"

"Iowa," said Jones. He looked homesick for just a moment. "I'm from Ames, Iowa."

"Never knew anybody from there." The boy's certain diffidence, his obvious loneliness, made Mando feel easier somehow. "So you're going to battle Roosevelt."

"I would in a minute. They won't let me. I'm to learn to play second."

"You don't like it much?"

"Not much." Jones had emptied the suitcase. He put it carefully in the bottom of a closet. He fastened his gray eyes upon Mando. "I'm not a tough guy. I'm no fist fighter. But I'd fight you or Roosevelt for your jobs."

"Jonesy," said Mando. "We haven't got jobs. Mr. Condor knows you? He don't know us, man. We're nobody."

"I'm Mr. Nobody," said Jones. "I just manage to get things done."

The door slammed open, and Roosevelt returned, briskly rubbing his thick body with the towel. He saw Jones and stopped.

"Hey, man, what you doin' here?"

Mando said, "He's the fourth infielder."

"Him? Why, he ain't goin' to make it. Hammer said he wasn't goin' to make it."

"Hammer's not running the club," said Mando. "This is Gilbert Jones. Another roomie. Haven't you got any manners at all, Roosevelt?"

"No," said the shortstop. He went to where his clean clothing hung and donned it. Then he paused and looked at the neatly hung slacks and jackets. "This here his stuff?"

Mando said, "Ask him yourself. I'm going to shower."

Roosevelt stared again at Jones. "One of them, huh? A rich dude. Man, I get all kinds. All kinds! Just like always, I ain't let off anything."

Jones spoke for the first time since Roosevelt had entered the room. "I didn't ask to room with you people. It's just one of those things. Maybe if you lay off me and I lay off you, we can manage what little time we have together. Right?"

32

Mando said, "That's the way I figure it. You two work it out between yourselves."

He found a towel and went down the hall toward the showers. The echo of the door he slammed behind him had not died when conscience struck him. He had deserted the newcomer, Jones, without thought. He had no illusions whatsoever about Sandy Roosevelt. He had come from a ghetto known as a *barrio,* he had been familiar with the Roosevelts whose skin was saffron to dark brown. These were recalcitrants, they had a hatred of society not excluding their own people. Jonesy represented the enemy.

Jack Kelly, finished with his bath, came toward Mando. They paused a moment in the hallway.

Jack said, "Hot water and everything."

"That kid, Jones, is with us," said Mando. "You know, the skinny second baseman."

"Surprise, surprise," said Jack.

"The Great Black One is on his back."

"Of course."

"Well." Mando hesitated. "There's something about Jonesy. I don't know. Like a stray pup from another world. More like your world."

"Man, I got no world," said Jack. "I got a first baseman's mitt. And you."

"Yeah. Okay. Check the kid, will you?"

Jack pretended amazement. "Mando the Man is adopting a stray?"

"No, damn it. Just check before Roosevelt eats him alive and we have trouble we don't need."

"Yes, sir, Mando the Man. Yes, sir!"

Mando snapped the towel at Jack's bare middle and ran into the shower room.

3

They were working the pitching machine. Hammer was working it, scarcely concealing his immense pleasure at their futile swings.

"You can't hit Iron Mike, how can you hit a real man?" he kept asking.

"I don't believe that thing is sixty feet, six inches from us," Jack Kelly said to Mando. "Look at the Great Rosey."

Roosevelt was hunched, neckless, glaring. Hammer pulled a lever. The ball came zooming from between two polyglass tires. The motor purred, the ball curved. Roosevelt swung and missed.

"Call yourself a hitter," said Hammer. "One more time. Just a nice fast ball."

Roosevelt squinted his eyes. He swung with all his might. He popped it up for a foul ball.

Hammer said, "Okay. We got Kelly, we got Mando the Man. You next, Jonesy. Step up and call your shots."

Jonesy picked up a light bat, hefted it. He minced to the imaginary home plate. He poised himself in a half-open stance. He held the bat high.

Hammer worked the infernal machine. The ball came in hard and straight, as it had for Roosevelt. Jonesy closed his stance and applied the wood.

A sharp shot sped into the net. It was a base hit.

34

Hammer said, "Oho. A smart guy. Try the curve, Smart Guy."

The curve slanted in. Jonesy slapped it for another patent hit.

Hammer said, "You got eyes or somethin'?"

But the behemoth coach was pleased. He pulled the lever, and Jonesy met the ball. The hits sprayed in all directions.

Hammer said, "That'll do it, podner. You do got the eye. Now, the rest of you. How did he do it?"

"He's a funky punk," Roosevelt muttered.

"Good eye, quick hands," said Mando.

"He didn't try to pull the ball," said Jack Kelly.

"What was that you said, Rosey boy?" asked Hammer. "I didn't quite grab that."

"I dunno," said Roosevelt. "It's just a stinkin' machine. Gimme a pitcher I can't hit, gimme that."

"If you live, you'll find plenty you can't hit," Hammer told him. "Okay, outta the way, roomies. There's others waitin'."

It was beginning to shape up, Mando thought. In a week the field had narrowed down. The four of them had hung on, with Jones improving so swiftly at second base that Hammer himself had uttered words of commendation.

Then there was Peck, thirty years old, a quick center fielder who had been up twice in the league with other clubs. He had been happy when the Gold Sox traded for him, and was fighting to make the team. His batting was hurting him. Now he was in the cage against Mike, and his wrist action was still poor, Mando thought. Good glove, no hitter, wouldn't cut it in the outfield, he had to hit to make it.

There was a kid named Downey next in line, about twenty, a country boy who resembled the young Mickey Mantle in all but skills. He too was an outfielder, a bit clumsy but eager. He had power and speed. He had a chance.

Acton, also an outfielder, was another veteran. He could hit, he could field, he knew the game. He had suffered a broken arm. If the arm came back, he would be an asset to any major-league team. They watched him closely, a clean-cut, serious man with a family.

There was one more sure bet, Mando knew. Dizzy Pazolla was a twenty-one-year-old catcher. He was a wild man. He was full of bubbling life. He had black, snapping eyes and an arm which cut down runners without effort. He could hit. He needed only experience.

This aggregation had played together in three-inning pickups. Mando had scrutinized them all. There was one more, a squat kid of nineteen, who had a chance. He was a third baseman. His name was Ely Zander. He had been born somewhere in Europe. He had come to the United States when he was nine, had fallen in love with a baseball.

Zander was next at bat. Mando watched him with a slight worriment in his middle. The machine sped the ball on its way. Zander took a full cut. He missed. Mando breathed a sigh of relief. Zander was a free swinger like himself, like Jack and Roosevelt. It would take a lot of practice to learn how to hit that machine with a free swing. Jonesy was a Punch and Judy hitter with a terrifically keen eye. Jonesy could hit it if he could see it, never for power, but always with assurance.

Still, that Zander was a good infielder. There was no question about that. He would not be in the next cut. There was no way to know who had the inside track, Mando or the immigrant kid. Nobody told anybody anything in this camp. Rumor ran like quicksilver, but nobody knew the truth. It all depended on Hammer, Ace Holder, the one they called Joker Wilde, another coach, and of course Manager Dutch Muller. Meetings were held every night behind locked doors. The cattle herd had gone; only those who might make a minor-league club were left.

Or the big club? Mando asked himself. As he saw it, looking over the regulars, none of them had a smell of a chance. It was an expansion team, veterans and youngsters, but it was just about set. The pitching wasn't too bad, but the rest of them were rejects and ambitious rookies. It was a last-place outfit, no question. But Mando wouldn't be on it, nor any of the others he had just run through his mind, he believed.

Zander missed his final shot. Hammer shook his head.

"Yawl are the worst bunch of bushers I ever seen. You gonna work on this here machine every day until you git to hit it. You gonna learn how to hit it. You gonna have to, because that's part of the thing we got goin' here. There's a reason for it. And I got another message for yawl. This afternoon you gonna play against the team." He pulled out a wrinkled piece of paper. He reeled off names.

They were the names Mando himself had picked. And Zander wasn't on it as a starter. Zander would sit on the bench with a few others. Was this a sign, Mando wondered? To be chosen to play against the big team, was that it? Would they all be assigned to clubs in the chain if they made good? There was no way to learn.

Clawhammer was booming, " 'Course you get pitchin'. We give you Grey, Cantor, Buchanan.' "

"Yeah, but who do they use?" asked Roosevelt.

Hammer snickered. "Guys you won't hit. You think you're gonna face old Ace?"

Sooner or later, Mando thought, it had to be learned who could really hit. The Iron Mike, the batting-practice ancients like Holder and Hammer, they were nothing. It was the big men who counted. Those named by Hammer would be working easy to get in top shape. The rookies would be facing people like Jay, the canny long reliever; and Tolliver, the short man; and worst of all, Oley Anson, the knuckle-baller. Mando had never in his life even seen a good knuckler.

On the other hand, neither had many of the other rookies, he told himself, certainly not Zander. In the two weeks they had been working out in the great camp at Goldtown, all had been accorded the chance to get in condition, to become aware, to learn the game. It was graduation day, and they had not even been allowed to mentally prepare themselves.

"Nobody ever said it would be easy," he told Jack as they headed for the training table.

"Don't eat much," Jack warned him. "This may be the day."

"Just what I was thinking."

The canned recorded music flowed through the commissary. The ballplayers were extraordinarily quiet this day. They had all been given the news, workouts against the big team, final checkouts of those not quite accepted or rejected, decisions whether they would be dropped or assigned to the lower leagues.

It would be frightening, Mando thought, to be dropped. But it could be depressing to go to an A league for so little money that he could not remain solvent. If he could make AA ball he would at least stay even with the world. He ate a salad and drank fruit juice and had a glass of milk. He had not eaten a refried bean since coming to the camp, nor had he seen a taco or a tortilla. In Arizona this food had been available because of the large Mexican-American population of the state. He had not realized before how much he missed the victuals to which he was accustomed, the home cooking. For a moment he felt alien, lost in the world to which he had come with such hopes for the future.

He looked at Jack and saw that he was not alone. Jack's expression was serious, his mind turned inward. He toyed with his food.

Roosevelt sat, as always, with the other black candidates. They chose to eat apart, a fact which made Mando often uneasy. He had heard of racial antagonism on ball clubs, he had expected to be, himself, a target. Since the initial clash with Hammer, nothing had occurred. Roosevelt's attitude was, Mando thought, unhealthy. But today the shortstop sat silent, a dark cloud of silence.

Oddly, only Gilbert Jones was, as always, quiet, unaffected, pleasant, but not offering anything. He ate a chicken sandwich and sipped iced tea. It seemed impossible that this slim, delicate youth could explode into meteoric action on the ball field.

38

Jack said, "You finished, *amigo?*"

"Right."

They removed themselves from the table. Jonesy drank the last of his tea and silently joined them. They walked out and across to the main diamond, the best-kept field, the one utilized by the big team. They were early. They sat on the bench together.

Jonesy observed in his mild manner, "I was so thirsty. I'm still thirsty."

"Don't drink any more," Jack advised with utmost seriousness. "It's not good to drink too much."

Mando said, "Yeah, you might founder like a horse."

Jack cracked up at his own solemnity. "A pony. Jonesy's a pony."

"But quick," said Jonesy.

"Quick," acknowledged Mando. "We'll be all right."

"You think so?"

"Us chicanos never admit."

"But you're scared?"

"Senseless," said Mando.

"You, Jack?"

"Scared silly."

"Then we're ready," said Jonesy.

"And here comes the big fella," Jack said. "The clawhammer. The old-timer. The learned veteran, see any sports columnists."

"And we got to go to work," said Mando. "Which is better than sittin' here scared."

The rest of the rookie team followed Hammer. Ace Holder was with them. Then the regulars, the sure-fire big-team individuals, came from the opposite direction, from their exclusive clubhouse with the carpeted floors and fully electrical training room and their deep lockers bearing their nameplates and all the other rewards of excellence. They were led by Dutch Muller.

Manager Dutch Muller, whom Mando had thus far seen only from afar, was gnarled, aged, a walnut of a man whose cap seemed a size too small. His eyes brooded, too close to his huge, broken nose. He did not speak to ballplayers unless it was absolutely necessary. He issued orders through his coaches. He never came off the bench except to remove a pitcher, and it was common knowledge that said hurlers received nothing from him but curses because they had allowed themselves to be knocked out of the game. Nobody ever accused the Dutchman of being a nice guy.

The rookies left the bench and began warming up, throwing the ball back and forth, keeping clear of the immaculate neatness of the main diamond where the groundskeepers had toiled to attain the geometric perfection of a big-league park. The red dirt, the green grass, the white lines, made a lovely picture beneath a cloudless blue sky devoid of the smog of cities.

Men and women drove around the winding road which bordered the field and parked behind the small but new and comfortable grandstand. These were the dignitaries, the people who had poured millions into the Bay City Gold Sox. Mando recognized two movie stars. All of them occupied the boxes, staying together as a group. They had been informed that this was the day the ax would fall, and they wanted, Mando supposed, to see where their money was going.

There would be no batting practice. The regulars in their close-fitting uniforms, designed to resemble as closely as possible the old Yankee pinstripes, but with golden trim, took the field for infield practice. There wasn't a rookie within sight who did not know every single one of them, know their strengths and weaknesses, covet their jobs. Mando watched the third baseman, Lou Libby, a hawk-nosed individual.

Libby was thirty-one. He was a black man. He had a fine glove and a good arm. But he had hit only .230 for his previous employers, the Braves. And he was thirty-one years old. Oh, Mando would watch him, all right.

Jack Kelly would be watching Bones Astor with the same intensity. The first baseman was a year older than Libby, a burly, red-faced, barrel-chested man. He hit the long ball. His glove was fair to poor. He ran fairly well for a two-hundred-pounder. He had been a big star and had saved his money and was known as wealthy but eccen-

40

tric. He had six children. He might retire if he suffered a bad year.

Jonesy would concentrate on the second baseman. His name was Monty Wells, and he was a .250 hitter and, like Jones, a lead-off man.

And Roosevelt? He would be scanning and scorning Al Gordon, the shortstop. Gordon was the best of them, Mando thought. He was in his prime at twenty-eight. He had a good arm, one of the best. He was steady and solid.

They were ballplayers picked up in desperation by an expansion team with very little range of choice. They paid their millions, Mando knew, and took what the established teams allowed them, which was next to nothing. Only the very rich could afford a big-league ball club as a toy and tax write-off. Which was bad for the game, he believed, diminishing the quality of play, the interest of the fans. Still, it gave a chicano rookie a better chance, however you looked at it. . . .

The baseball stung his hand. He saw Jack shaking his head as he steamed the throw. He nodded, agreeing that it was no time to be woolgathering, knowing that his friend was warning him. They knew each other that well, Mando thought; it was a fine thing to have a friend who knew you, understood you. If he was fond of your sister, that was good, too, a warm feeling. Connie was a good girl, the only member of the family he truly related to. He shrugged himself back to the present moment, to the battle to survive.

Hammer yelled, "Okay, you rookies, git out yonder and show your stuff if you got any."

They took the field in their makeshift uniforms, looking like a sorry group, Mando knew. The people in the grandstand would not be proud of this aggregation for which they had spent their thousands. They warmed up quickly. They then went to the dugout. The big team would be the home club, of course. The umpires who would be working the preseason games for the club were on hand to make it look official. It was all pretty cut and dried. Jonesy licked at his dry lips and took his

41

light piece of ashen stick to the batter's box to face the first Gold Sox pitcher, Sam Grey, the right-hand number-two starter.

Grey was a ten-game-winner, but he was a poised veteran. Like all hurlers, he had no mercy, nothing on his mind but his win-lose and ERA, both of which affected his yearly salary. He stared coldly at Jonesy, accepted Catcher Paigot's sign with a negligent nod, and came in with a straight, hard one, aimed for the outside corner in the strike zone.

Jonesy shorted up. He crouched, reached out. He dumped a spinning bunt down the first-base line and ran. He flew like the wind.

The regulars were caught flatfooted. Mando came up in the dugout yelling. Jonesy was safe by the proverbial mile.

Peck, the veteran center fielder, came to the plate. Grey regarded him with some attention. Coaching on first, Ace Holder talked to Jonesy, who took a fair lead, not a daring, attention-calling lead, just a safe one.

Grey toed the mound, glanced at Jonesy, pitched. Peck obeyed a signal from Hammer down in the third-base box and swung at a slider. The ball golfed weakly into right field. Jonesy took one look and was gone. He made second. Peck was easily on at first.

Roosevelt was breathing fire. His nostrils flared, he clenched his teeth. He went to the plate with a dark, heavily grained thirty-eight-ounce bat. He settled in, no neck showing on him, spreading his powerful, bowed legs.

Grey looked at the Gold Sox bench, at the umpires, at the grandstand, at the skies, as though to demand why this should happen to him. He squinted at Roosevelt and scented more trouble. He settled down to pitch the best way he knew how, with more skill than strength, with the knowledge that a workout with rookies before the distinguished assembly could result in something close to disaster if he did not settle down.

Roosevelt took a ball. He took a strike. Then Grey tried to sneak a fast one by him. It missed the corner and came in waist-high. Roosevelt came around with his bat.

The sound of full, good wood was on the air. The runners ran halfway down the baselines and turned to stare. In center field young Pascola was racing. Roosevelt, head down, turned first.

Pascola was home-run depth into the outfield. He turned at the last possible instant and leaped. He stuck up his glove. The ball nestled into the pocket. Pascola unleashed a terrific throw to the cutoff man.

The runners returned to their bases. Roosevelt had contributed only a loud, long out. He came back toward the bench with his teeth showing in a snarl. Mando wiped his bat with the tar rag and went to the batter's box from his on-deck spot. Roosevelt's blow would have been a home run in a half-dozen big-league parks, he recognized. And Pascola—Mando was glad he did not aspire to beat out the rookie for a job on the club.

Grey was not under the illusion that Roosevelt had been an easy out. He was shaken by the imaginative attack of the rookies. He had no way of knowing their weaknesses at the plate. Mando could see his mind working, and stayed loose at the plate. Grey had one more weapon, that of intimidation.

The pitcher threw from a stretch position. Mando was looking for it, and it came, right at his head. He leaned back, scorning to hit the dirt. The ball nicked his shirt.

Mando's neck began to swell. He hesitated, not looking at the umpire, who was boredly motioning him toward first, staring at the pitcher's box. Grey had thrown at him. Mando knew it. If he had been dug in, he might have been injured and out of the spring camp. He tossed away the bat, gently, without passion. He started for first base on the trot, paused.

He said distinctly, "You throw at me again, I'll beat your brains out, Grey."

The pitcher snapped, "You're lucky, rookie; just shut up."

Mando's pace faltered; then he went grimly on to the bag. Ace Holder moved in close, whispered in his ear.

"He's right. Shut up."

"The jerk threw at me."

"Where do you think you are, in the Little League?"

Mando shook himself. Ace was right. You had to take your chances up there. The pride of a pitcher was as the pride of a hitter. It was true; he knew it was true, but his blood boiled. It was an effort to be silent, to con the situation afield, to think about a sign from Hammer, to watch each pitch, to hope Jack Kelly, next at bat, would connect.

Three on, one out, he repeated to himself. A double play would end it. A hit meant two runs. Mando looked toward the plate. Jack was staring at him, knowing what he was feeling, what he was fighting. He lifted a hand.

The people in the boxes were stirring. Both Mando and Jack wore identical uniforms. There was a rustling of paper as the spectators sought the names of the rookies in the press handouts fashioned by the publicity corps of the Gold Sox. Theirs were not the decisions, but they were the money people; it would be good to be known by them.

Jack looked beautiful in the batter's box. He had the stance, left-handed all the way, tall, with the big, strong hands wrapped around the bat and the toed-in, closed position, all balanced, controlled. He was a picture, and Grey was staring hard at him. Mando took a good lead, since Bones Astor was not holding him on. The Gold Sox infield was set for the double play to cut off the run.

Jack took the hit from Hammer. He watched Grey with eyes which could spot the ball as it left the pitcher's hand. There was no sign of nervousness, no twitching of the wrists, no agitated swinging of the bat.

Grey looked around at the base runners. The sun hung high in the California sky. A hot breeze drifted in from Mexico, to the south. Grey threw from the stretch position.

The pitch was a curve. It was a very good curve, coming into the left-handed batter at the knees. Jack let it go by for a strike. This was the big league, but the law was the same: Wait for your pitch, guard the plate.

Grey seemed relieved. He took his time with the resin bag, with his cap, with the dirt around the rubber. He inhaled, threw again.

This one was a fast ball. It was also around the knees, cutting the inside corner of the plate. Jack watched it with detachment. Grey was now threading the needle. It was time to step back out of the batter's box, knock the clay out of spikes, shift the grip on the bat, slightly choking it.

Paigot was growling, "'At's the pitch, baby. 'At's a way to throw in there."

Doubt hung in the southern breeze. The nonprofessionals imagined they were looking at a scared rookie who couldn't get the bat off his shoulder. They began to check the lineup to ascertain who would be next to hit.

The pros waited. The base runners took their leads and watched. Mando waved a fist at Jack.

Grey threw another hard one, jamming Jack. The bat met the ball and fouled it off. Grey shook his head as though to intimate that Jack was lucky to have made contact with that one. He threw again.

He threw four good pitches, every one of them in the strike zone. Jack fouled them all into the stands. Mando began to grin to himself. Despite his power, Jack was always superb at guarding the plate when he had two strikes on him. Matching wits and skill with a big-league starter hadn't fazed him. Jack was doing his regular thing.

And Grey was doing his regular, big-league thing. He had lost his nervousness; he was matching wits with a young upstart. He knew full well what Jack was doing, that he was protecting the plate and awaiting his pitch. Grey was determined not to give it to him. He meant to keep the ball low and make Jack hit it on the ground for a possible double play to end the inning. All else was forgotten.

Grey began moving the ball around, trying to fool the hitter. He threw high, low, and wide in succession. Jack let them all go by. The count now ran full, three and two. Grey had to come in with his best pitch, and it had to be in the strike zone, or a run would be walked in.

Mando increased his lead, watching the pitcher, watching Jack, watching Hammer coaching at third. Grey ground a new ball in powerful hands. Jack showed no sign of trepidation, standing straight and strong at the plate. A peculiar silence fell on the field. There were no fans, no rooters, only critics, Mando thought. It was, this moment, a grim business. The game they had learned to play for fun had turned into an affair of life and death.

Grey was set to be the ace right-hander of the new club. He could fail now and survive, but the seed of doubt would be in the minds of the bosses if he gave up runs to yannigans in his first official start of the spring training session. He toed the slab. He came through with his best pitch, a courageous effort, a sharp curve ball designed for the inside corner.

The curve hung. Mando saw it and was off almost with the crack of the bat, holding up only long enough to gauge the flight of the ball. It cleared the outstretched glove of Wells at second. It ran into right field, not a power shot, a hard single. Gonzales came in fast. Two men scored. Mando held up at second as Hammer frantically flagged him down, lest the good arm of the Cuban outfielder nail him at third. Jack roosted on first base.

The silence grew more profound. No one cheered for unknown rookies beating the brains out of a first-line hurler, Mando thought. Jack was no hero; he was a killer. There was big money invested in Grey, very little in Jack, Mando, and the other rookies. The pitcher stood on the mound staring westward at the distant mountains. He removed his cap, wiped his face with his sleeve, and turned his attention to Jack. He shook his head in disbelief. Then he accepted another new ball. Downey, the kid right fielder, was at the plate swinging a stick and ready.

Grey struck out Downey. Then he made Acton pop to second. Then he walked very slowly to the bench. He had, after all, stranded two men. It was early in the training, he would have other opportunities. It was the new men who had to prove themselves quickly or be sent to places they did not care to go.

As he picked up his old worn glove, Mando said to Jack Kelly, "Why didn't you hit it out?"

"Chicken," said Jack. "I took a sure one."

"It hung there for you."

"Jealous?"

They exchanged grins and went to their positions. Jack began throwing the practice ball around the infield. Mando's returns were on the mark, swift as bullets. He had made two tosses before he realized that there had been a change in the pitching plan. On the mound for the rookies was none other than Blackie Schwartz, the star left-hander of the Gold Sox roster.

Management was going all the way, thought Mando. A show was to be put on for the visiting firemen. The rookies were going to have a chance to beat the regulars on even terms. And the two leading pitchers were being set against each other. It was, or maybe was not, smart baseball thinking. It was a test of who was in the best condition, probably no more. It also put the big team on its toes, served notice that nobody's job was safe, which also put the rookies on their mettle, showing them they had a chance. Maybe, he thought. Maybe.

The umpire called time, and he took his position against Monty Wells, the second sacker. Monty was a right-handed hitter but not noted for pulling the ball, so Mando gave him some of the baseline. He began barking in his customary manner.

"Let's get the leadin' lady in there. Let's go, let's go!"

Jonesy picked him up, and Jack joined in. Roosevelt was silent. Pazolla, the kid behind the plate, was a chatter guy also, and Blackie Schwartz grinned around at them.

Schwartz was a lean, round-shouldered, dark man, in his mid-twenties. He was known as an in-and-outer from previous experience, unbeatable when he was on. He had wild spells, like so many southpaws. He had speed, a curve, a slider, and a terrific overhand downer.

47

He said, "All right, kids. Let's stick it to 'em."

With that he walked Wells on four pitched balls, none near the platter.

Mando said, "All right, all right, get two, get two!"

Schwartz gave him a grateful glance, then settled down to pitch to the young new Pascola, a left-handed slugger who sprayed line drives all over the place. Mando gave some baseline and poised for a play in the hole if possible off this kind of batter.

It came, a sliced but hard-hopping ball to Mando's left. He went over and gloved it deep, then spun and made his short throw to second. Jonesy took the ball and pivoted to go to first for the double play. Wells slid into Jonesy and spoiled the timing. Jack stretched for the throw, but Pascola was safe on a fielder's choice.

Roosevelt was moving uneasily. He had been given no chance to shine, and his long out had not made him happy. Jonesy played deep for Al Gordon, the shortstop and righty hitter for the Sox. Jack held the swift Pascola to the bag as Schwartz pitched.

Gordon got hold of one and sent it hopping past the box. Jones came in on it, grabbed it, and went to second. Roosevelt, covering, made the force and tried for the double play. He also was slammed by the runner, Pascola. Again the throw to first was a bit off the mark, and again the runner was safe.

Schwartz looked at Roosevelt, then at Jones. Then he grinned. "Those punks are drop-kickin' you guys. Stick the next one in their teeth."

"One to go," Mando droned. "Two out, one to go." It was his natural manner; he was a take-charge man on the field.

Someone from the Sox bench yelled, "Listen at the chicano. Big deal, big deal!"

They chimed in from all over, "Hey, greaser! Hey, holler guy, who died and left you the king?"

Mando closed his ears. He knew the fate of ballplayers who listened to the taunts of the opposition. One split second of distraction, and the ball game could go away.

Cobbit, the left fielder, proved this by getting to an

48

outside pitch and driving it down the baseline. Mando hopped over; he had been giving ground to the left-handed power hitter. He grabbed at the ball. He stepped and extended his arm. A white streak steamed across the diamond and into the mitt of Jack Kelly.

"Yer out!" said the base umpire.

"Oh, nooooo!" came from the Sox. "You blind mouse!"

It had been close, but the man was out, Mando knew. The protests were automatic, part of the game. The Sox were already taking the field. He trotted in and sat beside Jack. Blackie Schwartz came over and donned a windbreaker, sitting beside them.

"You guys know how to handle that ball," said the star pitcher of the club. "I'm serious about those blockin' backs runnin' into you. Make them know you'll hit back."

"There's moves to be made," said Roosevelt, speaking for the first time that afternoon. "But I'd break a leg on 'em. I wouldn't want to break somebody's leg."

Schwartz stared at him. "No. That wouldn't cut it."

"You're on deck," Jones said to Schwartz. "It's a pleasure to play behind you, sir."

"Thanks," said the lefty. "I ain't so sure myself, not right now."

"You're good enough for us," said Mando.

"Wait'll you see me hit."

Grey seemed to have regained all his poise. Pazolla grounded out. Schwartz proved his point, swinging like a washerwoman at three pitches to fan. Jonesy went to bat.

Grey threw carefully to the slim second baseman. The count ran even. Then Jones slapped a curve into left field for a clean single.

Peck couldn't get a good whack and flied out, and the rookies were retired. Mando took the field again.

Now Schwartz seemed to be warmed up. He began throwing dazzling pitches, all flavors. He retired the side in order.

Roosevelt led off in the third. He waited, took a full count. Grey came in with his curve, game as always.

49

Roosevelt followed it, nailed it down the line at third for what seemed a sure hit.

Libby seemed to leap ten feet into the air. The ball stuck in the webbing of his glove.

Roosevelt, turning first, couldn't believe it. He walked back. He was muttering.

"You black thief, robbin' your own kind. I'd like to ram it down your throat."

Some of the players laughed, but Mando knew the shortstop meant every syllable. Roosevelt was a fighter all the way, every way, all the time. He wanted those hits on the record book kept by Hammer and the others. He would hurt anyone to make a place for himself.

Mando went to bat. He watched Grey's hand. This time the pitch came at him, but he had seen the betraying twitch of the wrist. He knew it was a curve when it left Grey's hand. He stepped right into it. He hit it over second base. He ran down to first and was safe by a mile, despite Pascola's swift throw.

Jack came up again. The duel resumed where it had left off. They were all watching Jack now. He proved the first time had been no fluke by again running the count full, again fouling off good pitches. Grey came with his hard high one on this occasion. Jack hit it into right field. Mando turned second, got the sign from Hammer, and slid into third. Jack remained at first as the cutoff man interposed.

Grey refused to again be angry. He worked on Downey. The kid right fielder banged one down to short, and the double play retired the side. The rookies still led by two runs.

This would be the last inning for Blackie Schwartz, Mando reflected, throwing the ball to Jack at first as the pitcher took his warm-up throws. Thus, in a way, this would be the actual finish to the little game set up by management. Grey had given up two runs, then settled down. But Grey had given the rookies a chance to hit.

On the other hand, Blackie had provided the opportunity to show fielding prowess. He was not sharp, he was a bit wild, and the bats of the regulars had been loud if unproductive.

Therefore management was probably correct. It had set up a miniature situation from which it would deduce certain facts, like a computer. The question was, how well had Mando done, how well Roosevelt and Jones? The one incontrovertible evidence was that Jack Kelly could not miss. Jack had come through in the clutch, and Jack reeked with class.

So there was one-half inning to go in this experimental battle. Astor, Libby, and Gonzales were the three Sox hitters, none of them truly great, although Bones Astor could hit the long ball sometimes. Schwartz toed the rubber, and Mando set himself for the left-handed batter. It seemed to him that the happy-go-lucky southpaw pitcher was amused. Schwartz's position was assured, and he was known to be eccentric. Mando shifted his feet, uneasy.

Bones Astor looked over a fast ball. Then he swung on an outside curve that did not break as it should have. The ball came down to third on a fast hop, close to the line.

Mando went over. He stretched. He gloved the ball, but the force of impact knocked him off balance. He threw with all his might.

Astor beat the throw by a fraction of an inch. Mando kicked the dirt. A left-handed batter had no right to smack with such power to the opposite side of the infield.

Schwartz called, "Nice try, chicano. No sweat."

A try didn't count, Mando felt. If he had not given so much baseline to Astor, he could have made the play. He fumed, crouching, watching Schwartz get ready to throw to Lou Libby, the third baseman of the Sox, the man who would be in Mando's mind all through the season, the man he hoped to succeed on the big team.

Again it seemed as though Schwartz was being either frivolous or careless. He gave Libby a waist-high ball outside. The right-handed hitter reached out and sent it

51

straight back through the mound. It was labeled hit all the way.

Jonesy never seemed to hurry. He drifted over behind second base. He gloved the ball. He slapped it to Roosevelt for the force on Astor.

Roosevelt was facing first base. Astor came in as runners do, trying to break up the double play. Roosevelt met him, braced, dropped his left elbow, made the throw.

Libby, not a fast man, was out. Astor rolled over in the dirt of the base path. His mouth was bleeding. Roosevelt had mashed him with the elbow. Astor came to his feet swinging both fists. Roosevelt stepped back, then dropped the enraged big first baseman with a stinging right to the jaw.

Jonesy, Mando, and Schwartz all seized Roosevelt at once. For a moment it seemed he would break loose and go after Astor again. Then he was still, his eyes red with anger, his mouth trembling.

"He tried me," he stammered. "Everybody saw him try me. No funky old man is goin' to show me up."

Hammer was on the field. He said, "Roosevelt, go on back to your room."

"Why me? You're as bad as any rotten boss. He started it. Why me?"

"You better do like I say, podner," said Hammer. "You don't like that, you can pack up and depart."

Mando thought Roosevelt was going to attack the coach. Then there was silence. The tough Negro shortstop's face became a mask.

"Yessuh," he said. "I ain't about to depart. When I flee a scene, it won't be for quittin' something I started."

"Okay," said Hammer. "Just do like I say."

Roosevelt walked, proud, head high, toward the distant dormitory. Hammer waved to an eager rookie aspirant to come in and play short. He walked back to third with Mando.

"That boy is trouble. T-r-o-u-b-l-e. Wherever he goes, whatever he does. Trouble."

"He's proud," said Mando. "He's black and he's proud."

"You proud, too, chicano," said Hammer.

There was nothing more to say. Gonzales was up, and Schwartz no longer smiled; he was all business. Mando watched in awe as the famous blazing fast ball rode across the plate. Gonzales never came close, and was kayoed on three pitches.

Hammer walked to the bench. He said, "Kelly, Jones, Cruz. Yawl go and take a shower; Zander, Hopper, Frederico, yawl go in and play infield."

Mando walked with the others away from the diamond. He wished he could stay and watch Zander. Zander was to worry about.

In baseball everybody was to worry about, he thought. A rookie coming up, he had the man ahead of him and the worriment of a Zander at his heels. The veteran had to worry about who was closing in on him.

Jack Kelly asked, "You think Hammer took us out because of Rosey?"

"Could be. He's always worked us together."

"We showed something. I guess. Three innings; you can't show much in three innings."

Jonesy asked, "Was my throw on the money, Jack?"

"Perfect," said Jack. "You know, Schwartz told us not to take any rough stuff. He laid it out for Rosey."

"Sure. But Rosey didn't have to stab the big fellow."

"Stabbing, Astor asked for that. Decking him, that was another thing," said Mando.

"He'll whack anybody who gets in his way," said Jack. "We all know that."

"But what'll it get him?" asked Jonesy.

"I don't know. He's tough all the way. Real tough."

"You think he's tougher than we are?" asked Jack.

"He's got his way. We got ours."

"He's not tougher," Jonesy said. "Different. Not tougher."

"It's a matter of definition," Mando said. "It's how you go about things that counts. I don't think the brass will hold it against Rosey for showing fight."

"Maybe not. I guess they like fight." Jonesy shook his head. "Not my bag."

53

"Rosey's what he is," said Mando. "I worry about Zander. Zander's a third baseman. Rosey's a shortstop."

Jonesy said, "I'm a shortstop."

They had forgotten that fact. They both looked at the slim infielder.

"Hey, that's right," Jack said. "You took to second so well it doesn't show on you."

"I think we did all right," Mando said, to reassure himself. "I think they know we can do the job."

"Who's 'they'?" asked Jack. "I mean, there were so many of them out there."

"Dutch Muller is 'they,' and you better believe it," Mando said. "The man you never get to talk with. If he knows you're alive, you may have a chance. A lot of good players never get to show what they can do, right? If you get a break, and he notices you, you've got a little bitty chance."

"You reckon he noticed Rosey?" asked Jack, imitating Hammer's Texas drawl.

"I reckon."

"Roosevelt must be sweating it out," said Jonesy.

Mando asked, "You want to bet?"

They went into the dormitory and up to their room. When they opened the door, they found themselves in a cloud of aromatic smoke. Rosey, neat in his one outfit, sat on a chair, his feet up, a long cigar in his mouth. He grinned at them in friendlier manner than they had ever seen from him.

"Hi, cats. Game over already? Five innings?"

Mando said, "Nope. They ran us off."

Roosevelt's feet came down, his eyes narrowed. "You got the gate for buttin' in on my bag?"

"Ask the bosses," said Jack Kelly. "They don't give you reasons; you know that."

Roosevelt carefully nicked the ashes from his cigar into a top removed from a tin can. In the can were eleven cigars to match the one he was enjoying. "Been savin' these. Friend of mine copped them some place in Newark. Couldn't afford to buy 'em. None of us could afford good cigars ever."

"Are you celebrating?"

He put his round head on one side. "Somethin' like. You got to figure. Either I made it or I didn't. Right?"

"Like what?"

"Like Astor come at me, man. Like I put him down. That could be good. It could be bad."

"So you celebrate."

"Yeah, man. It ain't up to me no more."

"You did your thing, is that it?"

"Somethin' like it. You dig those sports writers in the stands? Hangin' around the movie cats and all?"

"Well, they're always around the camp."

"Right, man. Today they saw us. You, me. They never did bother to look at us before, right?"

"They saw you deck Astor, maybe lay him up awhile."

"He got a fat lip is all," said Roosevelt. "I knock 'em out clean. He ain't real hurt. Me, I get my name in all the papers. Right?"

"You think that's good?"

"I tell you, men. I don't purely give a damn. All I know, he didn't take me outta the play. I made the play."

"You made the play is right."

"You didn't do so bad, you cats. They got to write it that Jonesy went behind second and gimme the good throw, don't they? They got to mention Jack Kelly, first baseman? And if they do—they got to take heed of Mando Cruz, the greaser kid. Right?"

Mando said, "Mando the Greaser and Rosey the Jigaboo?"

"Ho, you ain't gettin' me uptight," said Roosevelt. "Way I see it, we did good, and I made sure we got the ink, men."

"You did us a favor, then?" asked Mando, irked as always with Roosevelt's manner.

"You better believe it."

"I'm taking my shower," said Mando. "And, Rosey— don't do me any more favors, please?"

"Ho," said Rosey. "I didn't aim to favor you. It just happened that way."

They had to launder their own uniforms in the washing machines provided for that purpose. The three of them stripped while Rosey watched in a fashion most benevolent. They marched to the showers, leaving him with his cigar.

Jack said to Jonesy, "Sweating it out, was he?"

Mando said, fuming, "He did us a favor!"

Jonesy turned on the hot water, adjusted the cold so that he might not be scalded. "Unpredictable, isn't he?"

"You might say that," Jack agreed. "Also a jerk."

"Without prejudice," said Mando. "A jerk."

They washed themselves clean, draped themselves in towels, and paraded back to the room. Roosevelt was finishing the cigar. He was actually beaming.

Mando said, "Hey, where's our uniforms?"

"Gone, man," said Roosevelt happily.

"If you're playing tricks, you can have another go at belting people," Mando said. "Like me."

"Oh, no. Like I said, you ain't gettin' me today." Roosevelt waved the butt of the cigar. "You know that funky kid takes care of the regulars and all? Joey?"

"What about him?"

"Joey come and got the unies," said Roosevelt. "Like Mr. Hammer told him to."

"You mean he's washing them?"

"He ain't trimmin' 'em with gold lace," said Roosevelt.

They looked at one another. They were in. They had survived the big cut. They would be drawing Gold Sox trappings in the morning; that was the procedure; it had been gossiped around for a week that those who were retained would be notified by this unusual routine.

Roosevelt said, "You see what I mean? He asked for my unie, too. I already done it, but I gave it to him anyway. Now you believe I did you a favor?"

4

The uniforms they drew were traveling gray with gold insignia, "Sox" in script, gold jerseys and shirts, gold and black stockings.

Hammer said, "You gotta remember, these are the propitty of the club. Unless you make it to the team, you got to return 'em. Be lucky it's a new club, they ain't used before. Nobody here has got a chance for less'n A ball, that's for true. But nobody's got more'n a Chinaman's chance to go all the way. Nobody!"

Roosevelt muttered, "The sports-writer cats think some of us has."

Hammer turned a jaundiced eye upon the shortstop. "As for you, just look out for Astor. Or any of his buddies. You got a great start, you did."

"He come to me," said Rosey.

"You got you a cute elbow there," Hammer said. "Real cute. Just don't use it no more on our guys. You mind what I say, or you'll be in the boonies forever."

"I been there all my life," Roosevelt told him.

"Hittin' ballplayers in the jaw won't get you out. ... Now, the rest of you guys, I got news for you," Hammer said. "The way this club is gonna do it, you'll work out together. The training-season games start next week. We're tryin' to arrange for B teams to play against. Meantime, you work. Mornings you hit. Afternoons you field and run. Dutch has got a thing about conditionin'. I got to admit he's right. Ballplayers never do keep in proper shape. Dutch wants everybody to start the season, wherever he is, in the best shape. That's a tip for yawl. Everything everybody does is reported to Dutch, and don't you think it ain't." Again he turned his attention to Roosevelt. "Cigars ain't good for the wind."

Nobody replied.

Hammer went on, "So now here's the good news. You got the next two days off, and there'll be a check for each of you to go to town, over the border if you want, relax. You made the first step, you get to have fun."

They cheered. Mando realized suddenly that he had been under terrific strain since coming to the camp. He looked at Zander and wondered how the immigrant boy felt. It was fierce competition all the way. Every time at bat, every chance in the field, had been as in a World Series.

He thought about the two hits Zander had managed in the tryout game, the errorless ball he had played. When he walked with his friends to the cashier's office, he knew why they were silent. They were in the same frying pan with him.

Roosevelt said, "Men, I'm for town. I got me a lot of ideas what to do with some bread in the town."

"Just a playboy at heart," said Mando.

"The man give it to me about the cigars," said Roosevelt. "You heard him. Got to be a good boy in camp. Don't have to be good in town."

"The town's no place," Jack told him. "Better come with us over the border."

"Look, I got to room with you. I don't have to buddy up with you," Roosevelt said without rancor.

"You don't even eat with us," said Mando. He could not refrain from being irritated by the shortstop. "You're really exclusive."

They had come to the administration offices. Roosevelt paused and eyed them.

"You know what? I got a name. Sanderson Roosevelt.

They called me 'Sandy' in high school. White boys did. Black boys did. You never did."

He walked away, leaving them standing with their mouths half-open. They looked at one another. Mando kicked at a loose stone.

"He comes on so strong. How did we know he was sensitive about his name?"

"We didn't stop and think about it, did we?" asked Jonesy.

"Look, he's a tough guy," said Jack. "Let's leave it at that. He's just plain tough all the way through."

"Okay," said Jonesy. "But I'm calling him 'Sandy' from now on. I have to relate to him."

"That's right," said Mando. "Short and second has to relate. You have to know his moves, his thoughts on the field. He has to know yours."

"Right," said Jones. "He's a cat. He makes me look good. He may be a better shortstop than I am."

"But you don't believe it."

"I'd better not."

They went in and collected their expense money. Roosevelt went past them counting bills, his eyes gleaming, not noticing them. It occurred to Mando that the shortstop had been broke on arrival, that this might be the first cash he had seen in a long time. A voice spoke in his ear.

"Hi, Mando."

He turned, to discover Zander in line behind him. "Oh, hi. Hear you had a good game."

"Yeah. I was lucky."

"And good."

"Maybe good, too." Zander was taller and heavier, with straw-colored hair and the lightest of blue eyes. His smile was limited; his glance could be icy. "You did very well also. I saw you."

"I want the job," Mando said.

"Yes. We all want a job."

Jack moved aside with his money in his hand. Mando went to the window. He nodded to Zander.

"Good luck."

59

"Good luck to you, too."

Mando received his cash. He followed Jack and Jonesy. He and Zander had not been truly lying, he thought. They certainly could not be wishing that the other would prevail. It was a fine point, but well understood among the initiate.

Sandy Roosevelt walked down the main street. He had come through on a bus which took his last dollar. He had thumbed his way half across the country, saving for the bus ride so that he would not arrive in camp exhausted as well as broke in pocketbook. Waiting for the Gold Sox station wagon, he had walked the streets and come upon the place he now sought.

It was on a side street, a billiard parlor. He entered and stood a moment, hesitating as if at a disadvantage.

An attendant spoke to him. "You looking for a game? Want to practice? You're welcome here."

"Well, thanks," said Sandy. "I got a day off from the club, you know, the Sox."

"Yeah, we heard the ballplayers would be comin' in. You on the big team?"

"Not yet, but soon."

"What's your name?"

"Sandy." He let it go at that.

"Well, there's some sharks around. Wouldn't want a ballplayer to get suckered."

"Yeah, man," said Sandy. "I'll just watch awhile, okay?"

The attendant had narrow, slanting eyes and was chinless. "You shoot a pretty good stick, Sandy?"

"Just killin' some time."

"Well . . . okay."

He had already spotted the game. There were four men playing, one in his thirties and three around Sandy's age. He did not go directly to it; he wandered, watching some young girls who were taking lessons, a couple of well-dressed middle-aged men at billiards. This place was a far cry from the beer-sodden, poorly lit pool joints of Newark and his youth. He finally wound up on a high stool watching the money game.

They were playing odd ball, a quarter on each ball and a dollar on game. "Game" was won by the player with the most points, as designated by the balls he had sunk. The older man was winning. He was a crew-cut, thick-necked citizen in a loose sport shirt and tight pants. His thigh muscles bulged, and his forearms were thick and hairy, but he had a delicate touch with the pool cue. They called him Chuck.

The others didn't count, Roosevelt knew. There was a Mexican-American called Gómez, a skinny one called Willy, and a blond boy who was the big loser, a whiner called Hal. They were good shooters, playing combinations and cross-table shots with sure knowledge. Chuck moved quickly with seeming carelessness, knocking in the big ringers and the odd balls with ease. He finished off the rack and collected for game to add to his other winnings from the odd balls.

The last one to pay off was Hal, who said in his high, complaining voice, "I dunno, Chuck. I believe you're a ringer."

The big man leaned his cue against the wall. He counted out five dollars and thrust them at his accuser.

"That's about what you lost." He looked at the others. "You want him to quit? Or me?"

Gómez said, "Hey, *amigo*, you got my dough. He quits."

Hal took the five dollars. "And glad to get out of it. You guys are suckers."

"I think you'd better blow," said Chuck. "This here is a nice, clean place. I wouldn't want to splatter it."

"You try it, you'll wind up in the can." But Hal was on his way. He stopped and spoke to the attendant as he was paying his share of the time on the table. The attendant shrugged, then looked again, but at Roosevelt.

Rosey was saying, "Hey, men, how about me takin' his stick?"

Chuck surveyed him. "You know what we're playin' for?"

Roosevelt produced a ten-dollar bill. "Enough?"

"Okay with you guys?" Chuck was in charge of the game through sheer force, it appeared.

"Well, okay, sure." They were dubious, but they had lost money and were fascinated by Chuck.

Roosevelt seemed to pluck a cue from the rack at random. He showed them a mouthful of white teeth in an innocent grin. The attendant was making motions to him intended to discourage the play. He made the peace sign with his left hand. Chuck had the leather box of numbered pills and was shaking it.

Roosevelt accepted his pill. It was number four, as he had expected. Chuck knew his business, even to palming the pills. He drew number one for himself to gain the break. Gómez was number two and Willy number three. Rosey continued to grin somewhat fatuously as the balls were racked and Chuck took his stance. The attendant beckoned to him, and he walked over to the man.

"That Chuck is a shark," whispered the attendant. "I got orders not to let you ballplayers get taken."

"How about that? The bosses lookin' out for poor little us."

"You've got the warning. Chuck would break up the place if he knew." He said in a loud voice, "I guess it was another ballplayer they were callin' me about."

"Yeah, man," said Rosey happily. "Another guy."

He went back to the table as Chuck broke. The balls scattered as the cue ball, high-hit and following, plowed through the heap. The ten-ball fell. It was not a pay-ball, but it would count for high total toward game. The one-ball lay frozen against the side rail. Chuck banked for it and hit it, but did not drop another ball. He growled at himself.

Gómez could see the one-ball. He hit it, and that was all. Willy could not even see it, and played as safe as possible without scratching, just nicking the yellow sphere with a difficult bank shot.

Rosey surveyed the table. It was widely broken. He knelt and squinted. He could see the one-ball. He needed no further look to know his shot, but he walked around, chalking his cue, popping his eyes, grinning.

Chuck said, "You ever goin' to shoot, boy?"

Rosey stiffened, then relaxed. "Take your time, save nine," he said. "I ain't any expert, y' know. Just havin' fun."

Chuck made a disgusted motion with his hand. Rosey came back to the cue ball. He made his arch, and his right wrist moved in the telltale oiled smoothness of the pool player. He gently nudged the one-ball. The cue ball touched the twelve, which ticked the fifteen, which fell into the corner pocket.

"Well, whatcha know? A money ball!" Rosey's grin stretched. He collected a quarter from each of the three players. He looked again at the one-ball. "I do believe I can make that."

He sent it down to the same corner. He held his cue ball where he could see the two. He dropped the two with a sure, easy stroke. He never slammed the ball, as was the custom and style of Chuck and the others. He barely seemed to be making the shots good. Yet the white cue ball always drifted into position for the next shot.

He got the three, the four, made a combination on the seven. He banked the black eight-ball cross-corner, going down the table for the nine.

He said, "You ever see such luck? Just dumb lucky, that's me."

Chuck said, "Yeah. I see how lucky you are."

The balls were so well spread that Rosey could plan two or three shots ahead. Taking his time, appearing uncertain, hesitating, controlling the cue ball as though it was on a string, he ran the table. He collected nine dollars.

"Just plain lucky," he chortled.

Gómez and Willy were hanging up their cues. Chuck was eyeing Rosey. The attendant was doubled up with laughter. Rosey put the money in his pocket.

Chuck said, "Hey, boy, how good are you?"

"Not good, just lucky," Rosey insisted.

"Okay. How about a game of fifty for real money?"

"Ain't got no real money, mister," said Rosey. "Got maybe twenty-five. Plus nine. Thirty-four dollars?"

"That'll do," said Chuck. "Lag for break."

"Lag? What's lag?" asked Rosey.

Chuck shook his head. "Get another ball. Shoot down to the rail. Closest one to this rail gets to break."

"It's good to break? This ain't rotation, is it?"

"Straight pool."

"Well, okay."

They lagged. Rosey won by a fraction of an inch. Chuck took a deep breath.

Rosey broke. He nicked the outside ball, went to the rail with the cue ball, and came back to nestle against the scarcely disturbed rack of balls. Chuck called "safe" and tried to sew up the cue ball, and almost succeeded. Rosey walked around with the chalk again. Chuck sat on a high chair and glowered. Gómez and Willy were silent, watching.

Rosey said, "I been so lucky. I'll try the orange one in the corner yonder."

Now he hit the ball a sharp stroke. The five went in. The other balls scattered. Rosey chalked his cue.

Chuck said, "It was on."

"It had to be on," said Rosey. He walked slowly to position. Still in the most deliberate fashion, still coaxing the cue ball to the spot most advantageous, still grinning, he ran the table. He also left himself a break shot.

"Lucky, huh?" Chuck was growling now, a threat in his tone.

"Just plain lucky."

Rosey broke the heap once more. He ran the table, again leaving himself well. He made his ball. He began clipping them from the heap one at a time. Willy and Gómez were on the edge of their chairs, silent and wondering and admiring. Rosey ran fifty points. Chuck never did get a shot.

The big man put up his cue. He said, "You think you're goin' to get money from me? Boy, I know a shark when

64

I see one. You come in here and play the rube, and you're a pro."

"Pro baseball," said Rosey. "You owe me thirty-four dollars."

"Try and get it, boy," said Chuck. "You can't come in here and shark me outta no money."

"Thirty-four bucks," said Rosey. "I would've paid you."

"You never gave me a shot."

" 'Gave you'? In a money game, I should give you anything?" Rosey's grin had evaporated. He held the cue lightly in his hand. "You know, Mister Charlie, you ain't half-smart. You been takin' these locals real good. You figure to let 'em win a few, milk 'em, keep cleanin' 'em. I come along, you forget every man's got somebody can beat him. And then what you do ... you hang up your cue."

Chuck said, "You start anything in here, boy ..."

"And you gimme that Mister Charlie lingo. And I didn't hang up my cue." Rosey balanced the stick, butt end out. "Lay thirty-four on me, Mister Charlie."

Willy and Gómez were backing away. The attendant had his hand on the telephone. The other players in the room were listening, alarmed.

Chuck said, "You don't dare."

"I don't have to," Rosey explained. "After I get my dough, we walk outside without any pool stick. Then you can take it back. But first—the loot."

Chuck counted out the money. Rosey put it in his pocket and hung up the cue. He nodded to Willy and Gómez.

"I'm goin' out now. You can come along."

Chuck started to bluster. Then he said, "I know your kind. You got a shiv in your pocket."

Rosey laughed. "Yeah, man. And I got these." He held up two black, enormous fists. "You take a good look. Then you make your choice."

Chuck sat down. He averted his gaze. Rosey walked to the desk and paid for the time on the table.

The attendant said, "You're some pool player, believe me. I've seen 'em all. You're somethin' else again."

"Yeah, man. Tell it to Chuck."

"Chuck won't be around. You busted his balloon. Now they can see he ain't so tough after all. It was a good thing you did, Sandy."

Rosey blinked. "A good thing?"

"You can see this is a nice place. Families come in here. The mayor, the banker, everybody. Guy like Chuck, he can ruin it all. I admit, he had me scared. I call the cops—he lays for me, I thought. Not now. He's got crud, he won't stick around anymore."

"Hey, I came in lookin' for a guy like him," said Rosey. "I didn't aim to do any favors. Forget it, will you?"

He left the place in haste. He was scowling. It didn't make sense. He was no better than Chuck, just tougher and more skillful. His experience, plus a natural knack and a good eye, was enough to beat any but the best players on the professional circuit. He knew, because he had tried them, with fair results. He certainly did not want any credit for good deeds. He did not consider himself a good-deed man. He was mean and he was rugged, and he demanded a place in the world.

He went to the main street. There was another place he had located when he was walking the town. It was a first-class clothing store for men. He was still frowning when he went in through the big plate-glass door.

Gilbert Samson Jones III was having a good time in San Diego. He felt easier and more at home with Mando and Jack than he had ever felt with people before.

He was practicing a mild deceit upon them, but he did not feel guilty. It was self-protection. There was no profit in telling the story of his life. There was no reason why they should know he was heir to a huge fortune. He had been harassed often enough by people who knew which Jones family he came from. He wanted to be himself, he wanted to make it on his own in baseball; it was as simple as that.

Yet it was not simple, he well knew. Nothing was simple; everything had always been complex. The rich had their own problems. And when he was discovered,

66

which he must be if he made good, became prominent, what would they think of him, these youths who accepted him so casually and with such warmth?

He did not like to think about this eventuality. He had become attached to Mando and Jack. He wanted them to think well of him, Jonesy, the second baseman. He wanted to always remain on their level; he wanted that more than he had ever wanted anything.

Jack drove into the court of a motel. Mando and Jack had been here before; they knew the price, $16.50 per night for a suite with twin beds in one room, a double in another, and a bath halfway in between. Very low price, they assured Jonesy. Not a fancy place, but clean and comfortable for a night, they said. He eagerly agreed with them.

Their rooms were at the end of a long, undistinguished row of attached cabins. They parked and entered and relaxed, luxuriating in idleness.

After a little while Mando said, "It's about time to eat, right?"

"Pretty early," said Jonesy.

Mando reached for his jacket. "I saw a place across the way, there. Pancake house—they serve steaks just like any beanery. Okay?"

"I'm not hungry after the hot dogs and Coke," said Jonesy.

Mando threw him his coat. "It's mealtime. You're so skinny, we'll force-feed you if necessary."

It became apparent that Mando had a reason. Jonesy followed him out of the motel, and they strolled across a gas station toward the eating place.

"How come Jack isn't coming along?" He would not have asked in previous times. He felt free now.

"A gal named Connie," said Mando.

"Oh, he wanted to make a call."

"Right."

"You know the girl?"

"She's my sister."

"Oh. I'm sorry I asked."

67

"Why should you be? They're going together. It's a great thing for them."

"Well, sure. I should hope so."

"No, I mean it. When I first met Jack, he didn't know chicano from general training. Consuelo wasn't allowed to go out with an Anglo."

"I see."

"No, you can't see." Mando was kindly. "Nobody can understand unless he's been in the bag. Jack is middle-class, his father's a snob. Connie's from the *barrio*. Never the twain shall meet, right?"

"But they did meet."

"One of those things. Connie's only eighteen, but we grow up quick in the *barrio*. Jack's twenty, and he broke from his father. How it will turn out, nobody can know."

"But you have hope."

"I've got my chance to break out. Baseball."

"And the desire."

"Well, sure. And I'd like to do something for my family."

"Do you have a big family?"

"Big enough. Cousins by the carload. Big Talker Luis, the *padrone* uncle. Five of us kids. Big enough."

"It sounds fine to me."

Mando thought a moment. "Don't you have a family?"

Jonesy waved a hand. "In a manner of speaking. They're too busy to notice much. Oh, they're indulgent if absentminded. I'm just like the rest of you."

"Like we take our shots. In baseball."

"That's it."

They went into the pancake house. It was clean and well lighted. There were waitresses in short dresses over starched petticoats. They found a booth in the rear where they could save space for Jack. The variety of pancakes was enormous, to the point of bewilderment.

Jonesy said, "Holy cow, the hotcakes. Blueberry. Just right for me, since I'm not really hungry. Blueberry pancakes."

"Hey, man, how can you resist 'em? Next to Mexican

food, I dig them the most. Apple, I like the apple. With sausages on the side."

"Hey, sausage." Jonesy debated. "You think I got a tapeworm?"

"Just a healthy young athlete," Mando said.

"I think I'll have the sausages, too. You did threaten to force-feed me, right?"

"It'll never be necessary."

A waitress made her way toward them, pad and pencil in hand. She wore a ridiculous cap rakishly atop bright red hair caught back with a blue ribbon to match the short dress. Her legs were long and slim and tapering, her ankles finely made, her feet slender. Her eyes were almond-shaped, a surprisingly deep brown, her nose slightly snubbed. Her lips were full and red, and her teeth white and even as she smiled at Mando. Jonesy drew a deep breath.

She was not beautiful, he thought, she was—well, she was ravishing. He had never seen a girl more instantly attractive in his life.

She spoke in Spanish to Mando.

Mando said, "Don't tell me you're chicano?"

"Does Irish count?" She laughed. She wore a celluloid nameplate on her abundant chest which read "Ana Cassidy." She went on, "My mother is a Constanza."

"Beautiful," said Mando. "What are you doing tomorrow?"

"Do you really want to know?"

Jonesy was uncomfortable. He had never been able to carry on conversations ad lib with a girl. This one was instantly special to him. Yet Mando was trying to date her.

"Does a duck swim?" Mando asked, still grinning.

"Ask me later," said Ana Cassidy. "Are you ready to order now?"

They ordered. She went away from the table, hips swaying. Jonesy stared after her.

Mando said, "Maybe she'd like to see Tijuana. Maybe she comes from there."

"She's lovely," said Jonesy.

"Mexican-Irish is always lovely," Mando told him. "I think she digs me."

"Yes," said Jonesy. "I think she does, at that."

He watched Jack Kelly come into the restaurant, tall, handsome, blond, always graceful and poised. Jack spotted them in the corner and started their way. He almost ran into Ana Cassidy and a tray destined for a family of four. He smiled and apologized, and she smiled and apologized. Jonesy squirmed. He could never manage it the way his friends did it. With all his alleged advantages, he had never been able to manage it.

Jack squeezed into the booth and said, "Hey, wow. Did you dig that waitress?"

"We dug," Mando said. "Believe it or not, I asked her for a date."

"You did that already?" Jack was amazed. "Hey, man, that's not your life style."

"Ask Jonesy."

"He did. He asked her to go with us tomorrow."

"Man, you're growing up," said Jack. "I've been worried about you, not digging the chicks."

"How many do you find like her?" demanded Mando.

"Like instant love?"

"I wouldn't say that. But she's half-chicano."

"A Cassidy half-Mex?"

"So you grabbed her name. I'll tell Connie about that."

"Tell, tell, tell . . . Connie sends love. Your family sends love. Except Uncle Luis. He thinks you're a bum."

"I'm glad. I think Uncle Luis is a bum."

Jonesy wished he could manage the easy flow between them, the way they knew what to say to each other, the open and free camaraderie so evident.

They tolerated him, he thought. He was the second baseman. They asked him no questions about himself, about his past. They accepted him. If there was any fault, it lay in his own incompetence, he believed. He was simply not a successful social animal; he never had been. He was actually doing better now, with the base-

70

ball team, than he ever had before. Maybe he was improving.

Still, he never could have addressed the girl in Mando's style. He watched her come with their pancakes. She was really a startling female, shining with femininity. He wondered why she was waiting on tables in a place like this. Surely there was a better position in the world for such as she.

Mando said, "Hey, great, Ana. This here is Jonesy, and the big clunk is Jack Kelly, and I'm Mando Cruz. Okay?"

"I wouldn't change it for the world." She deftly placed the hot plates before them. "And does the big Irish eat also?"

"Steak and potatoes," said Jack. "Hash brown."

"New York-cut steak?"

"Right, nothing but the best. You are a doll, you know that?"

"He goes with my sister," Mando said quickly. "Forget him. Irish don't go with Irish anyway. Ask your mother or father."

"They know." She delivered a broad wink at Mando. "Coffee?"

"Coffee all around. How about tomorrow? We're going over to Tijuana. How about a date with three of tomorrow's great athletic stars?"

She said, "I'm thinking on it. Three of you, eh?"

"If you've got a girl friend. One. For Jonesy. I have to watch out for my sister's interests."

"I have a girl friend. Several, in fact."

"And boyfriends too, I betcha," said Jack.

"Also several." She nodded and left them.

Jack said, "Jonesy, you're zonked. The lovelies always pal around with uglies."

"Story of my life." He tried to pass it off, but it was true. He had been stuck with the plain friends of pretty girls before.

"We haven't scored yet," said Mando, pouring boysenberry syrup over his pancakes. "It's too good to be true, that doll and me."

71

"At least you took a good shot," said Jack.

They ate. Jonesy wondered if Mando had made the impression which he believed in. Time came for the check, and she was there, smiling gently, speaking softly.

"We're not supposed to date customers. But—a chicano? And I have family in Tijuana. I was thinking of visiting them tomorrow. It works out, you see?"

"We can pick you up," Mando said.

She wrote down an address. "What time, *amigo?*"

"About eleven?"

She said, "I'll try and get another girl." She hesitated, then added, "A nice girl."

Mando replied in Spanish, most courtly and serious, "But what other kind, *señorita?*"

She accepted him. Jonesy could tell. It was somehow touching and quite correct. They left a generous tip and paid at the counter and walked back to the motel suite.

Jack asked, "Anyone for a movie or something?"

"Better save our loot for tomorrow," said Mando.

"Jonesy?"

"I happen to have some extra loot," he said offhand. "Don't worry about tomorrow."

"Hey, man, a rich dude," said Mando.

"I don't have the responsibilities you guys do," Jonesy said quickly. "Anyway, you can pay me back later."

"Okay. A movie, then?"

Jonesy said, "I think I'll just loiter. Why don't you go?"

"You afraid movies will spoil your batting eye or something?"

"Just lazy tonight. You mind?"

"Heck no. See you, Jonesy."

They left. Jonesy sat for a moment remembering the color and shape of the girl Ana Cassidy. He had not dated a lot of girls, but he had seen aplenty, and she was, he knew, special. Unquestionably she had recognized something special in Mando. The Mexican blood, he thought, meeting and knowing that it was all right, that there was no cheapness in dating on first acquaintance.

72

What he could not divine was his own impulse toward the girl. He did not consider himself impressionable. Introverted, yes, and not easily engaged with females. Why had she so attracted him? He could not find an answer; he only knew he wished he had Mexican blood. . . .

Raucous was the word for Tijuana. And hot, Jonesy added. The main stem was jammed tight with hawkers. It was a Mardi Gras without music. The buses screamed without mufflers, splashing dust. There were tourists from every imaginable section of the United States and several foreign nations. The five young people strolled and window-shopped, buying nothing, availing themselves of the knowledge of Ana Cassidy and her cousin María Constanza.

María was short and plump and dark as night. She was a pretty girl without the trace of an accent, with laughter and unabashed gaiety. She clung to Jonesy's arm.

"Leave it to Annie-pie. Like wow! Three handsome baseball players. She's somethin' else again, now, isn't she? Always was. The family beauty with brains."

"Does she often gather guys for dates like this?" Jonesy had to ask. He wanted to know all about Ana Cassidy.

"You must be kiddin'. Ana's *wanted*. San Diego State where we go to school nights, you know, every dude's after Ana. Oh, no, Ana's no pickup. She just dug your friend, the chicano, that's all. She told me. He looked at her, she looked at him. You see? This is the first time she ever dated from the beanery, believe me. Not her style, not at all. And if our family hadn't moved up to L.A., she wouldn't have dared. Not one chicano to a pair of Anglos. Her people and mine would kill us."

"I believe you." He was vastly relieved. "And I agree with your folks."

She scrutinized him, looking up into his face. "Yeah, man. Ana doesn't make mistakes. You're nice guys. She said Mando wouldn't go for a girl to date Jack. Ana

73

liked that. We're modern and all that. We're not for the old customs. We get around with the dudes, have a lot of fun. But we're not with it all the way. You know what I mean?"

"Just what I meant."

"Right, man." She hugged his arm. "It's good to have fun. Me. I'm worse than Ana for fun and games. Lots of times it's Trouble City, you know. I'm not as cute as Ana in picking the right guys. No wonder she's a straight-A student."

"Is she working her way through school?"

"We both are. I baby-sit and do housework. It was do that or go to L.A. and start all over. We're sophomores." She was proud. "We graduated from high school at seventeen."

"Then you don't go steady?"

"No way, man. It hasn't happened to either one of us. Lots of kids just pick out a guy and make the scene because other girls do it. We're raised different. Lots of people think we're cubes. You know? But when it comes down to the nitty-gritty, we have more good times than they do—and no problems."

Jonesy said, "You're smart."

"Just the way we were raised," she said cheerfully. "You have to know, we can take care of ourselves, also. Karate."

"Karate?" He simply could not imagine Ana or this nice, plump little girl engaging in the skill.

"We took a course. Ana's papa insisted when we decided to stay in Dago. He was against it, our staying. We had to take karate, or they wouldn't let us. Funny?"

"Fairly funny."

"Don't be scared."

Jonesy had never met girls like these before; it was vastly interesting.

Jack strolled and laughed, but Mando stayed close to Ana and was attentive and polite, courtly. Jonesy watched as he walked behind them with María, and was disconsolate. There was no doubt about it, Ana had

74

taken that look, as María said, and that was it. Mando and Ana—he could see it building before his eyes.

María was rattling on, "You see, Ana's papa and mine are auto mechanics. They're real close. Like friends. So they got this chance to buy a gas station in the San Fernando Valley, and they took a chance. It was a bargain. I don't know, maybe it wasn't a bargain. But they thought so. Day and night. Twenty-four hours they work. Our mammas help, keep the books, they do everything they can. All the kids are away from home, and they just try to make it their way, hard work."

Jonesy said, "Mando and Jack are from up there."

"Yes. Well, maybe they can send customers. It's a hard life. Dirty hands. But they keep saying the money's clean. I think they're making it, just barely. It's what they know. Like we want to teach, Ana and me. That's our thing, what we want. I guess the world would be a good place if everybody got to do what they really want to do, wouldn't it?"

"Yes. I guess it would be." Two men in their forties, he thought, pumping gas and greasing cars and repairing engines twelve hours a day and deeming it a privilege, a chance for better living. It was a way of life he did not know.

The noise increased as they got deeper into the town. The shopkeepers and their shills became shrill, the voices more liquid, heavily accented.

At the curb on both sides of the street, strategically spaced, were strange contraptions, wide wagon seats high above miniature donkeys that could surely not have budged the vehicles to which they were loosely attached. Two young men attended each of these stands, waving on-the-spot photos, begging passersby to have their picture taken. Business seemed poor despite the vociferous salesmanship displayed by the gaily garbed, clean-cut vendors. Jonesy listened to María and wished that he had the courage to suggest a group photo. If he never saw Ana again, he could at least have a picture. . . .

He shook his head. He had never felt like this before; it

75

was strange, unnatural. He listened determinedly to María.

She said, "Ana doesn't look chicano, of course. She could pass for Anglo. But she won't do it. We're proud. Maybe we're not proud of some of us, you know what I mean. But who *is* proud of all of them? I mean, every group has problems, right? Hey, there's Caesar's across the street."

They dashed through dust and the milling tourists. Caesar's was a hotel with a long, dark, cool bar. They could see nothing for several minutes after coming in out of the brilliant sunshine. Jonesy found himself next to Ana Cassidy, tightly squeezed against her in the booth. He drew a deep breath and managed to get a grip on himself.

He spoke to María. "What do you drink in here?"

"Oh, the beer. You must try the Mexican beer," she said. "Carta Blanca, the light . . . but it is stronger than you're accustomed to."

Mando said, "Yeah, man. They don't ask for I.D. here. You can buy it, you can drink it."

"Beer is as far as I go," Jonesy confessed. "Hard stuff knocks me out. I haven't got the head for it."

"Chicanos are raised on wine and beer," said María. "Right, Ana?"

"Just about," said Ana. She smiled at Jonesy. "It is really strong here."

"That's all right," he said. A waiter had approached them, dapper in a white shirt, black bow tie, moustache, beaming smile. "Beer all around, please."

Jack said, "Whoa, not for me. Coke, please."

"I should've warned you," Mando said. "He's like that."

"Just an allergy," Jack said.

They accepted it, but Jonesy knew it was not true. It was because of Jack's father. It was because Jack was afraid to ever start drinking lest he become like his father. This had been discussed in the hours after baseball workouts. Mando and Jack had revealed themselves. Jonesy had not . . . nor had Sandy Roosevelt, it occurred to him.

76

The beer arrived, frosty, bittersweet, better than any that Jonesy had yet tasted. They had been walking in the heat of the border town, and they drank down the first bottle and ordered a second. Their voices rose, they laughed as they spoke together, they were happy and gay as they sipped the second round.

"What's it like in a baseball camp?" Ana asked.

"Rotten!" said Mando, laughing uproariously. "Just plain lousy."

"No," said Jonesy with great seriousness. "It's not. It's hard work, but it's . . . it's all right."

"Jonesy spent so much time in stir, he thinks everything is fun," Jack explained. "I bet he thinks we're having fun right now."

"Oh, no. He wouldn't," said Ana Cassidy. Her elbow gently nudged Jonesy. "Jonesy hates us all."

"Yeah," said Mando. "Jonesy's almost as big a hater as Rosey."

"Who is Rosey?"

"Our roomie," said Mando. "No neck, but plenty of mouth, that's Rosey."

Jack said, "He's a good ballplayer. He's black, and he doesn't believe Mando is as good as Mando thinks Mando is."

"The coke has got you, Jack," said Mando.

"Maybe, but Rosey's okay. He's a good ballplayer."

"That's right," Jonesy said. "He's good. I wonder if he can play second base?"

"Jonesy never gives up. Jonesy claims he is a shortstop," Mando explained. "Rosey is a shortstop. That makes Jonesy a second baseman."

"Baseball is hard enough to understand," Ana said. "You're not making it any better, you know."

"Inside stuff," Mando said. "Wouldn't expect you to savvy inside stuff. Only ballplayers dig it."

"I'm hungry," María said. "Two beers make me starve."

"We eat," Mando said.

Jonesy picked up the tab, pushed Jack and Mando away, paid the waiter, tipping him a dollar, and asked that they be shown a table in the dining room. The others did not notice, but the procedure was smooth and orderly. A squat maître d' in a dark suit with his hair oiled and waved escorted them to a leather-lined large booth. An aged, grinning waiter stood ready with menus. Jonesy slipped another bill to the maître d'. The beer was working in him, and he was determined to make certain that the party received nothing but the best.

"How about a Caesar salad for all?" asked Mando. "They invented it here. It oughta be good."

"How about *chile relleno* and *enchilada*?" demanded María. "You can get a Caesar in Los Angeles, anywhere. Eat *mexicano* now that you're here, why not?"

They debated while Jonesy mused over the menu. He decided upon something called "house special," which included beef taco, *chile relleno*, and cheese *enchilada*. It seemed very *mexicano* indeed. It was probably also hugely indigestible, and he was not one for strange, spiced foods. Still, it was a special occasion, and he now sat opposite Ana Cassidy so that he could watch her.

Ana did not notice. Ana looked mainly at Mando. She smiled and listened. María rattled on, but Ana listened. Mando was the Man. Jack Kelly responded to María, and Jonesy retreated, as was his wont, to his place apart, the observer.

He was safe in the role he had chosen for himself long ago. He was a spectator rather than a participant. Some inner factor insulated him from his peers. He could withdraw and smile and watch Ana and feel no pang as she continued to smile upon Mando. He tried the heaping plate of food, manfully swallowed a good deal of it, desperately ordered another beer to wash it down.

When they had finished, Jonesy again appropriated the tab and shooed the others out through a door into the lobby of the hotel while he paid from his hidden resources. He nodded at the *gracias* and followed his friends. It had always been part of his role to pay the check; only now it was all right, because he felt closer to

78

Mando and Jack . . . and because he had met Ana Cassidy.

Still sailing as they hit the street and the heat and the wave of noise, he said, "How about a picture? That's a real nice donkey. We put a hat on him, nobody'll mistake him for Mando, right?"

"Hey, why not?" María was agreeable, as always.

They dashed across the street. Jack, hanging back, tugged at Jonesy's elbow.

"Hey, man, you keeping track? I mean, you've grabbed it all up till now."

"Fine," said Jonesy. "I told you I had it today."

"Well, just keep track."

The two young Mexicans were bustling about. They produced sombreros with appropriate names printed in large letters according to gender, uncovered their small camera upon its precarious tripod. María questioned them in Spanish. They answered in heavily accented English, "One dollah, one dollah."

"You have to watch 'em," Ana said. "They're not doing so well this year."

"A dollar, that's easy," Mando said. "Come on, climb aboard. Close together, right?"

They squeezed as close as possible on the wide seat. They all grinned, showing their teeth, hats rakishly askew. People paused on the busy sidewalk to watch the merriment.

Then Jonesy was aware that María was suddenly silent. He saw that the photographer and his assistant were muttering to each other, glancing at the group as they set up for the picture. Ana frowned and said something sharply in Spanish.

The two young men were silent. They stood stiffly; the snap of the shutter was a clear click. Mando climbed down first, reached to help the girls. He took a quick step toward the two Mexicans and spoke. They hunched their shoulders, and Jonesy was aware that their staring displeasure was directed toward Jack and himself. Instinctively he took the girls by the arm and moved them

79

to the sidewalk, where the throng moved on, oblivious of the small drama.

Jack towered at Mando's side, asking, "What's their beef, *amigo?*"

"They don't say, but it's got to be the girls."

"Yeah, I get it."

"They think we picked 'em up."

"Uh-huh." Jack addressed the photographer. "Okay. Let's have the pictures, man."

The Mexican youth said sullenly, "Five dollah."

"Five? You said one," Jack snapped.

Mando said, "Let 'em keep the pictures. It's a bad town to be arrested in."

There was a slow-moving uniformed man across the street, slovenly but tough-looking. Jonesy stepped forward and took out money.

"Five dollars for five pictures?" he asked the two men.

"*Sí,* five dollah."

Jonesy said, "Okay, let's have them."

"I want to see a copy first," said Mando. He spoke to the two men in rapid-fire Spanish. He gestured toward the policeman.

The photographer hesitated. Then he grudgingly began to extract the negative. He washed it in a dirty solution. Amazingly, a shiny, identifiable print began to appear. Mando leaned close to scrutinize it.

"Okay," he said. "But who wants one? Everybody? Otherwise forget it."

"Five," said Jonesy. "It's okay, my treat."

"I don't like it," Jack said. "It's a holdup."

"I'll talk to the cop," Mando said.

"I'd like to rap these dudes," Jack said. "One thing I hate, it's a holdup."

Jonesy produced a five-dollar bill. "Like Mando says. Who wants trouble in this town?"

The assistant took the bill. The photographer busied himself with prints. Neither looked directly at Jack or Mando. The policeman moved on.

Jonesy said, "Why don't you and the girls take a small walk? Let me handle this."

They were reluctant. But they went to the girls. Jonesy stood fast, waiting. The five prints were forthcoming in a short moment or two. The sun was very hot, and the Mexican food plus the beer made him distinctly uncomfortable. He saw the assistant slip the five prints into envelopes printed crudely with the message, "If you don't like the picture, blame the jackass," and he was suddenly amused.

The assistant said, "Two bits each. One dollah twenty-five."

Jonesy took the five folders in his left hand. He looked hard at the two young men. "Who's the jackass?"

"One dollah and two bits," said the young man.

Jonesy said, "You want to give me back the five dollars?"

"You pay." The tone was threatening.

Jonesy looked at Mando and Jack, at the departing policeman. He grinned. He removed the pictures from the folders. He placed the folders on the footboard of the wagon.

"I don't pay," he said.

He walked to the group awaiting him and distributed the pictures. They were really not bad. He said, "The way I see it, you go so far, and no farther. Right?"

"Maybe I should crack their heads together," said Jack. "Just once."

"No," said Ana. "It would bring too much trouble. And our family is here, our cousins."

The two young men were talking together, their faces dark. But they made no move.

Jonesy said, "Let's flee the scene. What say?"

Ana said, "Right. You handled it, Jonesy, you're a great man."

"Yes," said María. "You did good, Jonesy. Let's move on."

They went toward the parking lot. There was a cloud over them, Jonesy felt. The fine edge of fun had been rubbed to a smudge.

Jonesy ducked into a store and bought envelopes to protect the still-damp photos. When he came out, the others were gathered at the edge of the parking lot. He distributed the envelopes, and they thanked him, soberly, the mood somber, he thought.

"They think we'd better not drive them to their cousins," Mando explained.

"I think they're right." Jonesy shook his head. "Discrimination raises its ugly little head in Mexico."

Mando said, "I could walk you to wherever it is."

"No. We're safe enough here," Ana said. "It's been fun. Let's not ask for more trouble. Mexicans are proud. Let it go at that."

"Chicanos are proud. I keep saying that," Mando said. "We'll call. It's a promise."

Ana looked at Jonesy. "Thanks again. Those two deserved a lesson. But you handled it."

"I'm peaceable," he said. He felt warm, rewarded.

The girls walked down the street. They looked lovely in the sunshine, their short skirts swaying.

Mando said, "Hell of a note."

"Let's split," Jack said. "Ana's right. It was fun while it lasted. She's some kind of a gal."

"Amen," said Mando.

They went to the car and drove out of Tijuana. It seemed tawdry to Jonesy, the scene en route to the border. But he would remember it without rancor, he knew, touching the envelope containing the picture. He would remember it well.

5

At eight o'clock there was no one on the entire playing field of the Gold Sox. A brisk March breeze was blowing across the flats, and the four infielders shivered in their windbreakers. They gathered at the backstop seeking shelter.

Mando said, "Rosey, what happened to your eyes?"

"I got 'em. You ought to see the insides of 'em."

"The idea is plain," said Jack. "Come in late at night, and you get an early call. But where is everybody?"

"The big team's playing the Angels this afternoon," Jonesy said. "They won't be around for a while. But where's everybody else?"

"Like the Claw," said Rosey. "That Texas stiff."

"Hasn't anybody got a ball in his pocket?" Mando demanded. "Can't we even warm up?"

"There'll be two workouts for us, no matter what," said Rosey. "I just as soon not have a ball." He slid down, sitting with his back against the boards where the sun could shine directly upon him, pulling the bill of his cap over his nose. "I can sleep some."

Mando said, "If it wasn't for you, we wouldn't be here."

Rosey yawned. "Big deal."

"We could run," suggested Jonesy.

"Yeah," said Rosey. "Show the man you're good li'l ole boys. Kiss him."

"I'm not thinking about him. I'm cold," said Jonesy.

"Rosey's thinking about him," said Mando. "Rosey is a tough dude."

Jack Kelly said, "Hey! Look what I found."

It was a dust-covered baseball stuck beneath the boards of the backstop, where it had been overlooked. Jack picked it up and wiped it off in the pocket of his glove. It had seen better days, but it would serve. Mando and Jonesy yipped and ran onto the infield. Rosey settled himself into a more comfortable position.

Hammer came out onto the field driving a golf cart. "I got some things to say to you hombres, the four of you. There's been some decisions made. That's why you're out here alone. I just come from a meetin'. Now, hear this: You four work good together. On the field, that is. You been watched. The thing is, a young infield is for the future. This here club we got in the league, it ain't goin' no place, which ain't news to you or anybody else. Not this year it ain't. So we got to look for futures. Well, there ain't a chance you start right in triple-A ball together. Not all four of you. Not four rookies on our top farm team. Yawl understand that?"

Mando said, "You're giving us bad news. I understand that."

"No, wait," Jonesy said. "What else?"

Hammer said, "They're givin' me a chance to manage." He drew a deep breath and went on defiantly, "I never ast for it. I know I ain't got the learnin' and all. I know I got to start at the bottom. Well, I did ast for yawl."

"You did what?"

"They don't know as much as I do about the rookies. Nobody does. If they're gonna gimme a chance, well, I wanted to start good."

"So you asked for us, all four of us."

"That's right." The big man shifted uneasily. They had never seen him at a loss. It was a peculiar sensation to them all. "Maybe you could go to AA or triple-A. One,

84

two, maybe all four of you. They seen you work against the big club. They got an idea what you can do."

"Are you asking us?" demanded Jack. "Is that what you're doing?"

"I'm askin' you," said Hammer desperately. "New Jersey. Little town called Mingo. The bushes. Forty miles south of Newark, New York, whatever. Near the Delaware River."

"No way," said Rosey.

"What you mean?"

"Not me. Not Jersey. I come from there."

"The cops want you or somethin'?" demanded Hammer.

"That's none of your business. Thing is, I don't want no part of Jersey. Count me out."

Hammer looked at the others. "Reckon you feel the same. Can't blame yawl. One thing, though. If we could show somethin' even in the boonies, we'd score with the brass."

Mando said, "Rosey? You're sure?"

"I ain't goin'. I'll take my chances. None of you is any joy to me," said he. "You dudes want to play sucker to Mister Big here, you go right on."

Mando turned to Hammer. "What about it if you don't get him?"

"Zander," said Hammer.

"Can Zander play short?"

Hammer shook his head. "Third base."

"Jonesy is a shortstop."

"No," said Hammer. "Not no more. Jonesy is a hell of a second baseman."

"Then I play short?"

"That's it."

Mando said, "Jack could make it bigger right now. We all know that. They all had their eyes on Jack."

"Uh-huh," said Hammer. "Kelly's got good marks. Every one of you got good marks."

"If Rosey splits, it breaks up the rhythm," said Mando. "You want a solid infield. You won't have it."

Hammer said, "I'll take Zander for third."

It seemed very odd, unbelievable. The Texan was on the defensive. It was because he had never hoped to manage a ball club in the wildest of his dreams, Mando thought. Every man has a dream concealed about him someplace. Hammer had been offered a chance, and he was grabbing at it the only way he knew how.

Mando said, "Maybe I'm a stupid slob. But I'll go if Jack and Jonesy will."

Rosey said, "Man, I thought you had guts."

"Everybody to his own kind of guts," said Mando.

"Huh." Rosey sneered. "Maybe you want to dump Zander this way. Maybe you figure he's too close on your heels. You cats. You gonna be big in Mingo? Ho! That ain't even big-time Jersey, man."

"Okay, you made your decision," Mando said to him. "Why don't you split? Go see what you can do for yourself? Go talk to Dutch or somebody."

"Nobody tells me to drag it," Rosey shouted. "Fine stinkin' thing. Break up an infield like this. One lousy note, this is."

"You're the one breakin' it up," said Mando.

"What's the matter, Sandy?" asked Jonesy in his quiet voice. "You figure to miss us?"

Sanderson Roosevelt slammed his glove to earth. He took off his cap and threw it down and jumped on it. He howled, "No!"

"No what?" demanded Mando.

"We could make AA or triple-A. All four of us. This ain't right! This stinks."

Jack Kelly said to Hammer, "I guess you got an infield. I guess you can send Zander up to AA or wherever. I guess your shortstop's going along."

"I never did have no sense. I been in trouble all my life because I got no sense," raved Rosey.

Hammer's expression changed. He seemed to grow taller. He said awkwardly, "Hey, I'm just a redneck Texan, right? I never went to no schools. But I can see through a knothole. That there Pennjersey League better look out. Here we come!"

"Pennjersey?" Mando sighed. "New Jersey don't even come first."

Hammer was going for the golf cart. "Yawl work out with the rest of 'em. I got things to do. We'll put a club together durin' the week, then take off. Start the second week in April. Just keep workin'. I'll be with yawl. And . . . hey, thanks."

He jumped into the cart, almost overturning it, and drove toward the buildings. The other players were straggling onto the playing fields. The sun was brightening and warming. The four players looked at one another.

Rosey said, "No plain common sense."

"Hammer gave us every chance," said Jonesy.

"He sure did," said Jack.

"He's rough, but he's on the level," said Jonesy.

"He knows the game. He knows players," said Jack.

"We have to start somewhere. Might as well be together," said Jonesy. "Right, Sandy?"

"Poop," said Rosey. "You let him con you."

"What about you?" demanded Mando. "Why didn't you take off?"

"You wanted me to! You tried to get rid of me!" Rosey grabbed up his cap and jammed it on his head.

"You're out of your skull," Mando said.

"You'll eat hamburgers and malts for dinner," Rosey raged at them. "You'll travel in lousy buses and sleep in dirty motels. You'll play on skinned diamonds. Oh, you're a bright bunch of dudes. Real heavy, you are!"

He stalked off to the field, dusting off his glove. His head was sunk all the way down into his shoulders. He was a perfect picture of high dudgeon.

Jack said, "Jonesy called him 'Sandy' and spoke quietly to him, and he stuck."

"He wanted to stick," said Jonesy. "Couldn't you see?"

"Not me, I couldn't see it," said Mando. "I'm beginning to think we made a big fat mistake."

"Well," said Jack, "we didn't sign anything."

"We could change our minds." Jonesy was solemn.

Mando stared. "We told him we'd go with him. We can't go back on our word."

"So?"

"Pennjersey, here we come. Like Hammer said. Ready or not, here we come."

They were packing in Room 16. They were not talking; they were remembering their days, good and bad, in the Gold Sox dormitory.

Hammer came into the room. He handed out checks, beaming. Rosey glared at him, mumbling what might have been thanks or might have been a curse.

Hammer said, "Yawl satisfied with your contracts?"

"Surprised," said Mando.

"Pleasantly," said Jack.

"This ain't no cheap outfit," Hammer bragged. "You're gettin' AA pay with options if we move up."

" 'We'?" said Rosey. "Where you get that 'we' stuff?"

"Oh, shut up," said Jack. "Thanks, I know you put in a word for us, Harry. We'll see you in Mingo. Wherever that is."

"Just be there," said Hammer. He stuck out a huge paw. "I think we got us a club can beat the tar out of the Pennjersey."

They all shook hands. Hammer departed.

They had the weekend to get rid of the old Ford and visit their families. Then they would take a plane, coach fare, and fly to Newark.

Mando said, "For the last time, Rosey, you're welcome to go with us. You can bunk with me."

"No way," said Rosey. Then he hesitated. "Uh—I never saw L.A. I might bum a ride with you."

"Okay. So you bum a ride. Jonesy stays with Jack. It'll work out." He was listless.

Jack said, "I'm all set and rarin' to go. What say?"

"Put your packages in the car, Rosey," said Mando. "Might's well leave now as any time."

He was the last to leave the room. He dragged his feet. He went slowly down the stairs. He was almost out the door when someone from the office yelled at him.

"Cruz! Telephone."

He dropped the barracks bag and stumbled to the phone on the shelf. He grabbed for the instrument and lost it, finally recaptured it.

"Hello?"

"Hello? . . . Mando?"

He swallowed hard and said, "Hi, Ana."

"I'm so glad I got you. Just had the word. María and I will be flying up to L.A. this evening."

"Hey, great!" He tried hard to be nonchalant. "I was just walking out of here."

"Well. I sure am glad I got you, then. You're sure you'll be free for a date?"

"Tomorrow?"

"Well . . . call me. Remember the number?"

"I remember. Sure sorry you couldn't get over here before we had to leave."

"It didn't work out. We're disappointed. Maybe next year."

"Well, sure. If we're not traded or something." Her voice sounded clear and sweet, and he hated to hang up. Then he said apologetically, "Hey, this is costing you. I'll call tomorrow morning, okay?"

"Okay, Mando."

"It'll be great to see you."

"Same to you, Mando."

They hung up. He turned and almost fell over his bag. He picked it up, shook himself like a terrier coming out of water, and walked out of the building and to the waiting car.

He said airily, "It was the gals."

"Girls?" asked Jack. "More than one girl?"

"I mean it was Ana saying she and María would be in town tomorrow." He put the bag in the rear deck with the others.

Jonesy said, "That's nice."

Mando got into the front seat with Jack. "They didn't know if they could make it. Ana called just as I was walking out."

"That's real nice," said Jonesy.

"Yeah," said Jack. "That's very, very nice. Mando the Man wasn't much worried, though. He really wasn't cut up when he thought they couldn't make it."

Mando said, "You going to drive the car, or do you want me to take it?"

"Can't wait to get home, huh?" Jack started the creaky old engine. "Can't wait to see the family?"

"Aw, shut up," said Mando.

Rosey said, "You mean you dudes are mixed up with foxes? Oh me, oh my."

"What's the matter, you don't like girls?" asked Mando.

"*Like* 'em? Man, I married one."

They all stared. "You what?"

"When I was seventeen." Rosey chuckled. He was in no way out of countenance. "Lasted a whole year."

"Then what?" asked Jonesy.

"She split."

"You had a quarrel?"

"Had a million of 'em. The relief people, her and me, around and around."

"You were on relief?"

"Man, you just don't know nothin', do you? A black boy in Newark. You couldn't know, could you?"

Jonesy said, "I'm sorry, Sandy. You're right. None of us could know."

"What about your folks?" asked Mando. "Couldn't they help?"

"What folks? I never had folks. I had a grandma, that's all. She tried. Washin' clothes for whiteys. Scrubbin' floors. Oh, she tried."

"You're pretty cool about it," Mando said.

"What's to be? That's the way it is, man. I wasn't the only one. Thousands of us. You remember the street fight in Newark?"

"The riots?"

"Riots to whitey. Street fights to niggers. I was there. Just a kid. They put me under the jail."

"Were you with the looters?"

"Who wasn't?" Rosey laughed. "Oh, I was there. And

90

they jugged me. And that did it. Black lawyers got the funky people out on bail. The leaders. Sure, they did. They left poor Sanderson Roosevelt right where he was. That taught me. Get out and do it on your own. Forget the slum, baby, forget it. That's when I started playin' ball for real."

There was a silence as Jack drove on the freeway to San Diego and Route 101. Each had his own thoughts, his own acceptance of Rosey's frank story.

Finally Mando said, "We had it rough in the *barrio*. But there was always the family. Somehow we stayed off relief. We ate a lot of fried beans. But we all pitched in. I guess that's the difference."

Rosey said, "Part of it, man, part of it. You'll never know the rest of it. Look, you know I wouldn't cry about it. No use to beat your skull, it's the way things go, man. You got to do it on your own."

Jack said, "That's what we're all doing. Trying to make it on our own."

"So we all wind up together in Mingo, New Jersey," said Rosey.

"We all *start* in Mingo, New Jersey," said Jonesy.

"Whichever way you cut it, I coulda done better," Rosey said. "I coulda made out better than the Pennjersey League."

"They're paying us enough," said Mando. "I'm satisfied."

"You can't never be satisfied," Rosey said. "You got to fight 'em down to the bricks."

Jonesy asked mildly, "Whatever became of your wife, Sandy?"

Rosey settled back on the worn upholstery of the old Ford. "Man, that's a story. I went back to school, see, to play ball. Grandma, she got on the relief. Long's I was makin' good grades and starrin' on all the teams, they paid. So Wanda, that's my ex, she went back to school, too. Then she went to the Normal School. Would you believe it, she's starting out as a teacher?"

"Did she remarry?"

"That chick marry again? She's too smart for that,

man. She can make a living now. She'll never hook up again until she meets a black man can make as much as she does."

"Do you correspond with her?"

"No way. Grandma kept up with her. Grandma did everything until she died just before I came out here."

"Oh, I'm sorry," said Jonesy.

"It's the way things are," said Rosey. "Just when I might could help, she ups and dies on me."

"That's too bad," said Mando. He was trying to think how it must have been for Rosey. He could understand better why there was so much feistiness in the man now. He could not quite condone it, but he could see the meaning of it. Rosey felt that he had to strike out at the world and everyone in it just to maintain his position. It would never be easy for him, because he would never allow it to be easy. But he had reasons, good reasons for his attitude.

"It's the way things are," Rosey repeated.

There were turns, there were side roads, there were meanderings which one had to follow, Mando thought. He had seen it in the *barrio*, in college, now he was trying to learn the way of it in professional baseball.

In the beginning he had resented Harry the Claw. He had believed Hammer to be an ignorant bully. It had developed that Hammer could learn not to call anyone a "greaser" or a "nigger," or even "boy." It was Hammer who had watched the four infielders and had estimated their value and had asked for them as a unit. Maybe the Pennjersey League was the low bushes—it was a start for Hammer as well as for the four of them. It all depended upon what they did, how they performed.

He did not mention any of this aloud. He knew Rosey would belligerently deny all, and it was not a time for controversy, it was vacation time, a prelude to a long, hard season of baseball.

Jack drove northward on the San Diego Freeway, keeping to the middle lanes where the old car could do a safe sixty miles per hour.

Mando was thinking about Ana Cassidy. When he had

been called to the phone, knowing it must be the girl from San Diego, he had felt all loose inside. He had stumbled, and he was not a person who was ever uncertain on his feet. He had dropped the receiver because his hand was shaking in anticipation of hearing her voice. Nothing like this had ever happened to him in his young life before; it was a phenomenon which needed exploration.

He had been startled to learn that Rosey was married at seventeen. The thought of marriage had never occurred to him. He had never been deeply involved with a girl. This was all new. He had been with Ana once. Now he could scarcely wait to see her again. It was a circumstance about which he knew nothing, completely outside his experience. He wondered anxiously if he would know how to cope.

Jack was silent. Maybe this was because he was going to see Connie, Mando thought. They had been going together for a couple of years now, Jack and Connie. Their relationship was established, as solid as it could be under the conditions. He had never thought about it much before; he had merely been pleased because he loved his sister, and Jack was his friend. He would have liked to ask Jack how he felt, if he had plans, what Connie thought about it all, but he couldn't. It was all too new to him. He was abashed at his own emotion whenever he thought of Ana Cassidy.

The miles ran under the wheels, and they came to the Ventura turnoff and made that difficult maneuver in heavy traffic. Now they were on the edge of Van Nuys, and a decision had to be made about Rosey.

"How can you know where you want to go?" Jack asked him. "You've never been here before. Why not go with Mando?"

"Because I'm me," said Rosey. "Just drop me off anywheres."

"In this megalopolis, you don't just drop people off," Mando said. "First we have to leave the freeway. Second there's almost no public transportation. The buses run now and then, and where they go, nobody knows."

Rosey said, "Hey, man, this here's the home of the Dodgers, the Lakers, the Rams, almost the home of the Angels, right?"

"We don't know any of those people," Mando said.

Rosey patted his rear pocket. "I asked people. Down at the camp, you dig? Black power. I got numbers to call. I get me some of those cats around a pool table, everything's gonna be all right."

They left him whistling on the corner.

It was a short drive to the familiar street where Mando's family dwelt. The houses seemed smaller and dingier, but the same youngsters were throwing a lopsided baseball back and forth. Mando was ready for them with three scarcely used league balls. They jumped up and down and yelled, "The Man. Mando the Man. Big-leaguer!"

He took the duffel bag from the car and said, "See you guys in a little while. Call me, Jack?"

"You know I'll call."

"Okay. Upward and onward."

They left him. Ricky came lounging out of the house.

"Hey, man. Connie's working after school, y' know."

"Yeah. You let her."

"She wants clothes." Ricky shrugged, indifferent. "Uncle Talker's inside. You okay?"

"How come you're not working?"

"Uncle laid me off." Ricky sniggered. "He had a little trouble with the Berets. He blames me."

"And you're as innocent as the dewy morn."

"Up Uncle Talker. I get unemployment. He'll need me, come the busy season. Hey, how about that Pennjersey bit? I looked it up. Nothingsville."

"I like it better than unemployment insurance," said Mando. He shouldered his way past his older brother and went into the house. All were there, Papa, Mamma, José, María, and Uncle Luis. They sat in a circle and regarded him with sympathy mixed with a certain amount of triumph. He kissed his parents and put the bag in the bedroom he would share with Ricky. He came back into the sitting room.

Uncle Luis said, "So. You're home. You will go back to the college."

"I'll do what?"

"Surely you have failed. Even Ricky, that ruffian, knows that you have failed to make good."

"My poor son," said Mamma.

"Tough goin', brother," said José, smiling, running his fingers through his mane.

"I did not spend all your money," said Papa. "There is enough for you to return to school with your scholarship. If you can regain your scholarship?"

Mando asked, "Are you all out of your minds? I'm going to New Jersey. I'm playing ball for a town named Mingo. That's an eastern Indian name. It's in the Pennjersey League. Now you know."

"But it is of the lowest!" cried Uncle Luis. "They do not pay enough to live upon."

"You will starve!" wept Mamma.

"Hey, man, the bushes?" demanded José. "You lost your pride?"

Mando surveyed them. "Ricky, he knows it all, does he? Uncle Talker and Ricky. They hate me worse than they do each other. They know nothing, do you hear, Mamma? Papa? Nothing."

"They read up on it," said José. "The *Sporting News*, right? The newspaper of the sports world. Pennjersey. Nowhere."

"Eight thousand dollars for the season," Mando said. "That's nothing? Since when are we all as rich as Uncle Talker?"

"Eight thousand?" His father did mental arithmetic.

"And maybe winter ball for another few thousand," said Mando. "That's enchiladas and fried beans?"

"Eight thousand," said Uncle Luis. "You didn't tell us."

"I didn't tell *you* anything. I just learned that they were going to pay us that well. All four of us. The infielders. So now will you climb down off my back?" He grinned to break the tension. "And now, Mamma, would you feed me? Could you spare a little real *mexicano* food?"

"Oh, my poor baby, he is starved!" Mamma clapped a hand to her head and fled to the kitchen, leaving a trail of liquid Spanish in her wake.

"Eight thousand plus winter ball," Uncle Luis said. "Ah, it makes me also hungry just to hear of it. Congratulations, nephew. We must speak together. It so happens I have inside information as to investments. You understand? Money to be made. Trust your uncle, we will become rich."

Mando said, "You are already rich. Do me no favors, Uncle Talker. Let us just eat and be happy."

In the ample kitchen the atmosphere altered, was warm again, the family talking together, overlapping each other's dialogue, laughing, merry. They were really like children sometimes, Mando thought, eating the food upon which he had been reared, enjoying. Even Uncle Talker had new funny stories, swallowing his taco and refried beans. They were good people, the best in the world, they were Mando's people.

Mrs. Marion Temple Kelly was a gentle lady, slim and white-haired but with style. Jonesy was attracted to her on sight and she was hearty in her welcome. They sat beside the pool and talked.

"I don't really worry about Jack," she said. Then she was suddenly vulnerable, looking intently at Jonesy. "He is happy, isn't he? Doing what he wants to do? I mean, he doesn't resent leaving college?"

"Jack is sure to make the big leagues," Jonesy said. "Sooner or later, he will be a star. He can pick up his degree anytime he wants."

"I'm so glad to hear you say that. I suppose you've discussed it."

"Jack, Mando, and I are going back to school. Baseball is a big part of our lives. It isn't all of our lives."

"I told Mr. Kelly." She broke off and was silent, biting her lip.

A big man came from the far end of the patio. He carried a highball glass in his hand. This had to be Big

Kel, Jonesy knew. His face was flushed and his expression blank. He sat down in a poolside aluminum chair which seemed scarcely sufficient to support his bulk.

"Jones," he said. "You're the second sacker."

"Yes, sir." The big man had not spoken to his wife, was ignoring her. She arose, smiled at Jonesy, and went into the house. It was a sad and touching moment.

"You didn't make it, either."

"I beg your pardon, sir?" His experience at home enabled him to remain blandly noncommittal.

"You and that greaser and a nigra and my Jack. None of you could make it."

"We're satisfied."

Big Kel took a slug of his highball. "I raised my boy to go first class all the way. Make all the teams, be a star. He was, too. Then he began running with that greaser. And the sister, the pachuca broad."

Jonesy swallowed his gorge. "Mando is a good man. Sandy is a fine ballplayer. We get along together."

"Oh, sure." He stared at Jonesy. "Where you from?"

"The Midwest."

"Yeah. Well, we travel with the best people, always did. There's no USC in the Midwest, after all. We've always had class. Jack went to private school. Agh ... you wouldn't understand."

"No, sir," said Jonesy, poker-faced.

"People with money. Professional people." Kelly waved a hand. "Looka this house, Olympic swimming pool, a Cad in the garage. Ten thousand in furnishings. And my son bunks in with the kind of people ... agh!"

Jonesy thought of the baronial splendor of the cold, luxurious decor which was his parental home, and could not repress a smile. He instinctively knew that Big Kel would give his eye teeth to be acquainted with the Joneses. But he merely said, "We get along."

"I just don't get it." He drank again from the glass. "You raise a kid, you teach him everything good. You coach him, make a champ of him. What does he do? He quits on you. He mixes with bums. He leaves school to become a lousy bush-league ballplayer. What's the use?"

97

There was the familiar sound of an auto horn. Jones arose from the chair.

"Mr. Kelly, with all respect, I must tell you that Jack is my friend and that I disagree with everything you have said and everything you think and everything you represent. Now, if you'll excuse me."

"You . . . you midwestern punk," shouted Kelly. "What do I care what you think? Or anyone else thinks? You're part of it, part of this youth thing, know-it-alls, turning on their parents that gave them everything. Go on, go with the pachucos, the nigras. You're all alike, ungrateful bums."

"Yes, sir," said Jonesy politely. He went into the house and picked up his suitcase.

They were all in the Ford, Jack and the pretty girl who must be Connie Cruz, and Mando and Ana, and María Constanza. Jack got out and looked at the bag, then at the house, then back to Jonesy.

"The pater got after you, huh?"

"You might say that."

They went to the rear of the car and put the suitcase in the deck. Jack banged down the lid.

"I'm sorry."

"Don't be. No problem."

"It's Mother. She likes you."

"I know. She's a lovely person."

"Is he into the booze?"

"Yes."

"One thing. He's always decent to Mother these days. He used to yell a lot. He stopped that, she told me, when I left home."

"I'm sorry for them."

"Yes. Both of them." Jack gestured. "Look, let's have fun."

"Okay," said Jonesy. "Let's have fun."

The first stop was at the service station on Moorpark Street in Studio City. A tall, gaunt, handsome man with sharp brown eyes, Ana's eyes, came to the car, leaned in on his strong hands soiled with grease and peered at them.

"Hi, boys. Who are those handsome chicks you got there?"

Ana said, "Always cute, that's my father. ... That is Connie Cruz, and this is her brother Mando. Jack Kelly and Gil Jones."

"Ballplayers, I hear. Good to meet you. Let me fill this old buggy with gas." His grin was warm and easy. He chatted with them as though he were a contemporary.

Mando got out of the car and prowled around the station. It lacked the architectural splendor of the major company outlets, but it had extra space for a repair shop. There was a young man beneath a car raised on the automatic hoist. He waved a hand.

"Hi, Mando."

Mando squinted. "Hey, Pasquale. A fotzadomotch."

"Haven't seen you since high school. Congratulations."

"Thanks, Patsy," said Mando. "What you up to these days?"

"Workin' for a couple of swell gents."

"You were always the automobile jockey. How's business?"

"Not great. But gettin' better. My bosses are top mechanics. So am I. We work like dogs, but we love it. Hey, ain't that Ana with you?"

"I get lucky once in a while."

The young man sighed. "You can repeat that, Mando. What a doll. What people, the bunch of them. María, her folks—the greatest."

"You repair trucks?"

"Does it run? We repair it."

"I was thinking of Uncle Luis. You remember Uncle Talker?"

Patsy made a face. "Mr. Cheapola. I remember."

"He runs trucks. And all the chicanos have cars, and none of the cars are new."

Patsy said, "It's an idea."

"Look, I don't want to come on strong with Mr. Cassidy. You dig?"

"I dig."

"If Uncle Luis shows—deal with him, huh? I mean, don't let him con you. One thing about him, he pays off. He argues for cash discounts, but he pays."

Patsy said, "There's ways of dealing with people like him. Mark it up a little, give him the discount. We could sure use some cash business, Mando."

"Okay. Just between us, huh?"

"Sure, Mando. Hey—knock 'em dead in Jersey, huh?"

"We do our best."

"You're the Man."

Mando returned to the car. He said, "Patsy and I went to high school together. He's a real nice guy."

"The best," said Ted Cassidy. He took the nozzle from the vent and replaced the top of the gas tank. "This is on me. You kids have a good time, hear? Don't be too late, Ana . . . María. Your mother worries."

"I suppose you don't worry?" Ana laughed.

"Not when you're with ballplayers. Not these guys. I'm young, but I'm old-fashioned. I think athletes are mainly clean. It may not be true, but I believe it."

"And he believes in karate," Ana told them. "For girls."

"Be prepared," said Ted Cassidy. "Boy Scouts are prepared. Why not girls? Hey—I got work to do. Have fun, kids." He leaned into the car and kissed Ana's cheek.

Mando said, "It's been a real pleasure. And thanks for the gasoline."

"I wish you'd let us pay," Jack said. "But thanks anyway."

"Just hit me a homer someday," said Ana's father.

They called farewells, and Jack drove eastward on Moorpark Street.

The Palladium was ancient, but the policy was new. Jack parked the Ford around the corner in a lot, and the six young people walked past the Brown Derby and the famed Hollywood and Vine, and they went down the boulevard and paid the admission fee and went inside.

They walked past the milk bar—there were several,

none of which served anything stronger than a cola—and the sound of hard rock assailed their ears. They made it to the huge dance floor.

There were two bandstands at opposite ends of the spacious floor. A group known as the Penitentiary was performing at full blast, completely electronic, the sound booming. On the dance floor were a multitude of couples expressing themselves as individuals, never touching one another, gyrating with elbows akimbo and feet shuffling.

Jonesy said, "María, are you up to this?"

She beamed upon him. "You know what, Jonesy? You're groovy. You're really groovy."

Mando watched them join the throng. Jack and Connie were already at it.

"He is, at that, you know," he told Ana Cassidy.

"I've noticed," she said. "The quiet man. He manages."

They took ringside seats. For a moment they watched the dancers. Then they looked at each other.

He had to lean close to her ear to make himself heard above the cacophony of the band. "You and your old man. You're too much."

She looked into his eyes without guile. "You're pretty much yourself, chicano."

"You don't know me."

"But you don't know me, either."

"You're mighty pretty."

"So are lots of people. You're handsome."

"Ho!" But he was pleased. No one had ever told him before that he was handsome. "What I mean, I dug you on sight."

"Yes. Me, too," she said. "It's a question of learning more about each other."

"But I have to go east. I have to play ball in New Jersey."

"Yes," she said. "And I have to finish school."

"I want to get my degree, too," he told her. "We owe it. Chicanos must become educated. I know that. Baseball's not a forever job."

"I want to teach."

He said, "I want to teach our own people if I can make it. Someday. Now . . . it's baseball. And you."

The rock band, as was their custom, ended abruptly in what seemed to be the middle of a phrase. Mando's last two words came out booming. People seated around them turned and stared; there were some snickers. He felt hot blood flooding his cheeks, but he did not turn away from Ana.

She whispered, "We have time. Lots of time."

"Waiting is a murderous time."

Now she flushed and said, "Careful, chicano."

The second band began to play a calmer rhythm. Ana came into his arms. He led her easily and purposefully. There was not the slightest hesitation, their steps matched as though they were a trained dance team, they moved bemusedly, wrapped in their close proximity. Her waist was slender and woman-soft under his hand. She touched his shoulder to keep contact as they slid, pivoted, glided over the waxed floor.

They made one long circuit of the hall; then she moved closer and was in against him, her cheek close to his. They danced slower now, in half-time, longer steps, graceful as gazelles. Each had the feeling for the dance, each had the music within, the response to the music. They saw no one, heard no one, yet they miraculously moved among the other couples without collision.

Someone said in Mando's ear, "Hey, man, how about you?"

Mando started almost out of his skin. "Rosey!"

"Who else, man?" The white teeth grinned at him. "Meet Rose Farmer . . . Mando the Man."

They circled once, and Mando said, "Ana Cassidy . . . our roomie we told you about, Sandy Roosevelt."

Ana said, "How nice! Are you with people?"

The beautiful dark-skinned girl in Rosey's grasp said, "Pleased to meet you. No, we ducked our crowd."

"Old heads," Rosey said. "They wanted to liquor up some. Rose, here, she's a juve. Like yawl."

Mando said, "Hey, look for us, huh? We're all here."

"*You* ain't all here," Rosey told him, grinning widely. "I been watchin' you. Half here would be too much."

Mando said, "Okay, knock it off."

"See you, man." Rosey whirled away.

Mando said, "What are you goin' to do about Rosey?"

"I don't think you need do anything about him. He's older, isn't he?"

"Twenty-one," said Mando. "He's been married."

"He's an attractive man," said Ana.

"You really think so?" He was surprised.

"Vitality," said Ana.

The music stopped, and they made their way back to the place where they had been sitting. The others were already there, looking for them. They sat together, elated from the dance, enjoying.

Mando asked, "Did you grab that Rosey?"

"And that chick," said Jack. "Is she somethin'?"

"She's beautiful," said Ana. "We asked them to join us."

"He won't do it," Jonesy told them.

"Why shouldn't he join us?" asked Jack. "He's our roomie."

"That's not the point," Mando said.

"No. He's like us," María said. "It's all right if we know everybody. But minority people are skittish. Maybe his girl wouldn't want to mix. There's always something in the way. Something."

"I didn't think of it that way," Mando confessed. "Like we're used to having Rosey around. He's one of us."

"How about a Coke?" asked Jonesy smoothly. "All this dancing around makes me thirsty."

Mando spied Rosey across the hall. He and his girl were standing with another Negro couple. They did not glance in the direction of Mando and his company.

They sat in the milk bar and chatted. The rock began to roar again. They moved upstairs to the balcony, deciding to sit this one out. Mando maneuvered Ana to one side where he could whisper privately to her.

"I'm sorry about your roommate," she said.

"Never mind him. He's cool," said Mando. "I'm glad he met you."

"Me? Whyever me?"

"Well, he and I—we're always ready to bicker. Seems like we can't get together on any subject, anytime, anywhere."

"Excepting on the field, you mean."

"Right. He's a cool cat. He thinks he can make it by fighting. Oh, he's tough. But he hits too quick and too hard. At least, that's the way I see it."

"And of course you fight back."

"What else?"

"You're chicano. But you're glad he met me. Why?"

"I guess I want him to think better of me," Mando confessed. "I guess I want him to know that if a girl like you goes out with me I must be somebody."

She said, "That's the nicest thing anyone ever said to me. It's not sensible—but it's sweet."

"It's true." He was aware, then, that Jonesy was listening. María was chattering away, and Connie and Jack were, as always, silent and pleased with each other, but Jonesy was looking at Ana and listening and smiling in a faraway manner. "Right, Jonesy?"

"Indubitably," said Jonesy. The jazz band had returned to action. "Could I please have this dance, Mando?"

"I don't follow real good, but if you really care. . . ."

Ana said, "Don't be a fool. Come on, Jonesy."

They left the milk bar and went to the dance floor. María hitched in closer to Mando.

"That Jonesy, he kills me. I dig him. But he's funny. Funny-peculiar, y'know? He says those witty things in that dry way, but his mind's not on it. Like he throws away the lines. And he's so polite, criminy, I never met such a polite fella in my life. Any girl could go for him. He does everything right, you know what I mean? Only when I try to get his attention, he gives me that absent smile. Like he's not with it. He doesn't really dig me, he's just being nice to me. Nobody's ever been nicer. Nobody could be. Maybe too nice? I don't know. It's like I'm

104

here and he's someplace else, you know what I mean? It's real strange, Jack's handsome and in love, and you're Mando the Man and Ana goes for you, and I'm right here able, willing, and ready, and it's like Ghostville. I've got chicanos with law degrees and medical degrees after me all the time. Maybe it's just that he's a gringo from up north or something? You think that's it, Mando?" She was half-serious and thoroughly plaintive.

"I wouldn't know," he told her. He could see the floor, see Jonesy dancing slowly with Ana, holding her as though she were a crate of eggs. He saw Rosey dance by with his pretty girl named Rose. He could not wrench his thoughts away from Ana.

María leaned even closer and spoke in Spanish. "Maybe we should remain with our own, Mando. My grandfather says we run to false idols, to foreign blood, that we are ashamed of our blood. I am not ashamed to be *mexicana*. But I am proud to be an American of the United States. Am I wrong, Mando?"

"You are right," he said in the same language. "We must not think of ourselves otherwise. It is to be proud of heritage but aware of today."

"Ai, this is not easy, Mando."

"Nobody promised us it would be easy."

A group of people in costumes which made it difficult to sort out male from female drifted past the milk bar. A tall, hulking man said, "Hey, Mando."

"Hi, Dolph." Mando watched them, recognizing them as part of a motorcycle gang some of whom had been in athletics during his high-school career. He said to María, "At least we are not as those. They are bad ones."

"Sí. They are dropout and make trouble within," she assented.

On the floor Rosey and Jonesy came together, exchanged partners. It was good to see Ana dancing with Rosey. Mando had a strong feeling that they would speak well of him, and this night he wanted that, wanted it very much. This was not his way, but tonight was roseate, he knew, because of Ana.

He said, "Maybe you'd like to dance, María?"

"I always like to dance." She dimpled at him, a pretty girl with dark and flashing eyes.

They went to the floor. Jack and Connie followed. The band was playing an old one, "Sweet Georgia Brown," and a singer was giving it a modern interpretation. Mando looked for Ana and Rosey.

He saw them at once. Dolph and his crowd had come onto the floor en masse. They were talking to Rosey, their voices were loud. The big man put out a hand to separate Ana from Rosey.

Mando said to María, "Get off the floor. Go to the milk bar and wait. Just keep quiet and wait."

He made his way through the crowd on the dance floor as well as he could without creating a disturbance. He saw Jack doing the same as Connie hurried away. It seemed forever before he got to where the bike people were milling around Rosey and Ana. His mouth was dry and his heart pounded like a triphammer.

He got a hand on the first of the crowd, and it was a female who spoke profanely to him, mouthing the word "nigger." He threw her aside and drove hard into the jostling bodies.

Rosey had Dolph by the wrist. A blow from another of the crowd struck Rosey behind the ear. He merely bent the wrist and twisted the hand of the big man. Jack was coming from a third angle. Mando sought Ana, saw that two of the enemy were trying to hold her. He sent one of them flying, took the other by the hair and sent her—it proved to be a girl—whirling in among her friends.

Dolph was going to his knees, his teeth showing in a grin of pain. Rosey rolled his eyes at Mando, winked, and said, "Right on, man."

Mando said to Ana, "The milk bar."

She was pale, and her nostrils pinched in with rage, but she nodded and left. Jonesy came sidling through, on the spot as usual. Mando slapped away a restraining hand and looked for the security officers always on the job in this place. Dolph collapsed as he uttered a high, shrieking cry of pain.

Mando said, "Hey, Rosey, let's flee the scene."

"For once you make sense." Rosey was grinning, but there was no mirth in him.

They blew their way through the disorganized motorcycle people. They picked up the lovely Rose, and at the milk bar the girls saw them and came swiftly to them. They went out the door with all possible speed. They walked without haste around a corner and into a shadowed part of the street.

Mando said, "Hey, Rosey, you were great. I mean, not clobbering that bum. I know that slob. He needs it, but it would've put us in trouble. All of us."

"Me and Rose, we'd be in the can," said Rosey. "You know it."

"You'd have had company," Jack told him.

"No way," Rosey said bitterly. Then he looked at Ana, and the grin returned. "Hey, you're somethin' else. You do speak up, don't you, lady?"

"I speak up, man," she replied.

"She laid it on him," Rosey said. "She really laid it on him."

"Look, why don't we all squeeze into the Ford and make Malibu?" Mando suggested.

"No way," said Rosey. "We got a date downtown."

The girl said, "Thank you. We do have a date with some of the Lakers. My brother is a basketball player."

"Too much," said Mando. He watched the couple swing off toward the parking lot.

Ana said, "He's all man, isn't he?"

"Quick, too," said Jack.

"He handled it well," said Jonesy. "His style is to swing hard and talk later."

They walked back to the boulevard and around the corner. Ana held Mando's arm warm in her grasp.

"Well?" she asked, smiling at him. "Aren't you going to ask me?"

"I heard Dolph yell at Rosey."

"Not that."

"Oh. You mean what did Rosey say about me?"

"That's what I mean."

"He didn't say anything."

She said, "Mando, sometimes I think you are the Man. That's precisely correct."

"Still," said Mando. "I'm glad he met you."

"I know what you mean."

He pressed his elbow against her hand. "You always dig me. Like you know what I'm thinking. It ... it makes me very happy."

"The moon is out," she said. "It'll be lovely on the beach at Malibu."

6

Mingo was situated in mid-New Jersey, an old town which had burgeoned with the coming of airplane industry but was still far from a metropolis. It was near the banks of the Delaware River and not far from the Jersey shore. It was fifty miles south of New York City but not on one of the throughways which bisected the state from north to south. The baseball field was small, poorly lighted, and not well supported, at least partially due to the fact that the previous year had found the local team hopelessly in last place.

The new broom wielded by the Gold Sox management had swept the decks clean. Harry the Clawhammer had brought an all-new squad to Mingo. They were housed in an ancient hotel. Partitions had been torn down, the upper and lower bunks reminiscent of the training camp installed. There was one big old bathroom per floor which had been partitioned to provide two sets of facilities, with showers replacing the old-fashioned tubs.

There was never any doubt that the four infielders would share a room. There was, Mando sometimes thought, an invisible chain binding them together. The Gold Sox management, including Hammer, had pasted them together, volume one of a story yet to be told.

Incredibly, it was May. Not so unbelievably it had rained during most of April, which to the Californians was at first mildly thrilling and later a pestilence. They had traveled Pennsylvania and Delaware and north Jersey and were now about to make a home stand. They had won ten games and lost two. They were leading the Pennjersey League by a game over the Yankee farm team of Mainville, Pennsylvania. The remainder of the teams were scattered helplessly in the ruck.

It was Sunday, and Mando was conning the first roster of big-league averages. He came to the name he sought and grunted.

"What's Lou Libby hitting?" Jack asked.

"Two-three-o," said Mando. "I don't wish him any hard luck. Only that he doesn't do any better."

"How about the shortstop?" demanded Rosey.

"Gordon? Let me see. Here it is—he's at three-fifty."

"Gimme that paper, you fink," said Rosey. He grabbed and squinted. "Two-eighty-one. That's bad enough. Any infielder as good as him can hit two-fifty and be a big man."

"What's Astor doing?" Jack asked.

"Two-fifty even. But with four homers."

"Nuts."

Rosey said, "Hey, Jonesy. Monty Wells is at two-five-two. Looks like Mando's man is the weak character."

"They're not about to send for me," said Mando. "If I don't shake this slump, even Hammer will give up on me."

"Yeah, man," said Rosey. "You're undercuttin', hittin' all those cans of corn."

"I think he's understriding," said Jack.

"Hammer thinks I'm trying too hard," said Mando.

"You started with six straight hits," Jonesy reminded him. "If you could think back to what you were doing. Concentrate. I wish we had films like the big clubs."

"Three straight," Mando groaned. "Horse collar for three games in a row. I'll kill myself."

"Hammer'll do it for you," said Rosey. "If you make one error he'll club you to death with the fungo bat."

Mando had not yet committed an error afield, but to him, like every other ballplayer, this did not count. Hitting was the name of the game. They lived by their averages. Jack and Rosey were around .400 against the Pennjersey pitching, which they had found to be not much above college level. Jonesy was safe at .290. Only Mando was down below that figure.

"It's early in the season." Jonesy was comforting. "You've got plenty of time."

"And that Yankee pitcher's got my number, too," Mando said. "Tonight could be just another bad dream."

"Positive thinking," said Jack. "You're wishing yourself bad luck."

"And Zander hasn't failed in a pinch yet. Four times at bat, a perfect sacrifice and three hits. A thousand percent."

"Zander can't carry your glove," said Jonesy.

"Only his bat," said Rosey.

The needle never stopped flying between them, Mando thought. They were natural enemies, the Negro shortstop and the chicano third baseman. It no longer came close to blows; on the surface it was just kidding back and forth. But there was a mutual lack of understanding, and they both were aware of it.

In a way it could be helpful, Mando supposed. He had learned to keep his mouth shut instead of responding to every cutting remark. He was getting his temper under better control. Possibly because of Ana he was becoming a more tractable person. He thought about Ana now.

She wrote to him twice a week. He had never been one for writing letters, but he faithfully answered. They exchanged more than sweet nothings; they traded ideas, philosophies. They wanted desperately to know each other better. It was a delicate and tremendously

111

important time for them, separated by a continent. They were trying to make the most of it.

Jack said, "Let's get dressed and take a look at our palatial stadium. The drainage is lousy. We might as well get used to the damp spots."

"Yeah, you can bet Zander's over there," said Rosey. "He sure knows how to make character with Hammer."

"He can carry my bat. You said so," Mando told him.

They began to don their uniforms, which were not too clean, white with blue trim, blue socks, and cap. Mando thought about Zander and admitted to himself that Rosey was right, the pinch-hitting third baseman did hang around and run errands for Hammer. There were always people like that, he knew. It was not his way, and never would be, and that could be costly someday. However, it was impossible for him to change; it would be an alteration of basic character.

The roster of the Mingo Skeeters was slim. Hammer had brought Green along to play center field, Downey for right, and the veteran Peck for left field. Dizzy Pazolla was the regular catcher, with Sonny Carey to back him up. Rock Roquero from Puerto Rico was an infield-outfield reserve. Biggie Howard was another young outfielder. Zander, of course, was infield, and twenty-one-year-old thin kid named Forest was the other outfielder. The pitchers were Page, Barone, Onslow, Terry, and Fargo, all of whom had talent of one kind or another.

Hammer had only one assistant, old Ace Holder, who had been the batting-practice hurler and a long-time friend of Hammer. It was a tight, skimpy organization, but at that the team lost money in the Pennjersey League. It was a farm club calculated to build for the future.

The quartet went downstairs to the lobby of the old hotel. One by one they went to the desk and asked if there was mail. They did this every time they left or when they entered the hotel. It was one of the few fun things to do in Mingo.

Behind the desk the manager stared at each of them in turn.

"The mail has been up for hours," he said to Rosey. "Besides, you have never yet received one piece of mail. Never!"

"All the more reason I should expect some," Rosey said solemnly. "You sure there's not a postcard, even?"

"There is not!"

"Well, when it comes, you be sure and let me know right away," said Rosey.

But when it was Mando's turn the manager reached behind him and said, "Yes. A special delivery."

Mando moved out of hearing. He tore open the envelope. The message was brief.

Dearest Man:

If there is anything I detest, it is being the eager bearer of ill tidings, but in this case it is mandatory. When you write again, please address the letter to our L.A. home. Last week Father was caught under a car and severely hurt. I have come home to help out. School can wait, everything can wait. I held off telling you as long as I could so as not to disturb you, but sooner or later ... This is later. Please do not worry too much. We are all working at the station, we'll come through ...

                                                            Love,
                                                            Ana

He folded the letter and put it back in the torn envelope, folded it over, and stuck it in his back pocket. He followed the others at a distance, his mind turning over. Ana had been serious about college, proud in her quiet way of her grades, ambitious for her degree.

And her father, with his friendly, outgoing grin—he had been proud of her, had worked as hard as he

113

could to make a place for her and her mother. Now he was injured. Mando's own father had been hurt, incapacitated; he knew about such accidents and the results in families living on the margin of stability. A few months of disability, and it would take years to catch up.

Now Ana was working at the station. Was she pumping gas? Ana? Could they afford a grease monkey, could they get enough work to keep Patsy working on repairs? A dozen problems presented themselves. He would have to put through a telephone call; he had to know the details Ana meant to spare him in her brief, dolorous message. The spring went out of his step as he approached the ball park.

The home field of the Mingo Skeeters had been a fairgrounds, but not an important one. The high fence was in need of paint. The entrance was through a wooden gate. The stands were of wood, somewhat splintery, holding two thousand people at most—and the ball team wished they could fill it at least once. Mando went through the gate.

Rosey said, "Like I told you. See?"

Zander was wheeling a barrow along the third-base line, dribbling sand into the dampness. Hammer was following him, spreading the dry sand with a rake.

Rosey said, "Better get out there and help, Mando. Zander knows his onions."

"It's not in my contract," Mando said. He was not up to bandying wisecracks with Rosey at the moment. His mind was back in California.

Jack said, "First team never does that kind of labor. Trouble with it is, if we don't, it'll never get done, and we have to play those dead grounders down the base lines."

"How else have we been playing them?"

Jonesy said, "It's not so good around second, either. Does it always rain in Jersey?"

"When it don't, it's miserable," Rosey told them. "Wait'll the mosquitoes come on us."

"Is that why they call us 'Skeeters'?"

"Well, the gnats are worse," said Rosey.

"Come to Jersey with Harry Hammer," said Jack. "You think we might've made some kind of a mistake?"

"We're leading the league," Jonesy said.

"By a game. And here come the Yankees," Jack said.

The bus came into view. It was a newer and sleeker bus than that of the Skeeters. It was painted with huge letters announcing that the Mainville Yankees were aboard. It pulled around to the other side of the stands. Players in their uniforms descended stiffly. They had dressed on the bus, Mando knew, like all the other teams in the league. Nobody, but nobody, had it fancy in the Pennjersey League. This was the bottom of the barrel in organized baseball.

Mando's competitive spirit was usually roused by the very sight of the opposition. Tonight he gazed gloomily at the stocky figure of Billy Fay, the left-hander who had kept him hitless thus far in the season. They said that Fay had a chance of becoming another Whitey Ford; he had the control, the sneaky fast ball, and two curves. And he was twenty years of age.

And he was playing right under the nose of the parent club, Mando added. What did they see of the Skeeters back in Bay City, California? They saw reports and read averages, that was all. The Gold Sox had troubles of their own. They were hopelessly in last place in their division of the American League.

Hammer glared around. Ace Holder was coming through the gate with several of the players.

"Where is everybody when I'm a-workin' my tail off out here? Ain't there nobody but Zander got this team's interest at heart? Yawl better look sharp tonight or there's goin' to be some all-fired changes, I tell you that."

"Maybe he's going to send us down to the Epworth League?" suggested Rosey. "How much lower can we get?"

"You Rosey, what you sayin'?" demanded Hammer.

Before Rosey could answer, Jonesy said, "He was just wondering about the field and all."

Hammer said, "It's lousy is what it is. And they got that runt, that Fay kid to pitch. And if they win, they're tied with us. And I ain't goin' to like that no way."

He stalked away from them. The bushes were getting Hammer down, too, Mando thought. Conditions were poor, the food was sketchy on the road, sleeping conditions were not good. But worst of all were the playing fields, the lights, the lack of crowds, fans, interested persons. It was like playing a round of golf early in the morning, all alone with par.

Mando went through the motions preliminary to the game. The two umpires appeared. A couple of hundred people scattered themselves in the creaking stands. His mind was not completely on the proceedings at any time. The old recording wheezed through "The Star-Spangled Banner," and he nearly forgot to remove his cap and stand at attention in the dampness around third base.

Hammer had decided to start Barone against the visitors. The wild lefty could be very good upon occasion. The plate umpire called time, and Mando mechanically took his position against Dore, center field and lead-off, a right-handed speedster.

Barone wound up and delivered. It was a clean strike which Dore took all the way. Under the dim lights a good fast ball could slip by the best of hitters.

Barone grinned. He was always happy and confident when he got ahead of the hitter. He came in with his curve.

Grey guessed curve ball and swung early. The pull was into the hole. Mando went over with a chance to make the play. His foot slipped on the muddy surface of the base path. He measured his length.

Rosey was over there, but far too late to prevent Dore from sprinting down to first. In the third-base coaching box Sullivan, the manager of the Yankees, slapped his hands together and whistled. It was a shrill, exasperating whistle. Mando rose, dabbed at his dirty uniform, and went back to play Portale, a lefty and the left fielder of the Yankees.

It was reasonable that on the heavy field Portale would sacrifice. It was up to Barone to refrain from giving him a good pitch. Barone laid one right in there.

Portale bunted down the third-base line. He should have gone the other way, Mando knew. He should have pulled Jack in and forced Barone to cover. Everything was mixed up this night.

Mando went in for the bunt. It rolled slowly in the sand. He picked it up with his bare hand. He had been a split second too slow, he realized. He whipped the ball underhand to Jack. Portale outran the ball. Dore was safe coasting into second.

Mando went to the mound, calling time, speaking to Barone. "My fault. Let's get two this time. They are yours all the way."

Barone regarded him with pain. "Rotten luck. I've been outta luck all season."

"The season just started," Mando reminded him. "Go, man."

Jonesy and Jack were talking it up. Rosey was waiting, silent as always, coiled like a black enameled spring. Behind the plate Dizzy Pazolla was shrilly calling for the pitch. Hammer walked up and down the length of the Skeeter bench, grumbling.

Andrews, the right fielder of the Yanks, was a big, strong farmboy with awesome muscles. Following him would be Hagney, the first baseman, who was also a behemoth. Barone fretted around the mound as he always did with ducks on the pond. Barone had natural talent, but he surely needed seasoning, Mando thought. They all needed experience, and he wished he could put Ana and her father cleanly out of his mind until he could get to a telephone.

Andrews picked on a Barone fast ball. He hit it hard, and it went over second. Dore scooted past Mando to score.

Portale held up at second as Green came in fast, despite the wet grass, and made the hard throw. Barone walked around the mound as if a tribe of Indians were buried beneath it. Hammer came out with fire in his eye. Mando and Jack joined the group.

Hammer stormed, "I admit Mando ain't been no bargain. But you're servin' it up on a platter, Barone, you hear me? On a platter with trimmin's. You git this next guy, or you come outta there."

Hammer stomped off. Sullivan was laughing at him— a lot of the sleek young upcoming managers laughed at Harry. Mando stayed a moment.

"Come on, *paisano*, you can get 'em."

"Don't you *paisano* me, you chicano," Barone growled. Then he showed the corner of a grin. "Us Latins."

"I'm with you, man."

"Okay. I gotta learn to bite the bullet, right?"

"Bite hard, *paisano*."

Mando went back to third. Hagney was a formidable figure with a big, black bat that was already a trademark. The Yankees had material, as in the old days. They were building another dynasty in the East. The Gold Sox were aeons behind them. There was no way to overtake the established clubs, the cards were stacked against the new owners. Money meant little. Talent must be developed, and the process was slower than molasses in January.

Barone stood on the mound staring at first one runner, then the other. He gathered himself together, visibly striving for control of his emotions. He went into the stretch.

He threw a brave fast ball. Hagney slashed at it. The ball popped off the big bat and went high in the night air. It arched foul, and Pazolla circled under it behind the plate. It was lost in the lights.

It reappeared. Pazolla made a sunfish dive. The ball came smack into his mitt. It popped out. Pazolla fell down, stretching. He caught it in the webbing of his glove as he rolled over. He came up without mask or cap, threatening the advance of the runners.

The always present computerlike baseball mind of Mando registered: One out, men on first and second, play at third, double play possible. He laid back a trifle for Terrill, the small second baseman of the Yankees, a deceptively strong hitter. He looked for a solid footing so that he might get a start on a ground ball. He yipped at Barone, "Stick it to him, *paisano*, stick it to him."

Barone was concentrating now. He tugged at his cap, did his ritual walk around the mound. He regarded the base runners with gravity. He toed the slab. He raised his arms, cuddling the ball. He threw as hard as he knew how.

Terrill swung and missed, knocked mud from his spikes, peered at Barone, stepped back in. He was ready for the fast ball. He was set to pull it, and he pulled well to left field.

Barone came overhand. He twisted his wrist. The curve did not break as sharply or as soon as it should. Terrill rapped at it.

The ball went to the left of Mando. He threw himself into the mud again, reaching. The ball escaped his glove.

Rosey was there. He got the jump on the ball, and he scooped it up and made the throw to second. The ball came to Jonesy's right. Jones whirled, escaped the drive of the base runner, and shot a perfect pitch to first. Jack took it, turned, and flipped it negligently to the Yankee first-base coach.

"*That* for your speed," Jack told him. "Shove it."

Mando came in as Jonesy went for his bat. Hammer was breathing easier, but not happy.

"They got the lead. You guys get that run back. Mando, it ain't all that sticky out there. You ain't payin' strict attention. Get on the ball, Mando."

There was no answer to this. It was true. He had contributed nothing to the inning. He was off balance, and even now, try as he might, he could not prevent his thought from straying to the service station on Moorpark Street in Studio City, California. Was Ana waiting on a customer? Was she wearing coveralls and ruining her lovely hands? She could be injured the same as her father; there was always danger around automobiles.

He wrenched himself back to New Jersey and the game. Hammer was coaching on third, Ace Holder on first. Jonesy was at bat. Hammer was giving signs with his Ping-Pong-paddle hands. Green was in the on-deck box rubbing his ashen stick. Fay was fingering the ball in his hands.

Fay had more grace than most left-handed pitchers. He moved easily despite his medium, square-built stature. He had a three-quarter motion. He came in swiftly on the corner.

Jonesy squared away. Hammer had given him the sign to lay one down. Jones dribbled the ball along the first-base line. He was off and running. The mud did not seem to bother him; he ran on top of it, flying lightly for the base. Fay came in to field the ball. He grabbed at it, missed the handle. He picked it up, glared at Jonesy, muttered to himself in the manner of pitchers the world over.

Hammer was bawling, "That's the swift, Jonesy. That's the way to show 'em speed."

This was to get the goat of Sullivan. It was also good baseball, well executed. Green was going to bat. Rosey was getting ready for his turn. Mando sucked in his breath and sat on the end of the bench. He was in the hole, and he watched every move Fay made.

Fay was a cool cat. He kept Jonesy on the bag, and he worked on Green. He ran the count even. Then he threw a lovely screwball. Green swung and missed it by a foot.

Rosey wandered to the plate. He never seemed perturbed by a situation. He thought about himself, what he was going to do, how he was going to do it. He was the closest thing to a rugged baseball machine that an individual could become. Mando selected his bat and knelt in the on-deck box, still with all his attention on Fay.

In the back of his mind he thought about Hammer and why he had not, one run behind in the first, ordered Green to sacrifice Jonesy along. He knew why. The Yankee infield had expected just such a ploy. They had been ready and in position, and with the uncertain footing it may have been possible to get Jonesy, even pull a double play. Hammer knew his baseball from A to Izzard. He was not asking Rosey to bunt, either. He was giving the "hit-away" signal. He knew his Rosey. He also knew that Rosey was the one hitter feared by Billy Fay.

The left-hander was very careful. He threw wide. He threw in close. He threw low. He threw high. Rosey walked disgruntled down to first as Jonesy went to second. Rosey always wanted to hit—hit—hit.

Mando gripped the bat and took his place. Fay grinned at him. Fay loved pitching to Mando. He began to pitch junk. If there was anything Mando abhorred, it was junk balls.

The first one came in twisting and turning and big as a balloon. Despite himself, Mando jumped into it with a full cut.

The ball tipped his bat and fouled back to the screen. He knew he should not have offered at it. He fell out of the box and looked apologetically down at Hammer. The manager made wigwagging signs, touching his shirt, his cap, his bare wrist. It took Mando a confused moment to grasp the sign. It was for the bunt.

This meant laying the ball down the third-base line to pull the fielder in and leave the sack open for Jonesy. It was a good notion, considering Mando's record against Fay. It also posed a problem.

Off a junk delivery the odds were that the ball would spin. If Mando did not meet it squarely, did not twist it into fair territory, it could be just another strike—or again, the double play. He sucked in his breath and went back to the plate.

Again came the slow, tortuous curve. He let it go in

121

the belief it would be a ball. It settled in on the outside corner. He gulped, turned to the umpire.

"Where was it, please?" he asked desperately but politely.

"In there," said the official. "Be a hitter, boy."

Mando gave him the hard stare but followed his rule of never backtalking the arbiter. He looked at Hammer. The manager was livid with rage. The sign was to hit away, for fear Mando would butcher it on third strike and be automatically out.

Mando heaved a sigh. The lights went down, then up, a common occurrence in Mingo. They were never bright enough, not that it mattered against the stuff Fay was chucking. Mando could see it—he just couldn't yet seem to hit it.

He settled himself. The only way to hit this slow stuff was to wait it out, meet it squarely, and shove it into right field, behind the hitters. Slugging was disastrous; the ball would not carry. He gritted his teeth.

Fay checked the runners. He seemed highly amused. He came in with his sneaky fast ball, inside, to make Mando hit to left.

Mando hit it. He drove it hard. He sent it directly to Terrill at second base. The play went to White, the shortstop, covering, then to first. Mando was out by a step. The inning was over, and the Yankees still led by a run.

Sullivan's derisive whistle hung on the night air. A few scattered boos came from the disappointed fans. Hammer came stomping to the bench as Mando picked up his glove. He had never felt more frustrated, been more humiliated on a ball field in his life.

Jonesy called to him. "Tough luck, Mando."

Jack said, "Next time, *amigo*."

Nobody else spoke to him. He went out to third with his ego lower than a snake's belly. He could not believe in failure, he was not accustomed to it, nothing had prepared him for it. He had always been the Man, the guy who came through in the clutches.

Against this chunky pitcher, this Fay, he was a bum. Inside he writhed at the spectacle he had made of himself. He took his infield throws with vicious speed so that Jack made silent protest, wringing his mitt hand. He assumed his position, hands on knees as Barone prepared to pitch to the bottom of the Yankee order.

Barone seemed to have gathered himself together. He was always behind the hitters, but he would gamely fight back for control. He walked Tilden, the shortstop, with one out. Then he struck out the burly Hooker, Yankee catcher, and made Billy Fay pop to Rosey for the third out.

Mando went to the bench in a daze. This was all too new for him to digest. He felt helpless, useless. He had not had a chance in the inning, nothing to snap him out of it, to make him feel a part of the game. He felt as though he was coming apart, that an essential factor had been amputated.

Hammer was bawling, "Get that run back. I want that run back. You lettin' that li'l old lefty buffalo yawll!"

The little old lefty did not need to buffalo anyone. He simply stood out there and did his thing, Mando thought somberly. He threw from all directions, and what he delivered was a confounding mixture of the best. Billy Fay would be up in the leagues before any of them. His catcher, Hooker, was another natural. They went together like tacos and beer.

It was a nightmare game for Mando. He came to bat twice more before the ninth without getting on base. He had one chance at third after Barone settled down and began to match Fay throughout the innings. In fact, it was a triumph for the wild, green, but game young Skeeter pitcher.

Jack got his hit. Jonesy got another. Rosey had three. But the Yankees snuffed out every rally. They led by that initial run as the Skeeters came to bat for the final inning. Mando still felt as though he was operating in some strange atmosphere. He came in to the bench knowing he would face Fay once more as Green led off the final raps.

Through the dismal evening Mando had managed one controlled reflex. He had watched every motion made by Fay. If the lights were better, he thought, he might learn more. But he thought he was beginning to pick up the rhythm of the effective Yank hurler. He could not see the left hand as the ball came toward the plate, but he was beginning to make guesses where before he had felt helpless.

He watched Green bite on a bad ball and go down on strikes. He watched Rosey, who went up with his customary nonchalance. Rosey simply refused to be awed. He settled in, wielding his heavy bat as though Fay was just another busher. He took a strike. He took two balls. Then Fay came in with his junk curve.

Rosey waited a moment as it sailed in toward him. Then he nailed the ball right on the nose. It went into left field for a sharp, ringing single. Hammer roared from third base as Mando started for the plate, running in to speak to the umpire.

"Zander! Bat for Cruz."

Mando could not believe it. Never in his ball-playing days had he been removed for a pinch-hitter. He looked at the bat in his hands. He looked at Hammer. His mouth hung open.

Then he carefully replaced the bat in the rack. He tucked his glove under his arm. He walked out of the park and toward the hotel. He was not fully aware of what he was doing, of where he was.

There were no telephones in the rooms at Mingo House, merely a pay booth in the lobby. Horace was kind enough to allow Mando to use his office with strict admonition to ask for the charges plus the tax. Mando dialed, and there was the usual tinkling, then the wait, then the ringing of the instrument at the service station in California. Finally Ana's voice came over the wire.

"Monarch Service Station."

"Ana! This is Mando."

"Darling! Where are you?" Her voice sounded tired, he thought.

"In Jersey. I just got your letter."

"Oh. I'm sorry to bother you, darling. I just had to tell you, I guess."

"What else? How is he?"

She sighed. "Not too good. It's his back. He's in a cast."

"I'm so damned sorry."

"Of course you are, dear. It's one of those things."

"You shouldn't be working in that station. It's ... all wrong."

"It's right, because it's the thing to do. You know that, don't you?"

He said, "Yes. I guess I do know that. But it's ... rotten."

"I'm making out. I'm learning about people. You ought to see me clean a windshield for a fussy old lady."

"I wouldn't want to.... Is Patsy still there?"

Her voice grew warmer. "You couldn't chase him away. He's working on commission. We offered to let him do better for himself, but he just stared at us. What a wonderful guy! He thinks you're the world, you know. Mando the Man."

"Never mind me, just so he sticks. Is business any good?"

"Not too good. Oh, your uncle was by."

"I see. No dice, huh?"

"Oh, we're servicing his trucks. But the prices. . . . That man argues over pennies."

"He's the world's greatest jerk," said Mando. "Can you make a nickel off him?"

"Nickels and dimes, and we need every cent. The insurance never quite covers the doctor bills, you know. But I shouldn't be telling you, darling. How is it with you?"

"Oh, fine."

125

There was a pause; then she said, "No, it isn't. Tell me."

"I had a bad night."

"What's one bad night to our hero?"

"It was a real bad night. Hammer sent in a pinch-hitter to bat for me."

"Is he insane?" she demanded.

"No. He was right." He gathered his forces and managed to laugh. "Never mind that. Look, I get paid the middle of the month, you know. I'm sending you a check."

"You are not!"

"A loan," he said. "To your father. Don't argue. You want to leave me out of things?"

She drew a deep breath, and then she said, "I couldn't, darling. I couldn't keep from writing to you. We're ... entwined."

"Yes. I like that. Entwined," he repeated. "Look, maybe it takes trouble. Anyway, I can say it. I love you."

"I love you, Mando the Man. I love you dearly." Now she was weeping.

"I wish I was there."

"I wish you were here. But you belong there. Do the best you can, darling. I know you'll be fine. Oh, dear. There's a customer. I love you, I love you, I love you."

"Take care, angel. Good-bye now."

"Good-bye for now."

He sat back for a moment. He was sweating. He had never been able to tell her that he loved her. Now the words had been spoken. He dialed the operator and asked for the charges. He jotted down the sum, added the tax. He gave the slip to Horace out at the desk. He went upstairs and took off his uniform and bathed. He heard the ballplayers coming into the hotel and went back to the room. He felt as though he had just waked up from a bad dream. He felt fine, as though he had escaped a great danger.

126

The roommates all stared at him. He waved the damp towel and asked, "Who won?"

"They did," said Jack.

"Zander?"

"Struck out," said Jonesy. "Jack got a hit, but Downey couldn't bring Rosey around."

"Zander fanned?"

"Fay made him look bad," said Jonesy.

Rosey said, "Hammer's looking for you. Don't you know better than to walk out?"

"I didn't know what I was doing," said Mando.

"Hammer knows. You better go see him."

Mando began to dress. "Hey, you're right. That was a dumb thing to do."

"You don't seem too upset about it," Jack said.

"I'm upset. I'm burned. Ana's father is bad hurt. She's pumpin' gas. How do you like that?"

They made loud protests; they were sympathetic, concerned. Jonesy and Jack immediately proffered any aid they could provide, including money. Mando waved them aside and left the room. He should feel differently, he thought, he should be completely distressed. He knew the reason he was not. It was in the three words exchanged with Ana Cassidy.

Hammer had a room on the first floor. Mando rapped on the door.

"Come in, whoever you are," growled Hammer.

He was sitting in his uniform, slumped, a bottle of beer in his fist. "Oh, it's you, is it?"

"I wanted to apologize," said Mando. "I shouldn't have walked off before the game ended."

"You know that much, do you?"

"I know it. I ... I had some bad news today from home. I'm sorry."

"Family trouble?"

"My girl's family." He had never referred to her as his girl before. It seemed odd but warm, satisfying.

"So you couldn't hit the damn ball."

"No, that wasn't it, Harry. He's had me fooled, that Fay. He's smart."

"He's some good, too, you better believe. I s'pose you know he whiffed Zander."

"The guys told me."

"I dunno." Beer gurgled down Hammer's throat. "The rest of this league, nothin'. Nothin' in spades. You bums kill 'em. But the only good outfit, what? You blow it."

"It looks like that, Harry."

"Looks like it? Listen, the name of this game is one, pitchin'. Two, knocking them runners home. So we had ducks on the pond, didn't we? Kelly and Rosey and Jonesy. Your buddies. And we got zero runs. *Nada* to you, chicano. Nothin'. Them Yankees might's well have Whitey and Mantle and Ruth and DiMaggio, far as you're concerned."

"Me. Not the other guys."

"Who else? Certainly . . . you."

"I was watching Fay." Mando kept his temper even under the attack. "He's so smooth you can't really figure him. But I thought I might be picking up on him."

"Uh-huh. So I shouldn't of batted Zander?"

"No. You were right. But we get to play them some more. I wish it could be daytime."

"Yeah? Well, it so happens we got a day game with them in two weeks. At Mainville. Some damn holiday or somethin'. And you know what? We'll still be tied with 'em, and Fay will be there with bells on."

"Well, I don't want to come on strong. I mean, I loused up the ball field tonight. You do what you think is right, Harry. You won't hear any beefs from me."

Hammer finished the beer. He straightened up in the chair. "You know what? I was settin' here wonderin' if I shouldn't give Zander a shot at third. You guys—well, you've maybe got into a rut. That's what I was thinkin'. But I wanta tell you, anybody comes to me and levels, it makes a difference. I bet on you four, you know that. I put this job on the line. To see you fall down against that damn Sullivan and his

128

bunch. It makes me sick." He scowled, shook his head. "Me. What I been through in baseball. Settin' here feelin' sick over one lousy game in the bushes."

"I guess that's it, Harry," Mando said. "I guess that's the whole *enchilada*."

Hammer considered a moment, then brightened. "Yeah. The whole *enchilada*. Any game."

"If you can't stand to lose, it's the thing. What it's all about."

The big man put the beer bottle on a table next to his report for the management of the Gold Sox. "Okay. We got the damn Yankees tomorrow night again. And the next night. See what you can do, chicano."

"Thanks, Harry."

"Never mind thanks. Show me some hits."

Out of the room in the lobby Mando exhaled relief. His instinct had led him to do the right thing. It was a narrow escape, and he was grateful.

Maybe the exchange with Ana had altered the flow of his life. Clouds were dispelled. He decided he wanted to be alone for a while.

He walked down toward the river. He bought a hot dog and a Coke at a tiny eatery. Then he walked along the river, his mind on Ana Cassidy. Things would work out, he would make them work out. Tomorrow was another day. Everything was beautiful. . . .

7

"The Yankees without Fay are not the same ball club," Jonesy observed. The second game of the series had ended. The score was 4 to 1 in favor of the Skeeters, and again the two teams were tied for the league lead. The infielders were relaxing in their room.

"We go better when the Mexican Tamale gets hits," said Jack.

"One hit." Mando was not satisfied. His home run with Green and Rosey on had been satisfactory, but in his other times at bat he had knocked the ball straight at a Yankee fielder.

Rosey said, "You don't fan, anyway. You get a piece of it, got to give you credit. It's just the ball ain't got eyes for you."

Mando regarded the shortstop. "That's the nicest thing you ever said to me, Big Shot. You gettin' soft?"

Amazingly, Rosey looked abashed. "Aw, what the hell? You gotta feel sorry for a hitter who ain't hittin'."

"I appreciate it," said Mando sincerely. "Believe me, I do. A slump is horrible. You try everything and nothing works. Nobody knows if it's in your head or your muscles. Talk about drags, this is the biggest drag of all."

"And tomorrow we get that other lefty, that Corrido," Jack said.

"He's been around," Rosey said. "He's from Panama by way of Mexico and Puerto Rico. He's about ready to go up."

"He's going up," said Jonesy. "Hammer heard it. He's going all the way."

"To the big Yankees?"

"Right."

"What about Fay? You hear anything about him?" asked Mando.

"No. You'll have to suffer some more."

Mando said thoughtfully, "You know what? I wouldn't want to see him go up now. Then I'd never know if it's him or me."

"I see what you mean." Jack was pensive. "I wonder how it feels to know you're going up?"

"I know it," Rosey said. "It's just *when* do I go up?"

"Yeah. But to have the word, man."

"Pitchers get it quicker," Rosey said. "They always need pitchers."

"The way you're hitting," Jonesy said, "you may be surprised."

"That'll be the day." But Rosey beamed, thinking of his .432 average. "I got to admit that Fay don't bug me any."

"Nobody's been buggin' you," said Mando. "Now if you'd just be a little faster taking my throw on the double play."

Rosey said, "Up the flue, baby. You can't get your feet out of that Jersey mud to make a good throw."

"That's better," said Mando. "I don't feel right unless you're on my back."

"I'm there, man. I'm ridin' you all the time."

Jonesy said, "You both do pretty good in that department. Maybe it's helpful."

"You think so? Then why don't he thank me for that fat average of his?" Mando asked.

"I ain't helping him," said Rosey. "He just can't hit anymore."

131

"It's pretty comical," Jack said. "Mando's all the way down to a three-hundred average. There are guys in this league would give their eyeteeth to be hittin' three hundred."

"Not on the Yankees. Not on this club," said Mando.

"Right. It's a two-team race."

"And Harry wants us to win it. You have to hand it to him. He's a competitor."

"He's a slave driver. What about that trip to New York? You want to bet we'll never make it? Forty miles away, and we can't make it," said Rosey.

"It can wait," Mando said.

"That's easy for you to say. You're not hittin'."

Someone rapped on the door. "Hey, Kelly. Long distance."

Jack turned pale around the gills. His mother had never fully recovered. He ran out of the door and down to the office of the hotel. He spoke fearfully into the transmitter.

Connie Cruz said, "Hello, Jack."

"Hey, angel. I was scared. Thought it was about Mother." Relief was plain in his voice.

"How are you, Jack?"

"Why, fine." Now his throat dried up. Something was definitely wrong. "Tough news about Ana's dad."

"Terrible. So you are all right?"

"Sure I am."

"You might let a girl know."

"Now, Connie dear." He had never been able to write letters. He could communicate orally with fluency, but paper and ink were not easy tools for him. "You know how I am."

"The only news I get is from Mando's letters home. And . . . from your darling father."

"My father?" He was incredulous. "You saw him."

"Oh, he came by."

"To your house?"

"Slightly inebriated. Full of his lovely notions. About his only son. Too good for chicanos. Couldn't

132

we see it?" The words rushed from her; he could feel the resentment and rage and humiliation. "Of course, Uncle Luis was here. It was a wonderful scene."

"Oh, no," he said. "Oh, I'm sorry, darling."

"And I don't hear from you. And the pressure. Uncle Talker and Mamma and Papa and my Brown Beret brother who hates all gringos. By the way, your father isn't as tough as he thinks he is. Ricky threw him out."

"He threw out my father?"

"On his butt, baby." Her voice came coarse and strong. "Right out and into his shiny Cadillac. You don't insult us chicanos in our homes."

Jack said, "This is awful. What can I say?"

"Nothing. But you can think. You don't know what it's like to be in a family like mine. They have their own ideas and ideals. Like father, like son, they say. He doesn't even write to you, they say. Oh, I don't know, Jack. I don't know how much of this I can take. Your father really blew my mind. I'm thinking . . . maybe he's right."

"He's the wrongest man in the world."

"He represents the part of the world that distrusts my world. No matter how you cut it, Jack, you can't really belong to my world."

"I belong to the world of you and Mando."

"You think you do. But what about children? What if we married as we planned and had children?"

"I'm not thinking about kids," he protested. "That will take care of itself in good time. Please, baby, I detest my father, and you know it. Have you talked to Mother?"

"I'm ashamed to talk with her."

"You shouldn't be. She's right, she's with us."

"Yes. Your mother, Mando, and us. Is it enough? I don't know, Jack. I don't know."

The worst part of it was the coolness, the lack of warmth and affection in her tone. He gulped and said, "I wish I could be there. You've got to know I'm crazy about you, baby."

133

"Crazy is the word. I can't talk anymore. You'll have to write me." She hesitated, then said, "Uncle Luis brought a man around."

"What?" He couldn't believe it.

"A chicano lawyer. The one who'll do for us what Mando gave up for baseball. He's a nice fellow."

Bitterness sprang from him. "And makes a good living."

"Yes. I'm going to the Ahmanson theater with him, Jack."

"You're dating this joe?"

"I've got to find out. I never went with anyone but you. I've got to learn about myself. Who I am. Lots of things."

He said, "Okay, Connie."

"Is that all? Just okay?"

"What do you want from me? My father is a fool. He acted like a fool. Ricky threw him out, good. But you—you strut out with the first guy comes along. What can I say?"

"You asked that before. I'm sorry, Jack. That's the way it is and the way it has to be. We'd better not talk anymore. I don't want to quarrel with you. I'm just telling you."

"All right. Leave it at that."

"Good-bye, Jack."

"Good-bye, Connie." He hung up feeling that it was really a good-bye. There had been a finality in her voice not to be misunderstood.

He managed to make his way up the stairs. He felt as if he had been double-teamed on the football field. His middle was missing. He walked stiff-legged to the room and opened the door and said, "Mando. Can I talk to you?"

The others looked their surprise. Mando arose from the bed and stared.

"Hey, man, was it your mother?"

"No. It was . . . I want to talk to you."

Mando said, "Right, man." He yanked on a sweater and followed Jack down the hall. "What is it?"

"Let's take a walk."

On the street Mando asked, "What makes, *amigo?*"

"Connie," said Jack. It seemed difficult to talk, to get it all out, to make it clear to himself and his best friend. "I blew it with Connie."

"You did *what?*" It was like toppling a California redwood. Jack and Connie had been one of the immutables; their relationship had seemed golden perfection.

"Well, the old man. He helped."

"Whose old man?"

"Mine. Not yours. Mine. The big-time Charlie Jerk. He went over to your house and played his game. 'It's better for us all if they break it off.' Meaning Connie's not good enough for the Kellys. Are you ready?"

Mando said, "I can believe it. Jonesy had a thing with him, didn't he?"

"Right."

"Jonesy sees the good in everybody." Mando still could not digest the situation. "Connie never fell for that jazz. I know Connie."

"Well, you know me, too. You know I don't write. It's just not my bag. 'Hope you are well. Wish you were here.' Hell, everybody *knows* all that. Why put it down on paper?"

"Look, *amigo,* you always hated paperwork in school. But Connie ... she has good sense. She ought to understand. I don't get it."

"Maybe I took her too much for granted." Jack was groping. "I mean, we figured someday we'd get married. Someday we'd have a family, all that. We didn't talk about it much. We were like—we were together. That's what I thought."

"Well, if your old man made a thing, it would get my family in an uproar, I know that."

"Ricky threw him out."

"Yeah. The Brown Beret. He would."

"And then who can blame your family? A damn Wasp comes in, throws his weight around." Then he added hopelessly, "But she's mad at me. For not writing or calling. I didn't know it meant so much to her, Mando. I didn't know."

"So you write her a long letter. Kill yourself already. Explain it all."

"She's dating another guy."

"Connie? She's puttin' you on!"

"Your uncle brought a chicano lawyer around."

"Uncle Talker. Wouldn't you know?" But this was serious. If Connie was convinced in her own mind that it wouldn't work out with the two families at odds, she would retreat, she would give in to pressure.

"She says he's a nice guy, the lawyer. He takes her to the theater, all that. I never knew she wanted to make that scene. We just noodled around. I thought it was enough to be together. I didn't write often from college. I just don't know, *amigo*."

"Hey, man, I dig." Mando was all sympathy. "Look, I just got it all straight with Ana. I know how it would feel if the balloon busted. I'll call Connie right away."

"No."

"Connie and I are close. I can talk to her."

"No good," said Jack. They came to the river and paused on the bridge watching the dark night water flow down toward the bay. This was Revolutionary War country, this was where Mad Anthony Wayne and George Washington had marched and fought and won a nation. They were silent, each with his thoughts. Then Jack said, "I just wanted to talk it out, *amigo*. You can't help. Nobody can help. I could tell by Connie's voice. She thought it out. She . . . she talked about kids. How it would be with her—your family—and mine. I never thought about kids. Women are different from us that way."

"Lot of ways," Mando said dryly. "But Connie doesn't dig that chicano scene, the *barrio*."

"With a lawyer she'll live in Beverly Hills maybe," Jack said bitterly. "The thing is, I can see her side of it. I can't ditch my rotten old man on account of

Mother. It would be there all the time, the clash, the hauling and pulling at Connie. That's what's buggin' me; I can see it."

"Ana's father made it."

"You want to bet he didn't have a father like mine?"

"Look, you're going to make it in baseball. You can live—you'll have to live—wherever you're sent."

"What about Mother?"

"Yeah. You got me there." He knew how much Jack's mother depended on him, that it was her only real interest, to see her son make good and be happy.

"No, it's between Connie and me. And she sure turned me off."

"You mean you got sore at her on the phone?"

"This joker, this lawyer, she shoved him at me. I lost my cool, *amigo*."

"Uh-huh." Supposing Ana had conveyed the same news, he thought. "I get it."

"I guess I'm wrong, but I just can't figure out how," Jack said mournfully. "I mean, where did it start?"

"With your father butting in," Mando told him. "We're proud people, like I always try to point out. Wrong, maybe, but there it is. Connie's one of us. She was hurt; and Uncle Luis being there—that made it worse. You'll have to put it all down on paper whether you want to or not, Jack. You'll have to think about it, then put it down."

"You think so?"

"Unless it's not worth it."

"Or unless I know it's hopeless."

"How can you tell?"

"The way she laid it on the line. She blasted me."

"There's a little of Uncle Talker in us all," Mando said. "We get upset, we holler a lot."

"That I learned. It's a rotten thing, my old man going there. But I still have to feel Connie would have been able to take that. I still feel I've been wrong. I missed out somehow or other, *amigo*. I wish I knew why." Jack braced himself. "I just had to

137

unload on you. I'm sorry about that. You want to go back and get some sleep?"

"Better had. We got those Yankees again tomorrow."

The third pitcher in the Mainville Yankee rotation was a giant youth known as Bubba Morton. Hammer went with Chick Onslow, a right-hander with some experience in the minors, another of the possible big-leaguers gathered under the wing of the Texan. Onslow, like Barone, had stuff but lacked pinpoint control.

Hammer talked to the team before the game. "This here Bubba, this strongarm, he'd stick it in his mother's ear on purpose to win a game. Like it is, he'll stick it to you without tryin'. So hang in there loose. Make him throw strikes. Don't dig in; I don't want nobody skulled. There ain't too many brains in this outfit like it is without gettin' skulled."

There were tiny lines at the corners of Jack's eyes that Mando had never seen before. It was evident that there had been little sleep the previous night for his friend. Jonesy noticed it and came to Mando.

"What's with Jack?"

"We had a late pizza," Mando said. "I guess he sat up with it."

"Jack? He can eat iron and spit nails," said Rosey. "Don't tell me."

"He'll be all right," Mando said. "Don't you worry about Jack."

The Yankees were boiling for revenge, Mando felt.

Most ballplayers are on their own, he thought. They think of the game in terms of their batting average, the number of errors afield. The pitchers worry about earned-run average. The shortstop–second-base combination seems like perfection in team play—but trade either of the two men, and in a week the new pair are doing their thing without discernible difference.

Off the field, they go their own way. Even Rosey went another path from that which Jonesy, Jack, and

138

Mando had thus far traveled together. Any day they would be split asunder by the business of the Gold Sox and forced to play among strangers for new bosses. It was difficult to maintain a closeness under these conditions. Sullivan had thus far succeeded in welding his Yankees into a team, but how long could it endure?

Mando went mechanically through the preliminary procedures to the game, worrying about Ana, perturbed about Connie and Jack. Beneath his concern was the nagging thought that he was not with it one hundred percent. He had come to know this was fatal. He began to haul himself together, to reassert the ego necessary to playing up to his potential. It was simple enough—he certainly could not help himself, nor anyone else, unless he played his best ball.

It was simple enough—but not so easy to manage. He had to make a tremendous effort. By the time the Skeeters took the field and stood hatless while the recording of the anthem wheezed to a close, he was still not altogether sure of himself.

The Yankee lead-off man, Dore, drew a walk. The clever Portale laid down a bunt, to put Dore on second. Strongman Andrews came up. Chick Onslow regarded him solemnly from the mound, rubbing the ball.

Jack retreated a step against the left-hander, guarding the line. Mando came in and moved to his left. Onslow stretched, pitched. It was a curve, and it hung.

Mando heard the unmistakable sound. The ball vanished above the dim lights of the home field. Downey in right field ran to the fence, then leaned against it, watching the homer drop beyond the boards.

That was two runs for the Yankees, one out. Sullivan's whistle sounded mocking and insulting. Hammer stalked out to talk with Onslow. Mando and Jack joined them.

"Don't you feel right?" demanded the manager.

"Certainly," said Onslow. "I would have informed you if I were ailing."

"You're throwin' like somethin's wrong. That curve."

Onslow said, "Unfortunately, it was not a good pitch."

"Yeah, I noticed," said Hammer. "One more hitter, you hear me? One more."

"Quite, sir." Onslow seemed in another world, one of his own making.

Mando said, "Make it good, Chick." The pitcher nodded absently. Mando went back to third with a premonition of coming disaster. Jack seemed to be in another world, not speaking, as was his custom, walking back to first with his head down. Remembering his own problem, Mando moved restlessly, concentrating. The hitter was the other strong boy, Hagney.

Onslow worked with extreme deliberation. He curved a strike low on the corner. He came in with his fast ball, and Hagney took his cut and fouled it off. Now the pitcher was far ahead of the hitter. Onslow tried a sneaky quick pitch on the outside corner.

Hagney came around with his full power. The ball went down on a line to first. Jack leaped.

The ball went into right field for a double along the line. Mando couldn't believe it. Jack usually gathered in those line drives with ease.

Hammer was on his feet, staring. Onslow held the ball and strolled around the box, not looking at Jack.

Terrill, the strong little second baseman, was at the plate, and Sullivan was whistling his head off. The Yankees were all shouting and laughing on the bench. Mando looked helplessly to the east. The clouds seemed to be coming closer. If it would pour down rain before four and a half innings were completed, he thought, it would be a miracle. Hammer did not call for a new man, but he had Terry, the husky Negro reliever, warming up.

With White and Tilden coming up before their heavy-hitting catcher, Holder, the Yankees would not sacrifice, Mando thought. First base was open, a hit meant another run. Terrill settled in, waving a lightweight, light-colored bat. Onslow looked more solemn than ever.

Pazolla was yelling his head off, trying to talk it up for his pitcher, who seemed not to hear. Terrill wagged his bat. Onslow pitched. Terrill met the ball well. It went bounding down to third.

Mando came in fast. The ball took a bad bounce and veered to his glove hand. He managed to make the stop. He was a bit off balance as he made the long throw to first base.

It was not quite on the mark, but it was good enough. Jack stretched, got his mitt on it. Then he dropped it.

Men were on first and third, with one out. Two runs were in. Hammer fidgeted on the bench. He could not blame his pitcher. He could not blame Mando under the circumstances. Even Jack's error had not been flagrant—many first basemen might have muffed the difficult catch. But put it all together, it added up to bad baseball.

Sullivan's ecstatic whistle did not aid or comfort Hammer, nor anyone else among the Skeeters. Onslow alone ignored it, ignored everything and everyone. White, the third baseman of the Yankees, was at bat.

It was a static time, Mando thought. Jack showed no expression of regret for his error; Jack's mind was elsewhere. Onslow's dreamy attitude was unsettling to the team.

Hammer waved the infield to double-play formation, but Mando had a notion. On Onslow's pitch he moved a bit forward. And White did square to bunt. Mando had his jump on the ball; he came roaring in. He grabbed the ball with his bare hand, bluffed the base runner, then went to first.

This time the throw was to the bag. Jack gloved it—and managed to fall down. Terrill was safe. Another run scored.

Hammer came raging onto the field. He waved his left hand to indicate that he wanted Terry to pitch right now.

Onslow said placidly, "It isn't my fault now, is it, Harry? I mean, what can a man do?"

"Throw the ball where they can't noodle it around," Hammer barked. "Nemmine. Just get outta my sight." He wheeled on Jack. "You!"

"Sorry," Jack mumbled.

Hammer regarded him closely. "Hey. You're sick or somethin'."

"I'm all right," Jack said without conviction.

Mando said, "He's sick, Harry. I can tell."

Hammer said, "Go back to the hotel. See the doc. You hear me?"

Jack nodded without replying, turned, and walked away. Hammer looked at Mando.

"Didja know he was sick?"

"No," said Mando.

"This ball club has got to stop playin' dead for these damn Yankees," Hammer said as Terry warmed up. "After last night, I thought we'd got better. Now, damnit, will you play your game, you jaspers?"

Mando spoke quickly, "It looks like rain, Harry."

"It better rain. That's all that'll save us now," said the manager grimly.

Mando went back to third. Trouble affected people in various ways, he was learning. Connie had hit Jack so hard he was clear out of key. He had even lost his graceful stride, shambling out of the park.

Roquero, the utility infielder, came in to play first in Jack's place, and Mando noted that Zander sulked on the bench. Roquero was taller and quicker than Zander.

The umpire called time. Terry looked at the runners, accepted Pazolla's sign, and threw his high hard one.

Tilden was no hitter. He swung with all the skill and élan of a rusty gate. Wood smacked against horsehide. The ball plopped over Jonesy's head and died in the grass before Green could come in and prevent a run from scoring.

Worse became worser. Every Yankee hit. Sullivan forgot to whistle as nine runs paraded across the plate. Hammer called in Fargo, his short-reliever, who had both speed and control for as many as three innings, sometimes. Fargo managed the two outs to retire the side.

Mando went to the bench feeling as though he had been put through a wringer. Hammer spoke to no one, stomping out to the coach's box on third; Holder went to first, also without giving orders of any kind. A nine-run handicap was too much.

Mando scanned the sky, said, "Hey, feel that breeze?"

"From the ocean," said Rosey.

"How about stalling some?" Mando said to Jonesy.

"Hey, righto."

Jonesy fussed with the tar, knocked imaginary dirt from his spikes, squirmed around before settling himself into the batter's box. Hammer came awake and began giving signs. Jonesy fell out of the box to peer down at Hammer, and the ump ordered him back. Jonesy went back and then felt around with his toe, lifted a hand to call time. He bent down and with great care removed what appeared to be a round stone. He tossed it toward the bench. Mando grabbed it in the air. It was neatly molded mud.

Rosey stifled a laugh and said, "Wait'll those cats figure out the wind is from the coast. They ain't onto Jersey weather. They'll blow their stacks."

Jonesy finally got into position to hit. Bubba Morton had a big windup, a high-flung leg action, and a lot of elbow. He threw sidearm for the most part, a tricky delivery for the hitter. Jonesy took a ball, then a strike, then fell out of the box again. The umpire ordered him back in. Jonesy ran the count to three and two.

Morton gamely tried his fast ball. Jonesy spanked it into left field for a single.

Green came to bat. Mando checked the clouds. If they were moving, it was with agonizing slowness. The wind died, then increased a bit. There was the slightest odor of salt from the sea. Green was not so adept at stalling as was Jonesy. But Bubba Morton

143

was proving not so adept at getting out Skeeters. Green hit a little blooper into left field and got to first, with Jonesy perching on second base. Rosey took his bludgeon to the plate.

Rosey stepped in briskly, as though anxious to hit. Then he suddenly fell back, pawing at his left eye. The umpire, perforce, called time.

"One of them gnats," moaned Rosey. "It hurts!"

"Dig it out," ordered the official. The caliber of umpires in the Pennjersey League matched their salaries—low. Still, Mando thought, Rosey was overacting. He ran from the on-deck box, and Hammer came in from third, and they stood close and dabbed at Rosey's eye.

Hammer said, "You ever try this in the big leagues, and you'll pay a fine. The idea's to keep the inning goin'. Go back and hit one, Rosey."

"How can I, with my eye and all?" Rosey was all seriousness. "Golly, Harry, golly."

"You hear me, you bum." Hammer was working hard to refrain from grinning.

Rosey wiped his eye one last time and went back to the box. Now Sullivan was on his feet looking at the clouds to the east. One of his men was from Jersey and knew about sudden cross-state squalls when the wind was right in springtime. The Yankee manager took a step toward the umpire, desisted as Rosey got up and faced the pitcher.

Bubba Morton threw a fast ball. Rosey struck it. The ball took off on a line. It slammed into center field. Jonesy came tearing around third and ran for the plate. The Yankee outfielder tried his arm. He was off the mark.

Jonesy scored. Green went to third. Rosey went to second. Mando went to the plate.

Sullivan was whistling again, but now there was a warning in the shrillness. Bubba Morton looked as though someone had taken away his candy. The Yankees all began to call encouragement. They did have nine runs, after all, And the clouds moved slowly but surely toward Mingo and the ball field.

Mando let one go by for a ball. Then he fouled off a good pitch. Then he fouled off another—and another—and another. Mando was very good at hitting foul balls. It tended to tire a pitcher, to annoy him, and to eventually force the pitch that Mando wanted.

Sullivan watched a few more fouls with suspicious mien, then came out to Bubba Morton. As he walked back to the bench, the first raindrops fell. The few remaining Skeeter fans huddled under ponchos and umbrellas. Most had gone home when the Yankees had scored their ninth run.

Catcher Hooker held his glove wide; Morton threw pitches beyond the reach of Mando. He was purposely passed to first base. Sullivan had recognized his ability to remain in the batter's box, and got rid of him, even though it meant filling the bases with one out and one run in. He was banking on his big lead and the fact that games in this league were not stopped this side of a downpour. Had they been, the schedule this springtime would never have been completed.

It was all plain and simple, Mando thought. It was all a part of the slightly sly strategy of baseball. He remembered the old anecdote about King Kelly in the halcyon days, sitting on the bench when an opposing batter hit a foul pop. It was a big one. Kelly had leaped up, howled, "Catcher Jones out, Kelly in," and had caught the ball, retiring the side and ending a rally. That was baseball. They kept changing the rules but they couldn't change the Yankee-like chicanery which was one of its basic tenets. He winked at Ace Holder and took a big lead off the bag, knowing that Bubba Morton dared not waste time—nor error—on a cut-off throw.

Now Hammer was in the act. He was calling time. He was walking as slowly as possible to the bench.

The umpire demanded, "What's this? I want you guys to play ball, understand?"

"I gotta have a pinch-hitter," Hammer told him. "My guy Roquero is a defensive player. Here we are, eight runs behind, I gotta get me a hitter in there, understand?"

"Don't tell me your troubles. Understand?"

"I'm answerin' your question, ain't I?"

"You play ball, understand?"

"I'm runnin' my club, understand?"

Ace Holder was holding his sides. Mando went back to the bag and also tried to control his laughter. The umpire was furious, and any minute could exercise his power in any of several directions, but it was a comical dialogue in a funny situation. The raindrops stopped falling. The clouds hung uncertainly over Princeton, to the east.

Hammer said, "Zander. You hit for Roquero." He turned to the umpire. "That's R-o-q-uero. Not g-uero. You understand?"

"I understand you're stallin'," cried the umpire. He pulled out a fat, old-fashioned railroad watch. "Play ball!"

Ace Holder said to Mando, "You better believe they got an understanding goin' there."

Mando said, "The rain's not coming fast enough."

"We do the best we can," said the pitcher-coach.

Zander didn't seem to be part of the ploy. He came to bat with all the seriousness of his rather colorless personality showing in his eagerness to hit. The Yankee pitcher threw him a curve, and Zander swung all the way around, as though trying to screw himself into the ground. He missed the ball.

Morton took heart. A ground ball might produce a double play to end the inning. He carefully aimed low to make Zander hit to the infield.

Zander golfed his swing. He caught the ball on the end of the bat, but with tremendous force. Mando took one look and began to canter down toward second. The Yankee center fielder put his hands on his hips and watched the home run disappear.

It was now 9 to 5, and the baseball minds among

146

the two squads altered slightly. Sullivan was not whistling. He was out talking to his pitcher. Bubba Morton was mortified. Sullivan took the ball and waved for another hurler. In from the bullpen came Amos Gross, a Brooklyn product, a lean, hard-boiled kid, right-handed and talented. A spate of rain greeted him as he warmed up.

At the Skeeter bench Hammer was saying, "Downey, you use your dome. If he gives you somethin', hit it out. Peck, you're on deck, you do the same. This here rain wouldn't break up a Sunday-school picnic."

The nineteen-year-old Downey grinned. "Do we get even, then what?"

"Pray a lot," said Hammer, and went back to the coaching box.

Fearing the rain, Gross warmed up quickly. Downey went to bat. He was a quick youngster, a Punch-and-Judy hitter, but consistent and brainy.

On the bench Rosey said, "Haven't had so much fun since the kids ate my pig brother."

"This is cute," said Mando. "Supposing we catch 'em?"

"Supposin' the moon is made of green cheese. Eighteen runs in one inning, even in this league?"

Downey hit a clean single. Peck followed with another, Downey going to second. Pazolla came to the plate.

Amos Gross had been working too fast against the rain. He thumped the ball into his glove and talked to himself. He needed, as had Morton, only a double play to get out of trouble. He pitched by the book, low and inside.

Pazolla snapped his bat, striking for right field, behind the runners. The ball skipped between first and second and through the hole. Downey scored. Peck went to third. The big noisy catcher perched on first, trumpeting the old, well-worn battle cry, "Everybody hits! Everybody!"

Now it was sprinkling, and the cold east wind

prevailed. Hammer allowed Fargo, the pitcher, to hit. He evidently agreed with Rosey: there could not possibly be eighteen runs scored in an inning—the first inning, at that.

Fargo struck out.

The rain stopped. Mando looked at the clouds, and it seemed to him they were circling southward. He nudged Rosey, the native son.

Rosey said, "Yeah, could be. I've seen it rain all around and never touch where you were at. It's the winds."

Jonesy was looking at Hammer for instructions. Hammer was staring at the sky. The umpire was yelling that the game must continue. Sullivan tried a whistle, not too successfully, Mando thought. Maybe Sullivan believed in the fact that in baseball anything goes. There was that fourth game of the 1929 World Series between the Athletics and the Cubs. The Cubs led 8 to 0 in the seventh inning. And the A's suddenly arose and tore into four pitchers to score ten runs. The final count had remained the same, A's 10, Cubs 8. If it could happen in a Series, it could happen anywhere at any time. It was now 9 to 5 for the Yankees, with two out—but two were on base.

Rosey said, "Hey, man. Just thought of something."

"Yeah?" Mando was watching Jonesy fiddling at the plate.

"If this game is called off, we lose those hits. They won't go in the records."

"So?"

"Dummy, every hit's a hunk of bread. You need yours. We all need 'em."

"Well, sure. . . ."

Rosey shouted, "Come on, Jonesy, hit it out, baby!"

Hammer glared. Jonesy showed no sign that he had heard. The runners took their leads. The pitcher threw the ball.

Jonesy clipped it on the nose. It rode smartly past the mound and into center field. Only the swiftness of Dore in rushing the sizzler prevented another score.

The bases were full, two outs, four runs to go, and the clouds were still drifting to the south, and the rain had stopped. The faithful few in the stands began to make more noise than the biggest crowd yet seen at a Skeeter home game.

Green came to bat. Gross was stamping at the earth. Sullivan started out, stared at the sky, then sat down again. Gross toed the rubber. The Yankee infield, with a play at any base, aligned themselves against a left-handed batter.

Gross threw his Sunday curve. Green followed it out and put his bat into it. The ball lined toward left. The shortstop leaped high. He couldn't reach the liner.

One run came in. Green roosted on first. Rosey was in the batter's box with his big bat. The score was Yankees 9, Skeeters 6. Mando knelt on deck, leaning on his stick. Hammer was clapping his big hands together now that the threat of rain seemed to be removed.

Rosey hit the first ball. It went into right-center. Two men raced in. Two were left on, and the Skeeters were only one behind on the scoreboard.

Now there was no question about it, Mando was in there to keep the rally going. Rain or not, it was an opportunity not to be avoided or denied.

Sullivan came running out, hand upraised. The umpire disgustedly called time out. Sullivan motioned for a pitcher. A sturdy, familiar figure came from behind the edge of the stands where he had been warming up. With only one day's rest, Billy Fay was coming in to pitch to one man—his favorite pigeon, Mando Cruz.

Hammer walked in circles around the coach's box at third. Aee came across to talk to him. They were looking at the bench, where they had Howard, Forest, and Carey for alternates. Mando gripped the bat and muttered to himself.

"This joker, this Fay, he threw nine innings the

149

night before last. He can't be quick. If it wasn't for these lousy lights . . . Oh, forget the lights, you hit these other guys in the same lights. . . . So he's sneaky, and he can thread a needle. What else has he got? I know, that junk, that slow stuff. That stinkin', lousy junk. . . ."

Fay took his five pitches. Mando looked at the sky. The wind had shifted slightly, and the clouds, black as ink, hanging heavy and low, seemed to have stopped heading south.

Hammer came in and asked, "How about it, chicano?"

"How about what?" He was trying to maintain his concentration.

"You got your eye back. Can you do it?"

"How the hell do I know?" Mando was suddenly angry.

"Okay, maverick. Dab it on him," said Hammer. He went back to third.

Mando faced the smiling, confident Fay. The runners took their leads, dancing, calling out to Mando the old cry, "Hit it out, man. Hit it out!"

Fay stretched, pitched. The lazy curve came tantalizingly to the plate. Mando restrained himself.

"Stuhrikeone!"

Fay nursed the ball. He threw another piece off the same cloth, a slow, twisting pitch to the outside corner. Again Mando let it go past.

"Stuhriketwo," said the umpire.

One more, Mando thought. But he knows I'm ready for it. He's a smart head, that one. He knows I'll poke at it. I've got to guard the plate. So maybe he'll waste one. . . . But he pitched day before yesterday. Maybe he'll try the sneaky one. And if he does . . .

Fay threw quickly. It was truly his change-of-pace fast ball. Coming atop the junk, it was a fine attempt.

Mando's last thought stuck in his skull. He was ready. Loose and easy he ripped through. He heard the sound, felt the solid impact down the bat to his

150

hands. He set sail for first base. The runners were in motion.

The outfielders ran. In center, Dore was nearest the ball. He made a diving attempt. The line drive escaped him. It went to the fence.

Both runners came in. Mando slid safely into third. The Skeeters, unbelievably, led in the ball game.

At that moment the skies opened up. The clouds had veered on a south wind and come rushing back. They hung over the ball field and poured down rain in buckets and barrels.

The umpires and players retreated beneath the stands. Not that there was a chance of resuming, Mando thought, plunged in deepest gloom. In fifteen minutes the playing field was a lake.

The miracle had been for nought. The game would be played over later in the season. Sullivan was now whistling a melody. Mando recognized the tune.

It was "You Gotta Have Heart."

From the show *Damn Yankees*.

8

In the morning the sky was blue at sunrise. And there was the bus. It was a veteran vehicle that had once run on the streets of Trenton. The springs were shot and the seats worn down and highly uncomfortable. The Skeeters, with an average of four hours' sleep per individual, straggled out of the hotel with their duffel bags and suitcases and climbed aboard.

Hammer began, slightly bleary-eyed, to count noses. Ace said, "There's one missin'."

"Kelly. Where's Kelly?"

Mando said, half-asleep, "He was—yeah. He was taking a shower. I'll get him."

He ran into the hotel and up the stairs to the communal bathroom. He knocked on the door. "Jack, you in there?"

No answer. He went to the room. Jack's traveling clothes, jeans and jumper, were on a chair. Mando descended the stairs and called the room clerk.

"Hey, you got a key to the bathroom?"

The room clerk asked, "Whatever do you want with a key to the bathroom?"

"I think someone drowned in there. Just tell Hammer that Kelly will be out in a minute."

He unlocked the bathroom door. Jack snored. He

was lying on the floor with his head on a towel, stark naked. His underwear was neatly hung on a hook. Mando shook a shoulder.

"Hey, man. You going on the trip?"

"Wha . . . what?" Jack came to his feet in one supple move. "What's goin' on?"

"The carriage awaits, me lord," said Mando. "Come on, get with it."

"Oh . . . yeah." Jack scrambled into his shorts and white woolen socks. "Didn't sleep a lot. Couldn't stop thinking about Connie."

"So?"

Jack wiped his face with his damp face cloth. "Finally figured it out."

"So?"

"I'll write the letter. Like you said. Then I'll wait for the answer. Then I'll worry."

Mando sighed with relief. "Okay. Now grab your clothes and your bag and let's *vamos, amigo.*"

He watched Jack glide down the hall with all his old grace. He went down to the bus and spoke to Hammer.

"He's fine."

"You sure?"

"Who knows him but me?"

"He'd better be all right. What ailed him last night, anyway?"

"You ever eat pizza before going to bed?"

"I can eat a horse. Mamma always said I had the stomach of a goat."

"Did you really have a mother, Harry?" Mando asked.

"Get on the bus, wisenheimer," said Hammer. "This ain't the hour for your clever sayin's."

Early in the season the four infielders had established themselves in the seats directly behind and across from the driver of the bus. Rosey and Jonesy sat together. The other seat was now vacant. No one presumed to occupy it. This had come about through the physical threat of Rosey and the fact that the

153

Skeeters knew the four had been sent to Jersey as a unit and that Hammer had plans for them.

Jack came panting, and flopped down beside Mando. Hammer and Ace came aboard.

They rumbled south toward the little state of Delaware. Mando moved over and sat on the edge of the seat occupied by Jonesy and Rosey, sharing the newspaper they were conning.

Rosey said, "The Gold Sox. Last place. No customers. See the story? Gordon's hittin' two-eighty, though."

"How's my man doing?"

"Nothin'. Here it is, Libby, two-thirty, and too slow, it says."

"Wells is at two-fifty," said Jonesy. "He's solid. And Astor knocked in another couple homers, so Jack's man is okay. Looks like you're the only one with a chance to go up, Mando."

"That's a good one," Mando said. "From the Skeeters to the big league in one swell foop. Big joke."

"It's been done," said Jonesy. "Hey, look at Jack. Asleep already. How does he do it?"

"He stays up all night," said Mando. He went back to his seat, careful not to disturb Jack. He wondered how it would be to go up to the big club, an unseasoned rookie. Then he laughed at himself. No way, he thought, not this year. Maybe later, if the Sox didn't trade for a third baseman of experience. Maybe someday. But not while he was in a slump in the Pennjersey League.

The bus rolled out of Delaware at eleven o'clock, the ballplayers still in their uniforms, sweaty and struggling inwardly with hot dogs, hamburgers, and various soft drinks.

Mando was trying to sleep. They had run more in the series against the Lions. Hammer had turned them loose, and they had actually stolen one game from the Delaware team's best pitcher. The guy didn't have the good move to first, and Jonesy had stolen him blind. Mando had stolen home on him after they got him rattled. And Mando had gone six for twelve at bat in the three games, which boosted his average considerably and made him very happy.

Tomorrow night they opened a series against the Lawton Rebels over in Maryland, where they might get an hour or so in a motel room to sleep and clean up. It was a great life in the bush leagues.

It was a four-game series against the Rebels of Lawton, Maryland, and before the final contest Jack Kelly was again becoming nervous. There had been no mail from California. His letter had been written in Delaware after the first game. He was stubborn about calling; he refused, and insisted that Mando not do so, either.

Barone, who was pitching good ball, beat the Rebels, but Jack went hitless. Page, the veteran, showed form in winning the second game. Onslow still could not apply his brain to his hurling, and narrowly lost the third contest. Afterward they rushed to a local newspaper office and learned the Yankees' Bubba Morton had also lost one to the Hazletown Miners, so that they were still in a tie for first place in the league.

Since it was three hours earlier in Los Angeles, Mando acquired a pocketful of silver and slipped away from Jack and the others. He did not quite feel it proper to call home against Jack's wishes, so he did the next best thing. He called Ana.

She said, "Darling, it's so good to hear your voice."

"I love you." Each time he said it, it was easier for him.

"I love you."

"Haven't got much time, I'm in a booth at the newspaper office," he said. "I wanted to ask about Connie."

"Yes," she said. "Connie and her lawyer."

"She's going steady with him?"

"Let's say she's not going out with anybody else. I

see her almost every day. She's a mixed-up kid, darling. Mr. Kelly really blew it."

"I know. Did she mention Jack's letter?"

"Again and again. And again. She doesn't know how to answer it."

"Look, tell her to write him, will you? He's going out of his mind, and he won't call her. I'll write to her when I can find a minute. She's got to take him off the hook. He's not playing his game. He's not sleeping."

"Poor kid," said Ana. "I'll do the best I can."

"Okay, darling. Hang in there."

"Hey, how many hits did you get tonight?"

"Three. But Jack went for the horse collar."

"I'll talk to Connie. God bless, dear."

"Good-bye, darling."

He hung up. He felt he had done the best he could. He went back to the dreary motel room he was sharing with Jack. When he entered, Hammer was sitting in the only chair; Jack was sprawled on the bed.

Hammer said, "I can't get anything outta this knucklehead. You want to tell me what's the matter with him?"

"How would I know? Anybody can have a bad game. Jack's okay so far as I can see." He did not include what he knew. Jack looked about the same, only a bit dragged out.

Hammer said, "It ain't his bad night. It's just . . . well, I know you characters pretty good by now. He ain't . . . right. Somethin's wrong."

"I'm all right," Jack insisted. "It's—well, this food on the road and that rickety bus and the push, push, push. I guess I'm not cut out for the bushes." He tried to laugh. "I'm a big-leaguer in my heart."

Hammer arose and started for the door, paused, came back, and sat down. "Look, I built this team around you four guys. I figured you two were the ones. Jonesy—he surprised everybody. That Roosevelt's no team man, but he did good. But first Mando goes into a slump, and now you, Jack. Maybe I better

156

let you in on somethin' just between us three. Plenty quiet, you get me?"

"Let me guess," said Mando. "There's trouble upstairs."

"How'd you know?" Hammer waved a paw. "Nemmine. I reckon anyone could guess. Yeah, the millionaire owners ain't happy. They want at least some local support. Not the dough—that's a tax write-off. But they get a lot of kiddin' from their rich buddies. Nobody cares about the team."

"The league didn't give them any players," said Mando.

"You know it. Anyhow, Buster Condor is gonna have to do somethin' or lose his job. And if he does, Dutch'll go with him. And if Dutch goes . . . I go, too."

"That figures."

"Well, the club's triple-A team's no better than the Sox. Double-A is better. You'd all four be double-A, wasn't for me. So there's things goin' on back in California. Nobody'll trade or sell; with expansion and all, there just ain't that many ballplayers. Every club needs every good man it's got. Now, we got a great win-lose record here. If it wasn't for them Yankees over in Mainville, we'd be standout, you know?"

"Like we have to beat their tail."

"I don't know the full score. But we got that series and that daytime doubleheader to play off the rained-out game. Five damn games against them, which means Fay pitches twice. You beginnin' to see how I'm thinkin' . . . hopin'?"

"A blind man could see it."

Hammer said, "That's why I'm worryin' about you two."

"We appreciate it," said Mando.

Jack said, "I'll snap out of it, Harry. Thanks a lot."

"Now, I'm goin' next door and tell the other two of you about it," said Hammer. "But nobody else, understand?"

"We promise."

"It'll break one way or the other after the Yankee series. Not because of it, but that's the time I figure somethin' has to happen. Get some sleep, now."

He left. Mando surveyed his friend. He started to speak just as the telephone rang. He picked up the instrument and said hello.

Connie's voice said, "Mando? Oh, I'm glad it's you. I'm so nervous . . . I just talked to Ana. I'm at her house. Is . . . is Jack with you?"

"Uh-huh. How are things?" He tried to be casual.

"Awful. He . . . he proposed."

"Oh? Your friend?"

"Yes. The family wants us to be married right away."

"What about you?"

She began to weep. "I had a letter from Jonesy. It just touched me, Mando, it really did."

"Jonesy?"

"He's such a sensitive boy. Ana says so, too. He's beautiful, Mando."

"He is, huh?"

"Look, Mando, I'll talk to Jack. I have to talk to him."

He turned and looked again at Jack. "Connie."

Jack's face turned white. "Connie?"

"Get on the phone, you jerk."

Jack scrambled off the bed. Mando went out of the motel and walked under the Maryland sky. After a while Jack opened the door, and Mando returned to the dismal room. It seemed somehow much brighter.

Jack was hugely excited. "Guess what?"

"You and Connie made up."

"That's not half of it. You know why she was bugged?"

"You didn't write to her."

"I never asked her to marry me."

"Now that's real strange. Us chicanos, we're very peculiar people."

Jack said, "So I asked her, and she said yes. Now she can tell the family."

"They'll be thrilled."

"No, they won't. So she wants to fly east and get married."

"You're underage!"

"There's Maryland."

"Hey, man, you're crazy, you know that?"

"I'm crazy happy." Jack beamed. "My next paycheck and her savings will handle it."

"You know what?"

"What?"

"You haven't asked my permission."

"Oh." Jack flushed bright red. "You're against it."

"No. But you could've asked. Us chicanos are very formal. I'm her brother."

Jack bowed. "I ask. I beg. Okay?"

"Well, I guess so. I thought it was arranged for the future sometime. Like Ana and me. But I know the family. A lawyer and all. They'll give her a fit."

"Now I've got to move up," said Jack. "A guy has a family, he has to make good, right?"

"Without a family, even."

"You know what I mean, *amigo*."

"I know what Hammer told us."

"Hey, yeah. How about that?"

"I don't quite believe it. But if it happens, we'll be back home for a while. Until we face some big-league pitching."

"We can't do worse than triple-A. Two can live on triple-A pay."

"Not very well," said Mando. "But dream on, lover boy."

"I can't miss. Now that we got it straight, I know I can't miss."

Mando said, "Let's not miss any more sleep. Control yourself, *amigo*. Tomorrow's another ball game."

He went to bed. Connie and Jack were too young to be married, he thought. If Jack had to fight his way up to the big leagues, it would be a long haul, with many moves around the country. A young couple shouldn't have to put up with all the disappointments, all the sudden changes of habitation, all the strains and pressures.

Then he wondered what he would do if circumstances had placed Ana and himself in a similar situation.

It was later than usual as they rolled toward Mountain View, Pennsylvania, to play a series with the Rams.

Jack Kelly smiled as he dozed. Mando turned to look across the aisle at Rosey sleeping and Jonesy with his eyes closed but not sleeping nor smiling nor anything, and he wondered what Jonesy was thinking.

He had said to Jonesy, "That was pretty swell about the letter."

"What letter?"

"To my sister."

"Oh. That letter." Jonesy didn't want to talk about it.

"Well, okay. But it worked, and they're going to get married. Only I'm kind of worried it's too soon."

"Don't worry. Just don't worry, Mando."

"Well, anyway, Connie said you're beautiful."

Jonesy had said, "Connie, Ana, María, they deserve the best in the world. The very best."

That was it. That was Jonesy. He was a strange one; there was something about him nobody knew. Mando was sure of that. He was also sure it didn't matter.

He struggled to get comfortable in the seat. There was a long trip, a hard trip before they met the Yankees for the important series. There was Hazleton in Pennsylvania and Mt. View and Denville in New Jersey, then away back to their destination in Mainville, all bad food and rotten sleeping accommodations. The Yankees would be enjoying a home stay, thoroughly rested and anxious and ready. The Skeeters would be road-weary and gaunt.

Nobody told you it would be easy, he reminded

himself. You must accept it, stand up to it. If you can't hit Billy Fay in this league, what would you do against top pitching?

He fell half-asleep—nobody ever really slept on the bus.

9

Sandy Roosevelt regarded his sleeping roommate, his friend, the only good friend he had ever owned. He could not display his affection for Jonesy. It was not in him to do so. He could not show his respect and regard for Mando and Jack. All that feeling had been kicked out of him long ago, or at least it had been beaten down in him so that it was submerged below levels of hurt and hatred and resentment of the world.

He was more aware of the problems of the others than they could know or believe. To him their woes were as nothing; he wished his own were as meager. He boiled within; he was never without hurt from the sword of his experience. He was a lion pacing the cage.

He was no militant for his race. He was born a loner, he believed. Everything in his past pointed to the fact that Sanderson Roosevelt had to get what he could on his own, over any obstacle put in his path.

He had been a weak fool, he thought, to assent to assignment to Mingo in the Pennjersey League. He could have done better. The other trio could have done better, too, if they had not listened to that racist from Texas, that mealymouth Hammer. They would have been scattered, but all would have been in better positions to be observed and evaluated for their true worth. The more he thought about this, the more rebellious he became. He got up from the chair and donned his best sweater and eased himself from the room so as not to disturb the slumbering Jonesy.

He walked. He seethed. He came to the bus station. He played a pinball machine with great shaking and tilting and obtained free plays and scorned to use them, presenting them to a wan and lonely-looking GI who had been watching in vapid admiration as Rosey beat the system.

A bus, panting in the station preparatory to departing, bore the destination in white letters, "Newark."

He did not consciously board the vehicle, pay the fare, sit alone staring out the window. It was the driving pain, the aching need which impelled him. He recognized what was happening to him, but there was no way he could prevent it. He did not recognize the consequences. He thought only of his need.

In Newark he knew the way. A taxi took him to the cellar known as Fats Noodles and Cats. It was off Broad Street, far from the neighborhood where he had grown up. The atmosphere was thick with the odor of illegal cigarettes and alcohol. A seven-piece jazz band walloped the walls with its solid beat. Rosey went to the bar.

The place was crowded. He found a stool from which he could command a view of the scene. People from all walks of life drank and smoked and talked and listened to the extremely sound jazz.

The bartender said, "What's yours?" Then he stared and said, "Hey, Rosey!"

"Hey, Papa."

"Where you been, Rosey?"

"Playin' ball. Gimme a beer."

"Playin' ball? Like where at, man? Cats been askin' for you."

"Never mind where. In a league." He could not resist. "On contract."

163

"You mean organized ball?" The beer was foamy and cold. Rosey put money on the bar.

"You know it."

Papa was aging and fat. He said, "Hey, man, that's somethin' else."

"You know it."

"What you doin' in town if you're with a club?"

Rosey said, "Cool it, Papa. Just cool it."

"Okay, Rosey, okay. You don't want it spread around."

"I don't want it whispered. Shouldn't have peeped. But you always been copacetic with me."

"I dig you good." Papa had been a ballplayer long ago.

An hour passed. Rosey drank another beer. The music did not soothe him; it was a driving, marching sound. Fats played "Sunny Side of the Street" for twenty minutes without repeating other than the basic four phrases. It was enough, he knew. He could catch a bus and be back at a reasonable time.

He accepted a beer on the house. The band finished the set, and Fats came waddling to the bar, a short balding man with a sad moon face.

"Great sound, man," said Rosey.

"Ain't no place for it," said Fats. "Howzit, Rosey?"

"Right on. You got the place right here."

"No recordings no more. Nothin'. Just these people."

"You makin' out?"

"Money ain't it."

"Right, Fats. I dig. Have one?"

"You holdin'? Last time I saw you, it was Tapsville."

"I'm holdin'." He paid for a straight shot for Fats. "Got to split soon. Sure good to hear it played right again."

Fats regarded him closely. "You got trouble?"

"Not so ever."

"I don't want trouble. Got enough with the snakes in the grass. The cops have to get with it once in a while. You know how it goes."

"I dig."

164

Fats went away. Now it was really time to depart. Yet Rosey waited.

A handsome Negro couple entered the place. Rosey saw them as they came in, watched them to a side table.

Papa said, "Oh-oh. Now, Rosey."

"No way," Rosey said. "Send over a drink."

"No," said Papa.

"Yes," said Rosey. He made his way to the table and stood looking down. The girl was tawny and beautiful, with bright, large, questioning eyes. The man was big and strong and well dressed. Rosey said, "Hi, Wanda ... Jerry."

She said, "Sandy!"

The man said, "Take it easy, now. ..."

"No trouble," Rosey interrupted. "Just wanted to say hi and all." He sat down. "Got a drink coming for you."

"Now, Sandy," said Wanda. "You're always trouble, and we all know it."

Rosey said, "No way. I'm doing okay. Wanted you to know it."

The man regarded him. "You're well turned out, I'll say that. Not robbin' banks, are you?"

"Jerry!" Wanda said.

"I'm carryin' scars from the last time we met," said Jerry.

"That was then," said Rosey. "You were up. I was down. Forget it. I wish you both happiness. I wish you a bluebird. You all married?"

"Not yet," said Jerry. "But soon."

Rosey reached into his pocket and took out a crisp fifty-dollar bill. "I won't know about it. So—a wedding present. Please."

Jerry said, "Not from you."

"Wait. Sandy?" She looked into his eyes; then she took the bill. "You mean it."

"Yes. I mean it."

"Something good happened to you."

He said, "Yeah."

"I'm glad, Sandy." She was friendly, warm.

"I met some decent people." Suddenly he could talk to this girl to whom he had once been married. He could talk in their own language, not the cant of the hip world. "I'm playing ball and making good. There are three guys—white guys. Well, one is a brown guy, a chicano."

"A what?"

"Mexican-American. He thinks he's got problems." Rosey found that he could laugh a little. "Anyway—we work together. They're not tough like me, but we work together. One of them is too much. Jonesy, you should know Jonesy. He's my roomie."

"A Charlie is your roommate?" Jerry snorted.

"He likes it that way," said Rosey. "Okay, you don't believe me. Anyway, I knew you came here. I took off and waited. I don't know why or how, I just knew you'd be here. So make what you want of it."

Jerry said, "I make you a big, fat phony. Now you've said your little piece, why don't you vanish?"

"Jerry!" said Wanda. "I know him. He's not lying."

Rosey stood up. "Thanks, Wanda. Like I said, no trouble. Any other time, Jerry. Anytime at all. Not tonight."

It was then that a warning buzzer sounded. The lights went down, then up. Then they went out.

Rosey said, "It's a raid. Follow me, I know the way."

There was an exit behind the dais on which the band played. It was covered by an innocent drape. Rosey took Wanda's hand, she took Jerry's hand. Rosey led them through, past and over people who were scrambling, muttering, cursing, shouting. He dragged them up the steps. He found the spot which he remembered of old. He yanked open a door.

A uniformed policeman barred the way. Rosey lowered his head and rammed with all his might. Wanda and Jerry flitted past him and the lawman and out an alley, free into the night.

166

The policeman hit Rosey on the skull with his blackjack.

Jonesy struggled from dreams of Ana Cassidy and his family and Mando and baseballs flying, and groggily answered the telephone. A soft voice asked, "Is this Jonesy?"

"Yes . . . yeah. Who's this?"

"This is Mrs. Sanderson Roosevelt."

"Wha . . . what?" Jonesy came wide awake.

"Rosey's in trouble. I was only able to get the phone number from him. I don't know exactly where you are, but he needs you. He needs you."

"Where . . . what happened?"

"He's in jail. First Precinct . . . Newark. He was trying to help . . . other people. . . . It'll take a lot to get him out. . . . It's real bad."

"Did he kill someone?" Jonesy was reaching for his clothes.

"No. Oh, no. . . . He assaulted a cop."

"I'll be there," said Jonesy.

"Oh, thank you. Thank you." She hung up.

He looked at his watch. It was midnight. He groaned. Then he went out of the motel and down the street to a garage where the bus was being repaired. He found the owner working on the bus. He waved a hundred-dollar bill, and the man gave him the keys to a fairly new Buick and promised secrecy. Jonesy picked out the route to Newark, driving swiftly but within the speed limits, lest he too be nabbed by the law.

The surprising thing to him was that Rosey should appeal for help. He knew his roommate, he sensed the unregenerate wildness of Rosey's soul. He had learned to understand the whys and wherefores; it had been a large part of the education he was gaining through association with the ballplayers. When he had awakened in the motel room and found Rosey missing, he had not been amazed. No behavior of Rosey could astound him. What he looked for was motivation;

upon finding it or even coming close to it, he had found he could reason with his friend. Not that Rosey would agree—but he would listen. Now, this cry for help was the first evidence that there was change in Rosey's heart.

The consequences, of course, would be dire. Jonesy was pragmatic, he saw the fact and accepted it, which did not prevent him from acting upon it. For himself he had worked out the creed that the greatest good must be accomplished at whatever cost.

Baseball, he thought, was surely the melting pot of young America. The four of them, all from different backgrounds, had been thrown together willy-nilly, and it had worked out. They understood one another as well as human beings, youthful humans, could possibly manage. He felt that if he had awakened Mando and Jack and asked them to come along on this excursion, they would have agreed—because they thought he needed them, if for no other reason. This was enough, he felt, to justify all.

There was a sergeant on duty behind the desk at the First Precinct. Jonesy approached him in his polite, subdued fashion.

"Excuse me. I believe you have in custody a man named Sanderson Roosevelt."

The sergeant bore a name plate, "Michael O'Leary." He stared stone-faced. "What of it?"

"I'd like to provide bail if I could."

"You know what that nigger's in for?"

"Not precisely." Jonesy's gorge was rising, but it was not distinguishable in speech or manner.

"Assaultin' an officer is what. Even if we could give bail at this hour, there wouldn't be no chance whatsoever, junior."

"My name is Jones. It is very important to me that Roosevelt be released tonight. Can you suggest a means?"

"You heard me, you ain't deef, are you? That jigaboo not only ain't gettin' out tonight, he's gonna be stuck *under* the jail for a long, long, time, buster."

"Jones, sir." He sighed. "Gilbert Samson Jones III."

"Gil . . . are you tryin' to kid me?"

"That's my name. Is there a pay phone available?"

"Gilbert Samson. . . ." The sergeant allowed himself a nasty chuckle. "Now, who in the hell can you call that'll do you or your jig buddy any good?"

"It doesn't matter, does it?" Jonesy smiled at him. "You're quite positive that he can't be released under any circumstances."

"Buster, you sure talk like a mouthpiece. You a lawyer?"

Jonesy said, "No, I'm really a shortstop. But they have me playing second base."

He entered the phone booth and left the sergeant staring in utter perplexity. He sat down and took out his wallet and found the number he wanted. He sat for several moments in thought. This would do it, he knew. This would end the masquerade. This would make the road ahead ten times as rough. He was not hesitating, he had visions of what could happen, what might already have happened to anyone in jail for attacking a cop. He had to act, and he had to move fast. He deliberately left the door of the booth open. Two other policemen came from the back room and leaned on the desk with the sergeant.

Jonesy deposited a coin and called New York. He got through to the Plaza Hotel. There was a bit of difficulty with the operator until he firmly pronounced his name and said, "I am the son of Gil Jones. I must speak to him. It is an emergency."

Now the extension buzzed. It was extremely fortunate that his parents were at the hotel. He hoped they were sober.

He heard one of the policemen say, "Hey, O'Leary, did you get that? The Plaza. Gil Jones . . . Gil Jones?"

The third cop said, "Holy cow! My wife, she's a nut on the social pages, y' know? If that's the billionaire Jones . . . wow."

His father's voice came clear and jovial to Jonesy's ear. "Hey there, son! What's up? You all right?"

"I'm fine," said Jonesy. "I'm in the First Precinct in Newark."

Hearty laughter assailed him. "You? You in the pokey? Why, I'm proud of you, Gil. Didn't know you had it in you."

"Okay, Dad, okay." Jonesy was patient. "I'm sorry, but it's a friend of mine."

"Sure, sure. I might've known. A friend. You're the biggest soft touch . . . well, never mind. What can I do?"

"They can't give bail. I thought if you knew a judge over here. You see, this fella—they say he hit a cop."

"Oho! Rough ballplayer?"

"Something like that. He's my roomie."

"Your roomie? That's different. Okay, son. Just stay where you are. By the way, how's the ball club and all that?"

"Fine. We're in a tight race for the lead."

"You playin' regular short?"

"Second base, Dad."

"Second? You let them shove you around again? How many times must I tell you to stand your ground? I taught you to be a shortstop, damnit."

"Now, Dad, it's the shortstop who's in jail. Please?"

Again the laughter. "Just hang in there, kid. . . . Here's your mother. . . ."

Her Vassar voice had not changed. "Son? Are you sure you aren't involved?"

"No, Mother. It's my friend."

"You are all right?"

"Yes, Mother."

"Well . . . I must say, you give me no cause for worry. And you always tell the truth. I'll hang up now and let Dad carry on. Good night, dear."

He hung up. He wiped his brow. It was always difficult to speak with them. They were completely indifferent to anything beyond their own particular desires. They were a happy couple surely enough, but they should never have bothered having a child.

The cop who had recognized the Jones name

moved toward him. "Hey, is your old man *the* Gil Jones?"

"Yes, sir."

"You hear that, O'Leary? Better get the turnkey ready. Boy, oh, boy. . . . Hey, Jones, is it true about your folks? How they travel with them Greek shipowners and all? And the Queen of England's sister?"

"It's true." No use trying to duck now, he thought. Get Rosey out, that was the point.

"And you're a ballplayer? Who you play with?"

He wished with all his heart he could dissemble, but the time for that had been past when he was forced to call his father. "The Mingo Skeeters."

"And this jig . . . this roomie of yours is the shortstop? Like we been readin' about the four of yez, the infield the Gold Sox is gettin' ready for the leagues?"

"You do read the papers, don't you, officer?"

"Levinsky's the name. Izzy Levinsky." He extended his hand. "Hey, this is somethin' on a dull night. You want some coffee, Jones?"

"That would be nice."

"Come on back with me. Hey, O'Leary, how do you like it? Is this a story? Is this somethin'?"

"That jig butted Sam in the gut," said O'Leary. "It'll take a helluva lot of grease to get him outta here."

"You got to be nuts," said Levinsky. "You ain't never seen grease like these people can handle. Come on, Jones. I got a million questions. My wife'll kill me if I don't bring home all the skam."

The coffee was very good. Officers on duty came and went. Levinsky was the hero of the occasion. It was no surprise when a reporter from the *Star Eagle* appeared. The fat was in the fire; there was nothing to do but make the best of it.

O'Leary appeared at the door of the day room. His face was flushed, his voice a deep growl. "Jones, whatever your name is."

"Yes, sir."

171

Levinsky chuckled, the reporter yawned, scribbling.

"Come get your buddy."

Levinsky said, "I told you grease. Awful quick, too, huh, O'Leary?"

"Shut up," said O'Leary.

Jonesy said, "Hey, thanks, you guys." He looked at the reporter. "No chance of covering it up, I suppose?"

"I wish I could," said the young man. "I really do. I see your position. But—too many around here know about it. Supposing Levinsky's wife tells her neighbor and it gets back to city desk, and they know I'm here, which they do already?"

"I know," said Jonesy.

"I'm sorry, kid. It'll be your tails, won't it?"

"Harry Hammer won't like it. The front office won't like it. Nobody is going to like it."

O'Leary said, "You comin' or ain't you?"

He went outside. Rosey had a bruise over his left eye, and his jaw was swollen. Worst of all, there was a subdued air about him, a diminution of ego, a sullenness.

Jonesy said, "Hi, man."

"Hi, pal. Let's get out of here."

Jonesy looked at O'Leary. "Anything to sign?"

"There'll be no charges," said the sergeant sourly. "Just take him away."

They walked out of the precinct and down to the Buick. Rosey got in and sat hunched, his head buried in his shoulders. Jonesy started the engine and turned the car toward Denville.

Rosey said, "How'd you do it?"

"My father did it."

"Your father?"

Jonesy sighed. "My father is Gilbert Samson Jones II—you might as well know. He could call the White House."

"What's that mean?"

"It means we're in bad trouble. The newspapers have got it. Hammer will have to know everything

172

about it. Everybody will have to know who my people are."

After a moment Rosey said, "I did it to you."

"No. You needed help. Did they hurt you bad?"

"Two of them hold you. The guy you hit gets to use a rubber-hose kinda thing."

"How did it start?"

Rosey told him slowly, thoughtfully, trying very hard the unaccustomed task of communicating, of making another person understand each facet of the happening. He ended, "Wanda—it took a lot of guts for her to come down there and make Jerry use legal stuff to get to talk to me. It took plenty of guts. They might've jailed her on suspicion of being the gal who got away, you see? And her about to start teaching school. It could've cost her."

"Yes. I see."

"I was punchy or I wouldn't have given her the phone number. They hit me in the head a lot."

"You had to get to me."

"I didn't even think you could do any good. I didn't think anybody or anything could do any good. I . . . I just knew you'd always been able to handle things. It was . . . it was like automatic to yell for you."

"That makes it all okay." Jonesy felt a load take wings from his shoulders. "That's everything that counts. If you believe that, then maybe I'm not really Gilbert Samson Jones III. Just Jonesy. You see?"

"I dig. Yeah. I dig that." A pause. "I did wrong."

"Right . . . wrong. If you have to do something, then you have to do it."

"I shouldn't have left Denville. I shouldn't have gone to the joint. Y'know . . . I didn't plan it. I just . . . went."

"So. It happened. No use to cry. What we'll do, we'll tell the whole story to Harry."

"He'll find out soon enough. The papers and all."

"It's always better to tell them first. He'll know we're not lying."

"Duckin' out on him. That's what he'll hate. With the games tomorrow and all."

"It wasn't smart," Jonesy conceded. "But it's done."

Rosey was quiet for a moment. Then, "No charges? Did that stinkin' sergeant say there'd be no charges?"

"That's what he said."

"Your old man must carry some weight."

They drove through the night, and they came to the town and parked the car and locked it in the yard of the darkened garage. They walked to the motel, and Harry Hammer came out of shadows wrapped in a raincoat over pajamas.

Jonesy said, "Harry, it's a long story."

"It better be good." Yet he was more bewildered than angered, it was plain to see. "You got your pals all awake and waitin'."

"I should have called you, but I thought maybe you were asleep," said Jonesy.

"Called me? From where? About what?"

"Let's go and talk."

He led them to the room occupied by Mando and Jack. Both were awake and worried. They crowded together and spoke in low tones so as not to awaken the rest of the ball club.

Harry said, "So tell me."

Jonesy put a hand out to stop Rosey from speaking. He told it all.

Then Rosey spoke. "I was wrong, Harry. It's all my fault. Jonesy—he's a stand-up guy. He blew his cover, everything, to help me. Lay it all on me. No other way."

"Yeah. No other way," said Hammer heavily. "Doggone it, I coulda killed you. I thought I'd fire you off the club as soon as the front office let me. I don't need no ballplayer that runs out on me after I tell 'em somethin'. I dunno. I just don't know."

Jonesy said, "I'm sorry about the newspapers. It couldn't be helped. They might have killed Rosey, you know."

Harry asked, "You need to see a doc, Rosey?"

174

"No. I hurt, but I'm tough. I'll be all right by the time we get to Mainville."

"It's a mess," said Hammer. "A real big mess. Jonesy, seein' the way things are, you did good. I got to admit, I'd of done the same."

"If I could just keep on being Jonesy who did what's right," he said. "They're going to be after me, you know it, Harry. I tried to keep it quiet. Nobody ever noticed me after I ducked and came to the tryouts. Of course, the front office knew, but they agreed to keep quiet, at least until I either flopped or made good. One of the owners is a buddy of my parents. Now it'll be field day for the press."

"That ain't gonna hurt the ball club," said Hammer. "Only you. I may be a redneck from Texas, but I see what you mean. It's a toughie, Jonesy, a real toughie."

"I don't want anything to happen bad to Sandy," said Jonesy. "It was a bad break, he was trying to help two decent people. Sure, he shouldn't have been there at that time. But ballplayers have gotten away with worse, Harry."

"The newspapers," Hammer said. "And the bosses. I'm finin' you fifty, Rosey. I gotta. And—you got it comin'. The rest is up to the front office." He arose. "Now, will yawl please get some little bitty sleep?"

10

Mainville, on the edge of but not part of the Pennsylvania anthracite region, lay among hills of variegated greens, a farming community, the only true baseball bastion of the Pennjersey League. The ball park was small but complete. The infield was manicured, the outfield grass cut to the quick. The stands were filled for every game with wild supporters of the Yankees. It was a bright, clear Sunday afternoon.

The home team took the field, and the fans roared and someone played "Charge" off-key on an old trumpet, a cheerful sound. Jonesy was at the bat rack. Billy Fay strolled out to the mound.

Mando said to Jonesy, pretending to examine the bats, "How's Rosey?"

"Beat. They hurt him."

"His eyes look bad."

"Yes. I'm worried about him."

"He must be worried about himself."

"I don't think so. He's quiet, but there's something in him that's different. He's real tough, Mando."

"I sure hope he's all right."

They stood at attention for the anthem; then Jonesy said, "Let's worry about that Fay instead of Sandy."

"We've been together so much," Mando said. "Almost like a family."

Jonesy brightened. "Nobody came down on me. You know?"

"Because you're a rich kid? Maybe in the beginning they would have. But you're one of us now, right?"

"Those newspaper stories. They were murder."

"Maudlin is the word. Forget 'em."

"I must forget 'em. Harry's been so decent. Too bad we have to go against that Fay in the first game."

"And the fourth," said Mando. "The bum."

The umpire said, "Play ball."

Jonesy swung his bat. "Well, here goes nothin'."

"Right on," said Mando. "Let's get it all together."

Mando went back to the bench. Green was in the on-deck box. Rosey sat quietly, his hands folded, an uncharacteristic pose. Down at third Hammer was clapping his hands, making a sound like pistol shots. Sullivan whistled from the Yankee dugout.

Mando said, "This is it, man."

"Yeah," said Rosey. His eyes were swollen, but there was fire behind them.

"You're goin' to be okay," Mando said in his ear. "Up and at 'em."

"Just knock me around. I'll be on." There were faint signs of the beating on his face.

"I'm with you."

Rosey nodded. Then they both turned full attention upon Billy Fay.

It was the first time they had seen the Yankee ace pitch in daylight. His style was smooth as silk, Mando conceded. He apparently gave nothing away, concealing the ball and his wrist behind an oversized glove. He could throw overhand, sidearm, and three-quarters. The trouble was that it was impossible to detect which pitch was coming from which angle. He seemed as young as springtime, as strong as a horse, and as confident as the perfect athlete could be.

The two teams were well matched, Mando thought, excepting that Fay was a nonpareil in this league. Barone had improved immeasurably and would be pitted against the Yankee star in both games; therefore it was just about up to the sometimes wild Skeeter hurler. Meantime, the hitters were the other key to success. Jonesy was poised, facing Fay.

Jonesy took a strike. Then he waited out the slow curve which missed the corner of the plate. Then he swung at the next pitch and hit it sharply down to third. White gathered it in and made the good throw, and Jonesy was out.

Green took his stick to the platter. The tall center fielder was a good hitter, but Fay had his number. Green fanned.

Rosey was next. He planted himself like a tank, the big, heavy bat poised like a wagon spoke. Fay slowed down. He knew about Rosey. His grin vanished, his eyes were slits. He threw a quick, sneaky curve.

Rosey hit it on the nose. The ball skied. Rosey ran down to first and headed for second.

At the fence in center field Dore jumped like a tuna. Rosey turned second at full speed. Dore slid and slammed into the boards. He fell down, rolled over. He came up holding his glove on high. The ball nestled like a white bird in its pocket.

Rosey turned, stopped, stared. It was an unbelievable catch off a well-hit ball. The first break of the game had gone to the Yankees.

Mando took his glove out to third. He had watched Fay, but daylight had not helped. He had learned no more about the crafty Fay than he knew before. He took his practice throws to first and prayed that Barone would be on his game today.

The old axiom of baseball, that the man who made the great play will lead off the following inning, held true once more. Dore was at the plate. The noise from the stands was overwhelming. The trumpet sounded; people stood and stomped their feet and yelled themselves hoarse. Nothing like this ever happened on the home field, Mando thought. These fans deserved a good ball club.

It could work both ways, he thought. The cheers were exhilarating. He had been weary from the events of the previous night, from lack of sleep, the bus ride. Now he was excited; he could feel the spirit flowing from his teammates.

Manager Sullivan's irritating whistle was in his ear. Mando's memory ran backward to a time when as a boy he had developed a talent. He stuck two fingers into his mouth. He blew, producing a sound not unlike that of a factory siren calling the workers to lunch.

He completely drowned out Sullivan's shrillness. Even the local fans laughed. Barone looked at Mando, and his grin spread from ear to ear.

The first pitch was a slow, tantalizing floater. Dore, eager to continue his great performance, swung with all might and main. The ball came down to Mando on one hop. He threw to Jack, and Dore was out by twenty feet.

"The way to go, *paisano!* Got the leadin' lady!"

The shout was from Sandy Roosevelt. It was the first time Mando had ever heard it. Jonesy chimed in; they all began talking it up, the outfielders shouting in at their pitcher.

Barone went to work on the dangerous Portale. He worked the count to one and two, then threw the best curve Mando had ever seen him deliver. Portale came around and fell, missing by a foot.

Big Andrews, the right fielder, regarded Barone with new respect. He stood in looser than usual. Barone fed him soft curves. Andrew picked on one. It went on a popping loop toward right.

Jonesy did not seem to hurry. He floated back onto the grass. He reached and picked the blooper out of the air. The Yankees had gone down in order.

Hammer said, "Come on, chicano. Let's see one, boy."

Mando faced Billy Fay. Both teams were at high pitch. He knew he would get nothing close to good from the stocky young hurler. He kept his eyes fixed on the left hand as Fay went into his brief windup.

The ball came spinning in. Again it was junk. Fay had seized upon the soft stuff as Mando's weakness, and his control was pluperfect.

Mando squared away. He bunted the ball down the first-base line. He saw the startled expression on Fay's face as he dug in with all possible speed.

He crossed first before Fay could handle the ball. Ace was laughing, and over on third Hammer was waving his arms. Mando roosted on the sack and paid attention to Hammer. He was giving the go sign.

Ace played along. "Hold up now, let Kelly knock one, hold up, watch his move."

Fay had recovered his cool, Mando thought. He looked the same as ever, confident and capable. He bluffed a throw, and Mando scuttled back. He faced Jack Kelly.

Now Mando sneaked an extra step toward second. He kept his center of balance, ready to dive back to first, but he edged with care to get an advantage. Jack had the sign.

Fay pitched, throwing hard with a man on base. Jack reached for a wide one and came slapping around on it, no power, just an attempt to get the ball on the ground and into right.

Mando was already going. Jack's puny hit did not get through. Terrill tossed him out, but Mando was safe on second.

Hammer was whirling like a dervish. Downey was at bat. Fay frowned. Mando held his spot, safely adjacent to the bag. Hammer was giving so many signs it was hard to distinguish which was the serious one.

Downey bunted toward third. Mando was flying as the hitter squared. Fay couldn't reach the rolling ball. White, knowing Mando was coming fast, hesitated a split second. Downey was safe on first.

Hammer bellowed, "That's speed, Mando, boy. That's runnin'."

Peck was up. He was no great hitter, but he was quick and full of the learning of his thirty years. Fay had to work on him with care. Mando took a good lead. Fay stared him back to the bag. Peck waited with the bat held high.

Fay pitched. Peck caressed the ball. It dribbled down toward first. Mando was in motion. Fay picked up the ball, saw he was too late, threw to first to get Peck. Mando arose from the dirt and dusted his pants. The Skeeters had scored a run without hitting the ball out of the infield. It was the kind of baseball that could discourage the best, most experienced pitcher.

Fay showed no expression. He bore down with terrific speed, then a change, then a curve. He struck out Pazolla. The inning was ended for the Skeeters.

Hammer came in, saying. "That's the way to go. That's what I calls heads-up baseball. Now hold them tarriers."

Barone proceeded to obey orders. He was hotter than firecrackers, Mando thought, exulting. He fanned Hagney, made Terrill pop to second, and struck out White.

Fay went back to the job. Showing no weakness, he made Barone ground out to short, struck out Jonesy and Green. Sullivan whistled. Mando promptly drowned him out with his built-in siren. Sullivan didn't like it, but there was nothing he could do about it. He was betrayed by his own arrogance, scowling, yapping at his hitters. It didn't work. Barone seemed in a world apart. He pitched as he never had before.

The game ground along, a pitcher's duel. Mando got a hit in the third, struck out in the sixth, doubled in the eighth on a fluke hit down the left-field line, but the Skeeters did not score again on Billy Fay.

Meantime, there was a strained silence on the Skeeter bench as they took the field for the ninth inning. Even the stands were hushed. It had slowly grown upon everyone in the park that Barone had not given up a hit. He had three more men to get out, and he would have accomplished that rarity in any league— a no-hitter.

Further, he faced the top of the Yankee batting

order, Dore, Portale, and Andrews. Dore had drawn a walk and had met the ball in his other turns without getting to first base. He was in there now, hugely determined not to allow his team to be shut out and humiliated.

Barone had to be tired, Mando thought. None of them had enjoyed proper rest for this game. But the big lefty was still grinning, possibly a bit pale around the gills, but showing no weakness in his demeanor. Hammer was hoarse from yelling. The Yankees began to bellow up a storm, and then the fans caught it and began exhorting their team to beat out Barone's brains, among other pleasantries.

"Keep chuckin', *paisano*," Mando begged. "We're behind you, baby, keep chuckin'."

Rosey was quiet now. He may have been waiting, saving his strength. Jonesy talked in his quiet way; Jack chattered as always. Barone toed the rubber.

Dore hit the second pitch. It rode down to third. It took a high hop. Mando's heart was in his throat as he jumped, grabbed, and threw all in one motion.

Dore was out by an inch.

Portale was next. Barone worked hard on the left fielder, recognizing his skill. The count ran full. Barone missed the corner. Portale walked, and the noise became riotous.

The infield gathered around Barone. He grinned at them. They patted him and went back to position. Rosey looked bad now, Mando thought. He looked entirely strung out.

Andrews, the heavy hitter, was batting left-handed. Mando figured the odds, moved over to give him the baseline; Jonesy played a bit deep and toward the right. Rosey moved toward second.

Barone threw a ball. Then he threw a lovely swift strike. Then he missed again. The tension mounted. Andrews fouled off two pitches in a row. Barone managed to throw two more wide ones, and the count was full.

Now Barone had to come in with his best one. He

looked at the runner. He took a stride and went overhand, game as a swordfish on a hook, straight down for the outside corner.

Andrews sliced the ball. It skidded for the hole between Mando and Rosey. Mando flung himself at it. He missed.

Rosey came from nowhere. He grabbed the ball. He shot it to second. Jonesy made the ballet pivot. He threw like lightning to first.

It was a double play. The game was over, and Barone had entered the minor-league hall of fame. He had shut out the mighty Mainville Yankees without giving them a hit.

The fans cheered him. The players mobbed him. They ran for the bus and climbed aboard.

They collapsed as they were driven to the motel, a bunch of worn-out youngsters, happy to delirium. They had time for a shower, then back into the sweaty uniforms for the second game of the double-header.

When they returned to the park, the four infielders sat together on the bench for a moment. Jonesy looked at Rosey.

"You shouldn't play."

"Don't fret yourself, pal," said Rosey. "I'll make out."

"I think Hammer's punishing him," said Mando.

"Could be." Jack was grinding his fist in his glove. He had hit into a double play and managed only one scratch single off Fay, and it had him angered.

"If old Page can hold 'em, we ought to be able to beat Bubba Morton," Jonesy said.

"I don't know. The team's bushed," Mando said. "These road trips!"

"We'll get 'em," said Jack. "I'm due. One for four. I can't stand going one for four."

Rosey was silent, occupied with his deep thoughts. The umpires appeared, and time was called.

Bubba Morton seemed easy enough. Jonesy got a hit, Green sacrificed, Rosey came to bat.

Rosey hit the first ball. It went over the fence, and the Skeeters had two runs. Mando hit a single. Jack followed suit, sending Mando to third.

Downey got hold of the ball, but it went to the shortstop, who started a double play to end the inning.

Page, thirty-five years old, felt the trip worse than any of them, Mando knew. The veteran simply did not have it. Dore, Portale, and Andrews all singled.

Hammer took out Page. He brought in Fargo, who was the short relief man and should have been saved. Fargo gave Hagney a good ball, and the big first sacker hit a home run. So then it was Yankees 4, Skeeters 2.

The fans loved it. The contrast with the first game gave them new life; they made more noise than ever.

Fargo continued to throw fast balls. It was all he had, Mando reflected; his stint was to come in and for two or three innings put everything into every pitch.

Terrill hit one to Jonesy, who threw him out. White lined to Green in center. Tilden rapped one at Rosey, who almost lost the handle, then made a great throw to retire the side.

Bubba Morton also became tough. The teams went through to the fourth without further score. Then Hammer had to bring in Terry, the long relief man who was sometimes a starter. This left the pitching staff, scanty to begin with, weakened for the remaining two games, but the manager had no choice. Fargo had thrown himself out with the fast balls.

The Yankees seemed to love fresh pitchers. They jumped on Terry for three more runs.

Then the Skeeters got to Bubba and made two runs, Rosey and Mando contributing long hits. But the rally was short-lived. The team was just plain worn out, Mando realized. They were going through the motions, but the road trip had taken it out of them. The game became a dragged-out nightmare.

The Yankees won, 14 to 8.

The Skeeters staggered to their bus, went to the

motel. The four infielders gathered in the room occupied by Jonesy and Rosey. They flopped down, too bone-tired to go immediately to the showers they sorely needed.

Mando said, "I'm so beat I don't think I can eat."

"We get a no-hitter, then we get a track meet. It's too much," said Jack.

"I was hoping we'd clean this series," Jonesy said.

"Not enough pitching. That sounds funny after Barone's bit. But it's true," Mando said.

"And tomorrow night we go again. It'll be Chick. He'd better be right," Jack said.

"We all better be right."

Rosey had not spoken. Mando regarded him. He was on his back, and his eyes were closed. The bruises were still noticeable. In a moment he emitted a slight snore. Jonesy beckoned, and the three of them went next door.

Jonesy said, "I'll shower with you guys, okay? He sure needs the sleep."

"He sure has the guts," said Mando. "Errorless ball, and five hits in the second game."

"That was no game—that was beanbag," said Jack. "Let's strive to eat and join Rosey in slumberland."

The next night Chick Onslow was on. The Yankees could get only five scattered hits. Rosey hit a double, and Mando knocked another one out of the park. The Skeeters won the game, two to nothing.

Hammer came into the room where Mando, Jack, Rosey, and Jones, cleaned and fed, were gathered. Barone was with him.

"Tomorrow it's that Fay," said Hammer. "We got to have this game. There's things goin' on out on the coast. Natch, they're excited about Barone, here. Anybody pitches a no-hitter—and the way their pitchers are goin' . . . The brass is completely disgusted with the team. This is somethin' I never seen in all my years. It's crazy. Anything can happen. Dutch was always the toughest, but I talked to him, and he's so uptight it's pitiful."

"How many have they lost in a row now? Twenty?"

"Twenty-one. Now, Rosey—that fifty-dollar fine? It's out. Get me some hits tomorrow, will you?"

Rosey said, "Thanks, Harry."

Jonesy's quiet voice interposed. "Why are you telling us all this, Harry?"

Hammer's big hand went to his head; he caressed his thinning hair. "Well ... You guys ... You're different than the old-time ballplayers. I feel like I can gab with you all. Barone, here, he's part of it, like he worked on his wildness and used his skull and come through. Ace, he's old-timey. I had him activated."

"Ace? He's past forty!"

"That's how bad we need another reliever. Well, he's like a kid about it. Can't get his head straight, he's so excited. Only talks about the old guys who have made comebacks with a knuckle ball. He ain't got a knuckle ball. And he don't believe in miracles."

"Miracles?"

"The leagues are overexpanded. The Sox are the worst, but the other expansion teams is likewise lousy. I tell you, Dutch is losin' his mind. Anything can happen."

Rosey said, "Man, you're telling us we might go up?"

"You been followin' the averages."

Jonesy said firmly, "We're not ready."

"Course you ain't. But Wells is hurt and hittin' two-oh-five, right?"

They were silent. Barone was sober-faced. Hammer got up and walked to the door.

"We need to take this series. We need to beat Fay again. Once ain't enough. This here's just among us, you know that. Keep it in your mind; we need to stick the Yankees."

He left. Barone sat down and wiped his forehead.

"I oughta be climbin' the walls with happiness. Instead, I'm scared."

186

"Miracles," said Rosey. "I don't believe in miracles."

"Gordon's batting two-oh-five," said Mando. "Libby's had it, can't go to either side and make the play. Astor hasn't hit a home run in two weeks. Outside of Blackie Schwartz, they haven't got a pitcher can hit a wall."

"Publicity," said Jonesy. "From the Pennjersey to the big league. An entire infield and a kid pitcher. They'd fill the park—until we bombed out."

"No way," said Rosey. "Miracles and fairy tales, I won't buy."

"Rosey's right," said Jack. "But I do want to take that smirk off Fay's face. That's something else again."

"I hit him, but I haven't solved him," said Mando. "We all want to get to him. It would be tougher in the league."

"What league?" Rosey shook his head. "No way."

Barone said, "I almost wish someone had got a hit off me."

The first intimation of trouble was when early the next morning an ambulance growled its way among the cabins of the motel. Everyone ran to the spot where it stopped. Hammer was shaking his head.

"It's Peck," he said. "Fever. He's plenty sick."

Downey, roommate of the man on the stretcher, said, "He's had a cold since the rainy spell. Me, too, but his got worse. We're gonna miss him."

That was the truth, Mando knew. The steady veteran was the key to the outfield. The rookies, Howard, Forest, and Roquero, could not replace him. The ambulance rumbled away, and they all returned to their rooms for more sleep. It seemed they could never get enough sleep.

Around noon there was a crash and a yell in another cabin. Hammer, wild-eyed, rushed to the scene.

It was Roquero, the most reliable of replacements for Peck. He had slipped and cut himself in the shower. His arm would be in bandages for a week, the doctor said after the stitching.

Hammer roared, "Now by the Lone Star they're tryin' to run a whizzer on us." He shook both big fists. "They can't do that to us now."

Mando said, "Harry?"

"Don't give me no more trouble!"

Mando asked, "Zander?"

"He's no outfielder. He's a third baseman."

"Okay, Harry, I was only thinking."

"Well, stop thinkin'. We got trouble enough. I was gonna play Roquero."

"Sure, Harry." Mando walked away.

In the cabin Jonesy said, "Anything less than full force against Fay and we're under the gun."

"Miracles," said Rosey.

"You look better," Jack told him. "That's a miracle in itself. You looked like a sick cat yesterday, the day before."

"Nature taking its course," said Rosey. "I still don't go for fairy stories."

"Okay," said Mando. Somehow he did not speak sharply in answer to Rosey these days. "But a couple of triple-A ballplayers are going to be demoted to the Skeeters to replace Peck and Roquero. That's at least a circumstance."

"A couple of 'em deserve it," said Rosey. "You been watchin' their averages?"

"You still think we shouldn't have come here with Harry?"

There was a short silence. Then Rosey said, "If I said I did, I would be worse than a rat. I'd be a dumb rat."

There was more meaning than the plain utterance of words, Mando felt. Rosey's bad time in Newark had altered him. It had much to do with Jonesy, but it affected them all. They were four together, now, all together.

Rosey said, not looking at the others, "Aw, I'm going to get more shut-eye."

"Me too," said Jonesy.

As they left, Mando looked at Jack. "I think I'll spend a few dollars this evening and call Ana when the rates are low."

"Y'know, I was thinking I'd call Connie. I guess that's what it's all about. You have somebody you want to call."

"When things get tight, there's somebody," said Mando.

"You think we're too young to marry, don't you, man?"

"Maybe. Maybe not. I know the problem. I know Uncle Talker and Mamma and Papa."

"I'm thinking about that miracle."

"Don't think too hard," said Mando. "You know what Harry said. Might strain something."

But he was thinking about it also, and how it would solve so many problems if it happened.

Hammer wrote down his opening lineup. The fans were again jammed in the stands. The lighting was better here at Mainville than in most Pennjersey parks. Zander came and sat alongside of Mando on the bench.

"Thanks," he said.

"For what?"

"Harry told me. You suggested me for left field."

"Well, you're a hitter."

"I couldn't hit that Fay last time."

"You're not alone, man."

"I know." Zander rubbed his big hands together. "Did you know I played some outfield in school?"

"How should I know that?"

"Well, if you didn't . . . thanks again."

"Forget it," said Mando. He felt relaxed. Ana had been warm and comforting and confident as usual on the phone. He had not told her of Hammer's hint of miracles. No use to raise hopes, he thought. He rather agreed with Rosey. It had never happened—although the Gold Sox, radio had told them, had lost another game that day. They were a laughingstock now. The problem was—would the calling up of four rookie infielders and a pitcher from the Pennjersey League not make them even a bigger joke in the game of baseball?

The Yankees took the field to the tune of blaring horns and honking klaxons and happy shouts. Fay took his slow, cocky stroll to the mound. Sullivan whistled from the coaching box at third, and Mando gave it back to him. Sullivan hadn't been using that annoying whistle so much since Mando had topped him.

Jonesy picked out his bat, waited for the anthem. Green moved restlessly, then went to the on-deck circle. Rosey crouched like a dark piece of granite at the end of the bench.

Zander said, "I got to say, Mando, you guys have swung it. I mean, you've got it together."

"Nothing counts, only tonight," said Mando. "If they're as good as we are, nothing counts."

"I know," said Zander. "It's a feeling you get. You got to beat them. You got to prove something."

"Knock it out, Jonesy," Mando yelled. "Shove it to him, man."

Fay adjusted his cap and rubbed up the ball. He would never lack for confidence. He was good, and he knew it. He nodded at Hooker's sign and went into his brief windup. He threw a soft curve at Jonesy. It went for a strike. That was Fay, ahead of the batter all the time.

Jonesy scraped the dirt and waited. Fay came three-quarters with his slider. Jonesy reached out and rapped at it. The ball soared foul off first, and Hagney took it in for the first out of the game. Fay could make it all look easy.

Jonesy came back to the bench and said, "Just like always, he hasn't got a thing. Only talent."

"The way he junks that ball past you—it murders you," said Mando. "Look at Green, there. Tight as a drum."

Green was taking his cut. He struck at the first two pitches, missing both. He fouled off two more. Then he fanned.

Rosey looked himself again, going to the plate with

that heavy, thick bat. Fay always took a little more time with Rosey. He fiddled and fussed, knowing he could not get this hitter off balance, but building his own concentration.

Rosey let two balls go past him. He was absolutely immobile at the platter, his eyes fixed upon Fay. The third pitch was a good curve ball.

Rosey hit it into left field for a single. Mando let out a yell and wrapped his hands around the handle of his bat. Fay regarded him with that thin smile of superiority which said, "Oh, it's you again, you're easy for me."

Mando watched the wrist as the Yankee pitcher came sidearm to him. He thought he saw the snap. He waited, then stepped forward. He caught the ball before it could break. He felt the solid sting of the impact. He sprinted for first.

Rosey turned second and went for third. The ball was in right field, where Mando wanted it, behind the base runner. The throw came into the cutoff man, and the Skeeters were in business with two out and men on first and third. Any kind of a hit from Jack Kelly would score a run.

Mando gave them his big whistle. He could see Sullivan scowling at him from the Yankee bench. He laughed with the sheer joy of getting the best of Fay and Sullivan.

And Jack hit a line drive which Terrill leaped and caught in the webbing of his glove. The inning was over, and the rally ended.

Mando's spirits diminished. Fay was handling Jack Kelly. In the earlier games Jack had hit freely off the wily pitcher. Fay must have brains along with his other obvious gifts.

Barone looked fast throwing his warm-up pitches. He was not a brainy young man, but he was a natural. He could learn, and he had plenty of courage. He had sense enough to be scared. He had enough ego, but not too much. Mando decided.

Dore came to the plate. The lean center fielder was typical of the young Yankees, smart and quick. He made

191

Barone pitch to him. One strike, one ball, two strikes, two balls. Dore looked them over without offering. Barone threw him a downer. It was a good pitch.

Dore had to take his cut. The ball popped over second. It was falling in. Jonesy made a sliding dive on his belly as Green came racing in to back up the play.

The ball fell into Jonesy's mitt. It stuck there as Jonesy, dazed for a second, lay still. Dore ran fast, turned at first, and was disbelieving as the base umpire waved him out.

Two good ball clubs, Mando thought. It was impossible not to be a bit proud of the Yankees, also. The Pennjersey League was full of nothing teams, but the Yankees and the Skeeters had proved themselves.

Portale was up. Every Yankee was straining to hit Barone. Good ballplayers respond to a no-hitter as a thoroughbred to the jockey's bat. Barone had only two days' rest, and despite his youth and his rubber arm, he could be vulnerable. Only the shortage of pitching and the importance of the game had forced Hammer to work him today. He would be using a lot of fast balls and his newfound control, sparing the twisting of his wrist required by curve balls.

Portale struck at the first pitch, waited out two balls, then took a strike. Barone came in hard, and Portale slammed the ball down the first-base line for what appeared to be a two-bagger.

Jack made one giant step and reached down. He trapped the ball behind the bag and ran, beating out Portale with ease.

Mando whistled, grinning at Sullivan in the coaching box alongside him. Sullivan was not amused. The heavy-hitting Andrews was next at bat.

"Wait him out," Sullivan was shouting. "Make him give you your pitch, Andy."

Andrews let two go by. One was a strike, the other a ball. Mando gave ground against the strong left-handed batter. Barone threw hard once more.

Andrews was a little late, but his swing was gigantic. The ball sliced down to short. Rosey should have been

192

handcuffed by its terrific force. He came in, caught the drive at his chest. Never losing balance, he threw Andrews out, laughing as he ran in toward the bench.

"Heavy, man," said Mando, running beside the shortstop. "Real heavy."

"You think Barone can last?"

"He's real strong."

"They'll hit him."

"No other way," said Mando. "We got to hit that Fay."

"We hit him. We just didn't score."

On the bench Hammer lingered. "You all right, kid?"

Barone said, "Lucky. Some fieldin' in there."

"If you get tired, you gimme the nod," Hammer ordered. "Don't try and be a damn-fool hero."

"Who else you got can go more'n a couple of innings?" asked Barone.

Hammer shook his head and stomped out to the coaching box. Downey took his bat to the plate. Zander picked out his bat and made ready to follow Downey. Fay tugged at his cap as usual and surveyed Downey, who had one of the hits off him in the opening game of the series.

Fay threw his quick fast ball. Downey hit it right back to the box. Fay gloved it and walked toward first base, tossing out Downey by thirty feet.

Mando said, "The guy can field, too. I'd like to smack one right through him."

"He'd catch it in his teeth," said Rosey.

Zander was grim-faced. The reserve third baseman had tried everything to make the team, even to sucking up to Hammer. Now he had his chance—as an outfielder. He waved his bat in a circle, crouching, a powerful young man.

Fay threw. Zander watched the soft pitch float in for a spinning strike. Fay grinned; he enjoyed making them eat the junk pitches, the triumph of skill over brute strength.

Zander stood in there, crowding the plate a little. Fay pitched to drive him back, a change pace swift on the inside. Zander came around on it. He got the handle of the bat on it. The ball took a curving course over Terrill's head, and the Skeeters had their first hit from a suboutfielder playing out of position.

Pazolla was at the plate. He bunted on the first pitch. Fay threw him out. Zander went to second. Barone went to bat. Hammer gave him a sign.

Barone bunted. White threw him out. Zander went to third. Jonesy went to the plate. It happened, then, for the first time.

A loud voice from the stands howled, "You got this baby, Billy. Gilbert Samson THIRD! He ain't no ballplayer, he's a bloody millionaire!"

The newspapers had hit the stands in Mainville while the Skeeter bus was on the road. Jonesy flinched at the sudden attack. Fay smiled and threw one down the pipe, and Jonesy did not offer at it.

"Strike one!"

Rosey said, "I want that bigmouth. I want him."

"No," said Mando. "Leave it to Jonesy."

It had been solid, big-league baseball, one man on, sacrifice him, let the pitcher push him along, leave it to the lead-off man, a steady performer who had no fear of Fay. It now remained to be seen if Jonesy could face the storm. Because it became a medley, all the loyal fans yelling, "Jones the Third! Third strike! Kill the rich kid!"

Fay looked at Zander on third. Then he threw his sharp breaking ball. It cut the corner for the second strike, and the Yankee rooters redoubled their cries for the third strike.

Jonesy showed no further sign that he heard. He tapped imaginary dirt from his spikes and stepped back in and faced Fay. The pitcher threw his best screwball.

Jones snapped his wrists. He cracked the ball on the good wood of the bat. Zander came running home with his chin on his shoulder. The ball went into left field between Terrill and White for a clean single.

Mando jumped off the bench and put his fingers in his mouth and blew a blast that rose above the crowd and mocked them. Rosey joined him, waving his arms at the section of the stands where the first loud sound had come from, yelling insults better covered by Mando's commanding whistle.

Green came to bat, and Rosey went to pick out his bat. Fay was still imperturable. He must have ice water in his veins, Mando thought. He thumped the ball in his glove and directed his stare at Green.

The unfortunate Green got the ace treatment. Fay tied him in knots and again struck him out. The inning for the visitors was over, but there was a precious run on the scoreboard.

Barone was still throwing aspirin. Hagney swung with might and main. He flied to Green in center field.

Terrill knocked one down to Mando, who threw him out. White came to bat. Barone eased up a bit, throwing low stuff. White hit one to Rosey to end the inning. Barone had pitched eleven consecutive innings against the Yankees without giving up a hit or a run.

Fay took his time, as always, in pitching to Rosey. Of all the Skeeters, the shortstop had given him the most trouble. Mando was on deck, watching Fay's every motion, but thinking of Rosey. He had thought that Rosey might go into the stands after the first offender against his roommate. This could never have happened as little as a month or so ago, he knew. Rosey had changed. He didn't snap back at Mando. He was quieter when off the ball field and noisier when on it. The tough guy wasn't wasting his strength on his teammates.

Fay broke off his good curve. Rosey swung on it. The ball shot on a line into left-center. Rosey was on first.

Mando went to try again against Billy Fay. Hammer was giving him a sign. He had to take it. Rosey was acknowledging it, Ace was waving his arms.

Fay threw the junk ball. Mando reached out, gently rotated the bat, and bunted toward first. Rosey was already on his way, obeying the bunt and run sign. Mando was out, but Hammer's strategy had a man on second with only one out and Jack Kelly at bat.

Jack came in with fire in his eyes. Fay had to throw hard, because Rosey was scampering off the bag, drawing the infielders out of position as they begged for a throw to nail him. The ball came in high and hard on the outside corner. Jack belted it over Terrill's head. Rosey came on the express, rounding third, sliding home as Dore unwisely tried to get him. Jack went to second.

Now Fay took off his cap and rubbed his hair. He walked toward the plate, then retreated. It was the first emotion he had shown them. Downey waved his bat, eager to run up a score on the Yankees.

Fay struck out Downey. Then he made Zander pop out to short. Then he got Pazolla on a long fly to center. He walked with head erect to the bench, put on his jacket, and sat with legs extended. He was a cool cat, Mando thought, the coolest. He had been proven vulnerable at last, and it did not faze him. He had been beaten by a no-hitter; now he was behind in the early innings, and it appeared that he might be taking a nap on the bench.

The bottom of the batting order faced Barone. He was still on top, still throwing. He lacked the finesse of Fay, but while he could shoot bullets at them, he could overpower them. He got Tilden, Holder, and Fay without trouble. He had gone twelve innings against them without allowing them a hit. Once more, Barone led off the Skeeter inning. The Yankee fans gave him a smattering of applause, but far from an ovation.

Barone pleased them by striking out. Jonesy knocked one down to Terrill, who got him easily. Green, with no one on and two out, hit a single into left.

Rosey was up again, and again Fay began to fiddle around, to rub a new ball, to tug at his cap. There was silence in the normally noisy ball park.

Fay threw his slow curve once more. Rosey met it flat and straight. It soared over the head of Tilden at short. Portale came racing in from left field. He dove forward and somersaulted. He came up with Rosey's sure hit.

The side was out, but they had touched up Fay again. Mando went to position and watched with one eye as Barone warmed up. Somehow there was the smell of danger on the Pennsylvania night air. It was cooling off, and a wind was beginning to blow.

Barone faced Dore. The determined center fielder hit the third pitch. Both Rosey and Mando went after it. The ball slicked through the hole. Zander came in and fielded it. The Yankee rooters stood up and rang the sky with their glad cries. The spell was broken. Barone had finally been tagged for a hit.

Mando went to him. "Okay, the pressure's off, goomba. Now you can relax and let us get 'em. Okay?"

"It's gettin' awful cold," said Barone. His face glistened with sweat.

Mando looked at the bench. Hammer was talking to Ace, who went to the bullpen with a ball in his hand. Fargo and Terry were up, a southpaw and a right-hander.

Barone looked down at Pazolla, who gave him a sign. He threw to Portale. The left fielder hit the first ball. The Yankees were no longer waiting; they were attacking. Portale was safe, and Dore went to third.

Again Mando looked at the bench, but the relievers weren't warmed up; the breeze had stiffened. Hammer let Barone pitch to Andrews.

Barone's wildness came back. He walked Andrews. There was a play at any base, but there were none out. Hammer now came slowly out to talk with Barone.

"I told you to tell me when you got tired."

"It's the wind," said Barone. "I feel all right, but it got so chilly."

Hammer said, "Okay. You did good." He took the ball from the pitcher and lifted his left fist, and Fargo draped his windbreaker over his shoulder and began the walk to the mound.

"You wipe yourself off and put on your jacket," Hammer said to Barone. "We got a lead. Fargo's good for a couple innings."

"Maybe," Mando muttered to himself, going back to where Rosey was waiting and watching.

Rosey said, "He's an in-and-outer. Streaky."

"Yeah," said Mando. "Well, what could you expect from Barone? He went twelve perfect innings."

"I don't expect anything. Not miracles either."

"Me neither, tell the truth," said Mando.

Fargo took his throws, went to the box. He looked around at the three Yankee base runners. He looked at Hagney, the redoubtable first-sacker. He toed the rubber. He showed no fear, no sign of the pressure. He either had plenty of nerve or he was phlegmatic, Mando thought.

Hagney was anxious to hit. When Fargo came in with his one valued throw, a fast ball, the first baseman was ready. He cracked it on the nose.

The ball skipped down to Jonesy. Without hesitation Jones gave it to Rosey. Facing first, Rosey made his strong, overhand toss. Dore came home to score. Portale went to third. But Andrews was forced and Hagney out at first on the double play.

It had been so lightning fast that Portale had no chance to ride home from second. It had been a perfect fielding play. Jonesy had deliberately given up one run. But two Yankees were out with the man on third, and the Yankees needed a hit to drive Portale home.

Terrill was at bat. Fargo regarded him as though he were just another manikin set up in order to be knocked down. He threw his fast ball.

Terrill did not try to hit it out. He met it. directed it with considerable skill into right field. Portale now was able to stroll in while Terrill roosted safe on first. The score was tied up at two-all.

Fargo shrugged. He lifted his arms, threw to White, the Yankee third baseman. White leaned on the ball. It rode down between Mando and the base.

He spun into the path of the bounding ball. He was actually off the diamond when he made his throw. Terrill was running hard. Jack stretched from first. The ball came low and hard. The umpire waved his hand. White was out, and so was the side.

"Lucky, lucky," said Mando, coming in. "They only tied us. Three hits and a walk, and they only got two runs."

"Get 'em back," growled Hammer. "Come on, now, you found out this guy can be had. Take 'im."

There was a rhythm to the pitching of every man, Mando knew. At no time was he aware that he had timed out Fay's deliveries. Yet when he went to the plate he had at last lost the feeling of incompetence which the lefty had formerly inspired. It was now an even duel.

He watched the usual junk flutter past him. A strike, a ball, another strike, another ball. He rippled his shoulders in tune with Fay's efforts.

The sneaky fast ball came. It seemed preordained. Mando hit it. The ball went into left field. Mando had another hit. He stood on first base, and this time he whistled in sheer relief that he had at last partially overcome the jinx.

Jack took his sign and laid down the bunt. He was out, and Mando was on second. Downey came up to bat.

Fay went on his unemotional way. He fanned Downey. He looked at Zander, whom he knew not too well, remembered that this one had hit him in the third inning. He began to move the ball around as he always did on strange batters. Zander worked the count even. Then Fay threw that low, sharp curve on the outside corner.

Zander took his cut. He got part of the fat on it. The ball sailed out into left. Portale came racing in and snatched it off his shoetops. The fifth inning was ended. Mando was stranded on second.

Fargo possessed enormous stubbornness to go along with his strength. He made Tilden ground out to Mando. He struck out the catcher and Billy Fay. He was working like a machine, but the results were satisfactory. It was a question of how long he could grind it out.

Pazolla led off the sixth. Fay got him to fly out to center. Barone again struck out. Jonesy flied out to right.

The top of the batting order meant no more to Fargo than the tail-enders. He just threw that ball. Dore knocked one to Mando and was thrown out. Portale fanned. Andrews hit one to the fence, but Zander pulled it in.

Fay showed no sign of weakening. A tie ball game was always tense, every play of seeming importance.

Fay continued to pitch his shrewd patterns. Green grounded out to Terrill. Rosey lined out to White.

Mando was loose and easy in there. Fay gave him nothing but soft stuff this time. Mando saw a floater turn over a bit too slowly. He rapped it into right field for a single.

Fay regarded him, shaking his head, for the first time in the season admitting that Mando was a live, breathing, moving human being. It meant that Fay realized he no longer had the Indian sign going for him, Mando thought. It was indeed all evens from now on out, a two-man battle.

Jack, who previously had no trouble with the Yankee left-hander, now stood in for a full count. Mando started on the next pitch.

Jack hit the ball high into right. Andrews got under it and despite the breeze made a catch, to retire the Skeeters. Again Mando was left on base.

Fargo went right on. He gave Hagney, the stalwart first baseman, a good ball, and the Yankee strong man hit it to Rosey and was out. Terrill tried to bunt. Fargo threw him out. White popped a foul behind third, and Mando took it off the edge of the grandstand for the third out. That was the seventh.

Fay had no trouble with Downey, but Zander scratched his second hit past the shortstop. Then Pazolla and Barone did their usual two-man stint, each striking out, each unable ever to do anything against Fay.

Now it was the eighth. Tilden, Hooker, and Fay were the hitters for the Yankees. Nobody ever had trouble with them.

So Fargo lost Tilden and walked him. Hooker hit the ball over Jonesy's head, and Tilden went to third. Sullivan, unwilling to remove his star pitcher, let Fay hit for himself with none out.

Hammer came from the bench. He lifted his right fist. Big Terry came onto the field. Fargo, still imperturable, strode off. He had done what he could for as long as he was supposed to go.

Mando talked with Rosey and Jonesy as Terry

warmed up. "Why didn't he let Fargo pitch to Fay? This is crazy."

"I think Fargo had it," said Jonesy. "He just had it."

"Fargo goes like that—quick," said Rosey.

"That Fay is tricky," Mando agreed. "And good."

He went back to third and played to hold the runner, watching Fay. Terry pitched hard and low.

Fay crouched. Mando started in. The bunt went in a perfect, slow, tantalizing line between Mando and Terry.

Mando grabbed it with his bare hand. Tilden was diving for home plate. Hooker was plodding toward second, a heavy-footed catcher, no speedster.

Mando threw out Hooker. Fay was safe at first. The Yankees were ahead by a run, and the fans were hysterical.

Terry now had to pitch to the top of the batting order. There was one out and a man on first. Hammer again stalked out onto the field. He took the ball from Terry.

Mando was astonished. When Ace came onto the field, he was unable to believe his senses.

Hammer said, "Okay. Now it's brains. That's all we got left. One out, remember. One out."

Dore was at the plate. Ace looked a hundred years old to Mando, a batting-practice pitcher, a has-been.

Dore was at the plate. The Skeeter infield set up for a possible double play. Ace held the ball loosely, but his eyes gleamed. He checked Fay, who took no lead at all buttoned into his windbreaker. He threw with an easy, sidearm motion.

Dore jumped at the ball. He nailed it on the fat of the bat. The grounder came roaring down to Mando. He threw it to second. The double play consumed no time at all. The Yankees were out of the bottom of the eighth with their one-run lead.

Ace said as they went to the bench, "Keep it low and turn it over. They can't do much with it, can they?"

"They didn't," said Mando. He wondered if Ace could

go a full inning. With that easy move he might well do so. Respect for Hammer mounted with each new day.

Fay was as calm as a pond facing Jonesy. He threw the soft stuff, then came in with the nearly fast ball. Jonesy knocked it down to short and was out.

Green again tried too hard and did not get the good wood on the ball. He flied out to center.

Rosey was the last hope. Two out in the ninth, the fans were still waiting, still shouting, still making the stands rock with stamping feet. Fay mused, looking at the night sky, at the bench, at anything but Rosey. Then he pitched.

Rosey hit the ball into left and went racing down to first. The noise diminished as Mando came to bat. Still Billy Fay did not turn a hair. Sullivan did not come off the bench. Supreme confidence abounded in the Yankee camp.

Mando watched. Fay must have the strength, the stamina of a bull, he thought. The motion was the same, the wrist snapped, the curve was perfect. If anything, the lefty was sharper under the gun, it seemed. He had his balance, he had the beautiful rhythm.

It was the rhythm that counted, Mando knew. The curve, the change, the quick fast one, all delivered in that almost mystic fashion, all well designed to a purpose. The count ran two and two, and Mando almost went for the junk ball which missed the edge of the plate by a hair.

Now it was down to the last pitch. Mando fouled it off rather than try to hit the screwball. He wiped his hands on the resin bag. He came back in, and his brain was functioning and his eyes were narrowed under the lights. He was looking for something. He was looking for the last piece of the pattern.

Fay pitched. It was the fast, sneaky ball, with something of the slider to it but not much hook. It was a lovely pitch.

Mando anticipated it. It was the missing piece of the jigsaw. He took a long step. His bat flashed. He got it just

202

before it broke. He hit it with all the pent-up strength he had been withholding because of Fay's brilliance.

The ball took off. It began to rise after it passed over second base. It went up and up. It soared over the head of Dore. It took wings and disappeared into the night beyond the stanchions of the overhead lights.

Rosey trotted, Mando scampered, then slowed for the circuit, carefully touching each base. The Skeeter bench was up and waiting for him as he crossed the platter. They were making so much noise that the reaction of the fans could not be heard.

Fay watched it all the way through. Then he accepted a new ball. He rubbed it. His face did not change. He waited for Jack Kelly to get into the box.

Then he struck out Jack.

Mando said, "He's going to be one of the greats. Nothing, but nothing daunts that cat."

"Who's going to get Portale, Andrews, and Hagney?" Rosey wanted to know. Old Ace had to face these most dangerous hitters.

Ace wandered out to the mound looking as though he was a tired old man. His warm-up tosses were anemic straight balls—but each was over the plate. His control had made him a perfect batting-practice pitcher, Mando remembered. In his day he had been one of the best, a twenty-game winner three times in his career. But he was over forty, and the Yankees were the best in the league, and this league was all youth and fire.

Ace looked around the infield. He winked. He toed the rubber. He seemed to merely flip the ball at Portale.

The left fielder slammed at the low straight ball. It rode down to Jack, who stepped on the bag. One out.

Ace sighed, used the resin bag. He squinted at Andrews. He pitched.

Andrews hit it to Jonesy. Two outs.

Now it was Hagney, the strong first-sacker. Ace blinked at him. He threw a strike that skittered as Hagney swung. They were all swinging. It looked too easy. They all knew they could hit this old character.

Ace threw one for the inside corner. Hagney heaved

at it again. There was the solid crack of a well-hit ball. Jack jumped. He stretched. The ball landed in the pocket of the mitt. The game was over, just like that. The Yankees were beaten.

As they were hugging him, Ace said, "When they get eager, you just let 'em hit it."

The stunned fans lingered, not quite believing what they had seen. The Skeeters had come in as underdogs, they left as conquerors. Hammer urged them to the bus. It was a long ride home, and another game tomorrow night. It was life on a treadmill.

11

In the background Eydie Gormé sang her hit song, "It Was a Good Time." A saccharine song, Jonesy thought, but apt.

The lobby was jammed. Harry was mysteriously absent, but then the word was out, and it was good—wonderful, in fact—publicity for the parent club.

The man from the *Star Eagle* in Newark was slightly apologetic. "Look, it had to come out sooner or later. I had to print it, you know. Your folks ... well ..."

A weekly news-magazine man asked, "What, precisely, is your relationship to your teammates ... to Roosevelt?"

Jonesy said, "They're my friends."

"But you must have some deep reason for being here. Something must have driven you to drop out of sight, then turn up in the bush leagues."

"I wanted to play ball."

They weren't satisfied with the simple answers. He was just off the bus, he needed rest before the night game, which they all would attend. The pressure was building; it was worse than it had ever been, even in the other times. He moved his head restlessly from right to left. It must be a dull time for news, he thought, to have so many here. Sports writers, yes, but all these others ...

"Your parents have left New York. Where are they?"

"I can't say."

"You mean you won't say? Are they in Europe?"

"I can't say."

Now the crowd moved in closer. He felt smothered. It was all over, the flight, the wonderful vacation. The brief yells in Mainville had been only the beginning; he was the rich kid again, the millionaire in his own right. Nobody would treat him as before. They might try, but they couldn't. It was not their fault; they all believe "the rich are different from us." They knew all about Scott Fitzgerald. They might like him, but they couldn't treat him as they had before the blowup.

The Newark man showed penitence in his concern, "Will you be able . . . will you stay with the Skeeters?"

Jonesy said wearily, "I guess that's up to you people."

"But you have your own money. No one can prevent you from taking whatever course you decide upon," said the news-mag man.

There was a disruption, a flurry, people were jostled. Then Rosey stood alongside Jonesy's chair in the lobby. The reporters started to crowd in again, now more than anxious.

Rosey said, "Hold it right there."

"We have some questions to ask you."

"I've been listening. Don't ask them."

"Now, just a minute, Roosevelt. . . ."

Rosey's voice lowered, became cold. "You cats blow. Out! You've done enough to him."

"You can't tell us . . ."

"Can't I?" He turned to Jonesy. "You had enough?"

Jonesy smiled at his friend. His head was suddenly clear. Front office, his fleeing parents, what did it matter? Why was he sitting here taking all this? They had just said it themselves; he didn't have to take it.

"Hey, man. Let's go."

Rosey said to the assemblage, "How would you like to stop us?"

They fell back. They couldn't believe it. Rosey and Jonesy walked through them, up the stairs. On the steps behind them they left Zander, Green, Pazolla, Barone. The ballplayers had heard it all. They massed, regarding the people from the press with hostile eyes.

The news-mag man said, "We'll wait for Hammer. We'll see about this."

"You do that," Barone told them. "You want to talk to me about my no-hitter? Great! Ask anything. But leave Jonesy alone. Jonesy's *our* boy. Jonesy ain't your boy. Dig?"

They retreated, scrambling for the phone booth. Hammer came from the rear. Before they could get to him he had bustled through his ballplayers and up the stairs.

"I'm calling the Gold Sox office," said the news-magazine man. "This is ridiculous."

"I fanned eight," Barone told them. "Only walked two. I used to have trouble with my control, see, but I only walked two of 'em. . . ."

Only the man from Newark was listening.

In the hallway Hammer said to a passing ballplayer, "Go down and tell them people to see us at the ball park. Then get some sleep or whatever. We got a game tonight. Tell 'em I got a story for 'em will harelip the sports pages."

He went into the room and said, "Jonesy, I was on the phone. Sorry." He was bursting with news. He wiped sweat from his broad face. "Mando, get packed."

"Packed?"

"You heard me, chicano. You take off from Newark on the nine-thirty American flight to L.A."

"I *what*?"

"Lou Libby broke his leg slidin' to a base today. They'll use Andover, but he's a bum, and so is Tilley, and Dutch knows it. Go up there and show 'em you can take over."

"You're putting me on!"

"Ha!" He grinned at the others. "The chicano's scairt."

Jack said, "You think so? He's numb, that's what he is. Come on, *amigo*, get packed!"

"I ain't through," said Hammer. "Dutch is sore as a bear with a wounded paw. He says if Mando makes it, we all got a chance. He says the sports writers are tearin' him up, the owners gettin' the ax ready. He says to hell with it all, give him a week. He says he needs an infield, and he don't care if it's from the Epworth League, it can't be no worse'n what he's got. He says Barone's to be next, maybe tomorrow if he can make arrangements. Then he said a lot about this whole expansion thing which ain't nice to repeat. And then . . ." Hammer paused for breath. "And then . . . he said I get to come back up as a coach with yawl. He said I earned it."

They all cried out. They had never heard anyone in their lives speak with such pride. They felt the thrill that comes with knowledge of a job well done. They pounded on Hammer's back and shoulders.

And Rosey said, "Now, pal. Y'see? If we go up—what can they do you? They got all sorts of crazies in the big leagues. You'll just be one more."

"You don't believe in miracles," Jonesy reminded him. But he was smiling. Hammer's story would take the bloom from his own. The furor over bringing up a Pennjersey busher to the parent club, the prospects of a whole kid infield for the Gold Sox would tie in, thus diminish, his own problem.

Hammer said, "Okay, now. I got a million things to do, gotta see Zander, talk to them people, keep 'em quiet. . . . Mando, do us good, will you, chicano? Show 'em for us?"

Mando said, "I'll murder 'em, Harry."

But Hammer had been right. He had butterflies. He snapped his bag shut and looked at his friends. His eyes were wet.

"This is no good," he said. "I wanted us to go together."

"That's not baseball," Rosey said. "You know it. Lucky they didn't trade you off."

"They would if they weren't desperate," Mando said. "I guess maybe we're lucky, at that."

"Lucky? Man, you're going up!"

"I just don't believe it."

Jack said, "Hey, I forgot your gloves and your spikes! You'll need another bag."

"Take mine," said Jonesy. "The small one."

Mando looked at him. "Always on the spot. That's you, pal. Hey, what can I tell you?"

Jonesy said, "I'll see you in California."

"You'll call us? About everything?" Jack asked.

"About your wedding? Think not of it," said Mando. "I'll handle everything."

He got away. It was too sudden; he could scarcely grasp it.

Bemused by the long trip by airplane, his ears buzzing, swallowing hard, Mando walked up the ramp and into the arms of Ana Cassidy. His life immediately fell into place.

She said, "Darling, darling, darling . . ." and other things.

He said, "I love you . . . I love you . . . I love you . . ." and other things.

They walked toward the ramp leading down to the luggage department. They both talked at once, overlapping; they kissed twice. Then they became, with an effort, something resembling their everyday selves.

She said, "It seems so silly to go all the way to Bay City when the team is coming to Anaheim to play the Angels."

"That's day after tomorrow," he said. "They . . . we . . . wow! . . . *we're* off tomorrow."

She said, "Well, the family thought they could wait so that I can drive you to Bay City. That's good."

"That's perfect. You got my wire, then?"

"Of course. Pop's so excited, you can't believe."

"Is he better?"

"I think your good news helped a million. His eyes are brighter, he moved better when he heard. It's . . . it's . . ."

"A miracle Rosey didn't think could happen," he finished for her. "It's really because of the expansion. There just aren't enough ballplayers."

"And you did your job in the Pennjersey."

"We did our jobs. All of us. And Harry Hammer turned out to be at least an uncle. A baseball-smart uncle."

She said, "Ricky's working the gas station for me tonight."

"The old Brown Beret? That's something else."

"Ricky's given up the beret. The violence turned him off. Ricky's going to work steady with us."

"He quit Uncle Talker?"

"He found out the way we were being squeezed by your uncle. You don't know it, darling, but Ricky's awful proud of you. He's been wonderful to Pop and to me. He's peculiar . . . you know."

"Chicano," he told her. "You ought to recognize that."

"Maybe. . . . Anyway, what about Jack?"

"He wants to get married. Right now, if not quicker."

"So does Connie."

He looked at her. "And you?"

"I can wait." She squeezed his arm. "I think we've all learned a lot this spring. The station . . . Pop's station . . . it's important to him, to the family. To Patsy and Ricky and me. We're building something."

"Is it going better?"

"Ricky helped. Patsy's dragsters. Maybe people like me a little. Uncle holds us together with his experience. When Pop gets well . . . we can think about it later."

"But we'll think about it."

"We'll think about it."

They reclaimed the luggage. They found her father's car in the huge parking lot of Los Angeles International Airport. They drove south toward Bay City. They filled each other in on all the little intimate details. He sat close to her and touched her, and the muscles of his belly loosened and the butterflies were stilled for the first time since Harry Hammer had told him to pack his bags.

The Pennjersey Skeeters demolished the Newton Lions in short order that evening. They then rushed to the radio station outside Princeton and en masse, by local courtesy, they listened to the broadcast of the

210

game between the Bay City Gold Sox and the California Angels at Anaheim.

Jack said, "That's a great ball park. Cozy-like. Great lighting. Beautiful decor."

"Yeah," said Rosey. "I betcha Mando's not looking at it that way right now."

The radio announcer for the Angels was chatty in a rather superior manner. "The Gold Sox have yet to win a game against our Angels. In all fairness, the Sox have had the worst of luck—besides being the newest expansion team in California. They recently lost their veteran third baseman, Lou Libby, and have brought up from the Pennjersey League, their Class A farm, a youngster from Los Angeles named Mando Cruz. Cruz is nineteen, has been hitting over four hundred for Mingo—MINGO?—New Jersey. . . ."

Jack said, "I never heard of it, either."

"They'll learn," said Harry Hammer.

"If only Mando gets to hit one out," said Jonesy.

The announcer was saying in wonderment, "We've just got the lineup. The kid from California is going to start! The old Dutchman is making a bold move to infuse youth into the sad Gold Sox. This is interesting, folks. We'll be telling you about the debut of Mando Cruz as the game progresses. . . . Now we return to the studio for a brief message."

Jack said, "I'd give almost anything to be there. Even my old man is at the game. . . . All of Mando's family, Ana, everybody. It's *the* day."

Harry Hammer said, "Expansion. The Dutchman's job shouldn't be on no line . . . but it is. Mando should have another year. Yawl should have another year."

"We've learned a lot from you," Jonesy said.

"We got two hands and two feet," said Rosey. "Age don't count."

"You don't believe in miracles," said Jack.

"It's no miracle. The Gold Sox got handed a bunch of has-beens and never-wases," said Hammer. "And some never-will-bes. Expansion."

"And now 'The Star-Spangled Banner,'" the announcer was saying.

Automatically the Skeeters arose and stood at attention. The room was electric with tension.

Mando sat on the bench alongside the wizened, tobacco-chewing Dutch Muller. The butterflies were gone, replaced by burning resentment and a loneliness he had never before experienced.

The old manager said, "Burned, huh, kid?"

"To a crisp," said Mando.

"You got to look at their side. Their jobs are in danger. Vets always hate rookies."

"Even Gonzales gave me that chicano routine—and he's a Cuban. The hell with 'em."

Dutch said, "Either you can take it or you can't."

"Yeah," said Mando. "I know."

"Harry says you got the guts." He spat brown juice. "I put a big store by Harry."

Mando did not reply. He was batting sixth. The Angels had their good right-hander, Hacker, in the box. Monty Wells, the aging but still quick second baseman, led off for the Sox. There was a scanty crowd in the fine stadium—nobody was interested in the dull, no-talent Bay City visitors.

The regulars, the reserves, all the Sox had been brutal in their treatment of him. He had expected some hazing, but the spirit of these hapless ballplayers was so low that they lashed out at the nearest target, he imagined. The rage simmered in him; his Latin blood boiled.

He watched Wells, Pascola, and Gordon go down in order before Hacker's assortment of stuff. The three of them seemed listless, helpless, uncaring. Wells and Gordon were veteran journeymen, but Pascola was a youngster and should have been anxious to make good. It was a sad situation. Mando took his glove and went onto the field and began warming up with his throws to Bones Astor on first. Astor was a mediocre glove man, with none of the grace of Jack Kelly.

Blackie Schwartz was pitching for the Sox. He had

been the only one to give Mando a grin and a wink. He seemed more alive, alert, determined to preserve his own record as a pitcher.

The first Angel hitter knocked the first pitch down the third-base line. It was skimmer, headed right over the bag. Mando jumped like a big cat. He gloved the ball, threw off balance with all his might and main. He had the runner by a step.

Astor dropped the ball.

Mando roared without conscious thought, "Heads up, there. Come on, play ball, you guys!"

The Sox jumped as though shot, every eye turning hard and cold toward the rookie who dared to shout at a veteran.

In New Jersey Harry Hammer said, "Some first inning. Two unearned runs off Blackie."

"Mando must be steamin'," said Jack.

"They make more errors in an inning than we do in three games," Jack said.

"Them bums," said Harry Hammer. "Them stinkin' bums."

"Mando gets a rap this inning," said Rosey.

"I sure wish I was there," said Jack again.

"We all wish we were there. On the field," Rosey said.

"Blackie don't give 'em a hit, and they get two runs," Barone said. "I don't think I want to go up to that club."

"Mando had two assists," Hammer said. "Should've had three. They're whackin' 'em down to the rookie."

"And he's showing them something."

"They'll either hate his bones or he'll pick 'em up," said Hammer. "Long as he proves out for Dutch, he's okay."

"He won't stay quiet," Rosey said. "He's got the big mouth. He'll make or break; he won't quit."

"Yes," said Jonesy. "That's the way it is, Sandy. That's really the way it is."

They were all hunched, tense, fists clenched. The radio announcer chattered on.

213

"The infield stinks," said Rosey. "You heard it. They blew two runs to the Angels."

"You don't believe in miracles," Jack said.

"Like Harry said, no miracles." Rosey grinned. "Expansion."

". . . Strike three . . . Hacker got Astor on a good curve ball. . . . And now the rookie, Cruz, comes to the plate. He's a muscular young man. . . . He looks aggressive. . . . He faces Hacker with a closed stance, swinging a medium-weight bat. . . . Strike one. . . . Strike two. . . . Hacker's in great form today. . . . Here's the pitch. . . . It's a good one. . . . Cruz fouls it off. . . ."

"Guard that plate," Hammer breathed. "Stand in there and protect that damn plate."

"Here's the next pitch, a fast ball," said the announcer. "Cruz swings. Again he fouls into the stands. . . . This boy really seems to know his business. . . . He's cool. . . ."

"He's mad," said Jack. "I know that. Ravin' mad at his dumb bunch of bums. That's Mando."

"Make him give you your pitch," Hammer said. "Make him come to you, boy."

"And here's the pitch. . . . It's a curve ball. . . . Cruz steps, swings. . . . Did you hear that, fans? . . . Going, going . . . touch 'em all! His first time at bat in the big leagues, and young Cruz from California knocks it out. . . ."

They danced up and down and around. They hugged each other like girls. They yelled and screamed and batted each other on the head. Hammer was yowling, "Cooeee, coooeee, come on, you hawgs, coooeee, root, root, root. That's our boy!"

In a field box Ana Cassidy was hugging the entire Cruz family. Tears ran down their cheeks. Even Mamma, who wouldn't know a home run from a touchdown, was weeping with joy. Papa and Rick were screaming.

Down on the field Mando was sitting on the bench. Blackie Schwartz walked along the line of Sox players and paused, grinning his offkey way, his eyes snapping.

"Kid, you're somethin' else. Lemme tell you, win, lose, or draw, I'm with you."

Cobbit, his black face shining, followed Schwartz. "Man, you got me with you. I don't know when anybody's knocked me in with a shot like that."

One by one their voices came. "Nice goin', kid." "You're with it, chicano." "You got it all together, man."

Dutch Muller said, "Okay. Now how about playin' some damn baseball?"

In New Jersey Hammer said, "No matter what happens now, he done it. First time out, he done it."

The game was over. Mando had managed a single to drive in the winning run for the Sox and break the losing streak.

Jack said, "I'd give a farm to be there."

"We'll be there." It was Rosey, speaking flat out. "I don't believe in miracles. I believe in Harry. And I believe in what Mando just did."

"We'll be there," echoed Jonesy. He was thinking about Ana in the stands, how she must feel, how marvelous it was for her. Friend of the family, Gilbert Samson Jones III, that was the way it would be. Time would take care of the pain, he supposed. People always said that time cured everything. It was another lesson he would have to learn.

Mando was talking to the sports reporters. They were crowded around his cubicle; he couldn't get to the showers. He was answering questions about the Pennjersey, about Harry Hammer, about Jonesy. He was happier than any man had a right to be, he thought. He wished he could get away to be with Ana and his family, but it was sweet to hear the compliments, to hear Dutch Muller say that there were other young infielders in Mingo who would be brought up as soon as he could make arrangements.

The reporter who followed the Sox asked, "Just how good are these other kids, Mando?"

"Good enough to make this team," said Mando, pull-

215

ing no punches, uncaring who heard him. "Wait'll you see 'em. Harry Hammer brought us along fast."

Dutch said, "Harry'll be coming up with 'em. Harry's been my man for many a long year."

A reporter asked, "What did you think of the big-league pitching—besides tearing into it?"

"The Yankees got a kid named Fay as good as he is."

"Would you call yourself a cocky rookie?" asked a local man.

"Call me anything you want," said Mando. "I am proud I am chicano."

"Hey, chicano, that's tellin' 'em," yelled Cobbit.

On the instant he was "Chicano Cruz." It would stick with him as baseball monickers always did, he knew. It was wonderful.

He said, "Excuse me now, please." He ran through the crowd to the showers. He wanted to think of the guys back in Jersey, of his family, of Connie and Jack ... and of Ana Cassidy.

ABOUT THE AUTHOR

WILLIAM R. COX's interest in sports began when he was four years old and his father presented him with boxing gloves, a baseball and a bat. He played baseball through high school and on semipro teams, often covering the games in which he played for the Newark *Sunday Call.*

His family was in the ice, coal and wood business, and he says that from hauling, lifting and shoveling he developed muscles "coming out of my ears . . ." But, realizing that a writer can't live by sports alone, Mr. Cox began writing crime novels and westerns. Only recently has he returned to the sports scene for his themes.

Mr. Cox has written thirteen sports juveniles, including *Five Were Chosen.* He now lives in Sherman Oaks, California.

REACH ACROSS
THE GENERATIONS

With books that explore disenchantment and discovery, failure and conquest, and seek to bridge the gap between adolescence and adulthood.